THRONE
OF POWER

RINA KENT

Throne of Power Copyright © 2021 by Rina Kent
All rights reserved.

No part of this publication may be reproduced, stored or transmitted in any form or by any means, electronic, mechanical, photocopying, recording, scanning, or otherwise without written permission from the publisher. It is illegal to copy this book, post it to a website, or distribute it by any other means without permission, except for the use of brief quotations in a book review.

This novel is entirely a work of fiction. The names, characters and incidents portrayed in it are the work of the author's imagination. Any resemblance to actual persons, living or dead, events or localities is entirely coincidental.

To strong women.

AUTHOR NOTE

Hello reader friend,

If you haven't read my books before, you might not know this, but I write darker stories that can be upsetting and disturbing. My books and main characters aren't for the faint of heart.

Throne of Power is the first book of a duet and is not standalone.

Throne Duet:
#1 Throne of Power
#2 Throne of Vengeance

Don't forget to sign up to Rina Kent's Newsletter for news about future releases and an exclusive gift.

When powers clash...

In the mafia world, women don't reign.

I'm the exception of that rule.

I didn't choose this life, it chose me.

I have a legacy to protect, a power to snatch, and no one will

stop me.

If an arranged marriage is what it'll take to lead, then so be it.

What I don't count on is that my chosen husband is a ghost

from my past.

Kyle Hunter.

He was once my guard, my protector. Now, he's after my

kingdom.

The road to the throne is paved with thorns, blood, and

casualties.

To win, I'll risk it all.

My heart included.

PLAYLIST

Throne—Bring Me The Horizon

A Little Wicked—Valerie Broussard

Monsters—Shinedown

Kingdom of Cards—Bad Omens

Start a War—Klergy & Valerie Broussard

I luv that u hate me—Story Untold & Kellin Quinn

Let Down—Dead By Sunrise

Scars—No name faces

Tell Me Why—Dream on Dreamer

Not Afraid to Die—Written by Wolves

Legends Never Die—Solence

Shotgun—Spoon

Far From Any Road—The Handsome Family

I'm a Wanted Man—Royal Deluxe

Cold Blood—Dave Not Dave

Bad Man—Blues Saraceno

This is War—Thirty Seconds to Mars

Dance With The Devil—Breaking Benjamin

Monster—Colours

The Resistance—Skillet

Cut the Cord—Shinedown

Hard to Love—Too Close to Touch

Kerosene—Vanish

You can find the complete playlist on Spotify.

THRONE
OF POWER

ONE

Kyle

THE TRUTH ISN'T WHAT YOU SEE. IT'S WHAT YOU make of it.

There's no such thing as a wholesome truth or a perfect reality. There are people and agendas.

There is peace and war.

There is losing and winning.

I have come a long way in my search for the actual truth—my own truth, the one they stripped me of thirty years ago.

When they made a machine out of me, they never thought it would come back and destroy them from the inside out.

They underestimated me.

I love it when they do that. It means I will have the best time ripping them apart, crunching their bones, and watching blood ooze from all of their holes.

That's my system, my reality. And no one will be able to stop me.

Not even death.

It can try, but I've come too far to be intimidated by something as insignificant as death.

When I go down, I'm taking every last one of them with me, their names and titles included.

If I will be erased from this world, so will they. If I've become a shadow, so will they.

This is my resurrection.

I stand in front of the huge mansion in a secluded area in Brooklyn. The walls are high enough that no one can peer over. There are no tall buildings nearby, which is a tactical move to eliminate the threat of snipers. Wires surround the walls' edges like in a military camp, and several cameras placed at regular intervals along the walls blink red.

If I take a step forward, I'll be swarmed by guards who won't hesitate to shoot me a hundred times just to make sure I am indeed finished.

They're so serious I can't even play dead with their kind.

When they committed their crimes, they knew they had to hide in palaces like these, palaces where they're completely safe from the world.

But not from me.

Never from me.

I step forward so I'm directly in front of the gate. It doesn't open, but as expected, booming, unsubtle footsteps come from behind me. They never learned to cover their tracks as I taught them.

Oh well. I guess you can't make any soldier into an assassin.

"Put your hands up in the air," one of the guards booms in a thick Russian accent.

I do as I'm told because, while death doesn't scare me, it would be a fucking waste if my cause of death were holes in the back. Not only that, the one who would get the credit for killing the legend that is me would be this Russian tool. Fucking shameful, I tell you. I wouldn't be able to look my godfather in the face anymore.

Not that I have in the past couple of years. But that's another tragic story not fit for the present.

The sound of a clicking gun comes from behind me before he speaks again. "Hands behind your head and turn around slowly. One wrong move and I will spill your brains on the ground."

I spin around and, sure enough, there are three of them. Two are holding guns to their sides while their leader, a senior guard with grim features and an asymmetrical mustache that's more comical than intimidating, is pointing an AK4 in my direction.

His weapon of choice is sure as fuck not comical.

Upon seeing my face, his eyes widen in clear surprise, and he falters for a fraction of a second.

That's the only opening I need.

I charge forward and elbow him in the throat. The moment his hold loosens on the AK4, I snatch it then pull my gun from my waistband.

The two other soldiers spend a long time pausing in shock. By the time they point their guns at me, I'm already aiming the AK4 and my weapon in their faces.

"Didn't I tell you a moment of hesitation is all it takes for you to get killed?" I stare at their senior guard, because I recognize him—and his hideous mustache—from before. These are new recruits, looking barely out of their pubescent years.

He curses in Russian then goes back to English. "What are you doing here, Kyle? You couldn't stay the fuck away?"

"Pay respect to a Vor, peasant." I smirk as he curses again.

They all hate that a British person—and therefore non-Russian—was given that title by their previous *Pakhan*. The fact that no one can take it away makes them hate me even more.

Hatred doesn't matter. My goal does.

Becoming a member of the elite group in an organization I don't give a fuck about is all part of a plan that's finally coming to fruition now.

I motion at him with the tip of the AK4. "Now, take me to your boss."

He puffs his chest out, and his mustache twitches as if participating in the action. "Why should I?"

"Igor and I have a war to start."

TWO

Rai

IF POWER ELUDES YOU, THEN YOU HAVE NOTHING. It's not only about being at the top. If you're high enough, no one touches you or those close to you. No one dares to look at you, and when they do, they are blinded by the non-negotiability you project back at them.

That's why I don't and will never stop.

The higher I go in the ranks, the more they respect me, and one day, they will all bow down to Grandpa's family name.

"We're Sokolovs, Rai," he told me once. "We don't bend the knee. Everyone else does."

With his words engraved deep in my heart, I take the stairs down.

The house is huge, as expected of the Bratva's compound in New York. The sweeping marble stairs lead to a grand hallway that has light marble flooring. Gold rims the chesterfield sofa in the middle, the pillars, and even the carpet. The ceilings are vaulted, and there's a painting of angels fighting demons in the middle. That usually gets visitors to stop and stare at the intricate detail put into the image.

On the other hand, that's also usually the last thing they see before they're 'taken care of'. While we invite our associates here, we also invite our enemies.

Heaven and hell. Angels and demons.

Dedushka—Grandpa—was poetic that way, which shouldn't have been a surprise considering his origins. He was not only the leader of one of the most successful Bratva branches in the States and Russia; his roots go back to the beginning, dating to the end of World War II.

I am part of that bloodline.

In fact, I'm the only one who can protect it anymore.

Today, I opted for black suit pants that give me a sharp edge. My beige coat hangs on my shoulders without me having to wear it. It's a quirk I learned from *Dedushka*. My blonde hair is twisted in an elegant bun. My makeup isn't loud, but it's a few layers thick, making me look like I'm in my thirties instead of twenty-eight.

Being young is a weakness in the Vory world, and there's no way I will let them exploit any of my shortcomings.

I'm stopped by a radiant face at the bottom of the stairs. Anastasia, my great-cousin, smiles upon seeing me, revealing perfectly straight—and petite—teeth. In fact, everything about her is, from her nose to her lips and her frame. The only thing that's big are her huge green eyes. It's like staring straight into the calm of the tropical ocean.

She's wearing a modest long-sleeved dress that stops below her knees. Her blonde hair, a few shades lighter than mine, is gathered in a low, neat ponytail by a long ribbon. As usual, no ounce of makeup covers her face. Her smile falters for a second, and my red alert goes up all at once. The bloodthirsty mama bear in me comes out to play.

"What is it, Ana?"

"It's…" She shakes her head. "Nothing, Rai. Have a nice day."

"Ana." I speak in my no-nonsense tone that she knows no one should challenge. "You can either tell me now, or we can stand here all day until you do."

She bites her bottom lip, peeking up at me from underneath her naturally thick lashes. That should mean she's close to letting it out.

Ever since I was brought into the Vory world, I always thought I only had *Dedushka*, and that was enough considering he was the Bratva's *Pakhan*.

But then, my great-uncle Sergei, *Dedushka*'s youngest brother, brought in Anastasia to live with us. The first time I met her, I was thirteen. She was only five years old. Back then, she looked up at me as if she saw the world, as if I were her savior from whatever life she used to live before.

We instantly became best friends—or more like I became her protector, as she's too fragile to be out there in the world.

Fifteen years later, she still considers me the same way she did before.

I step closer to her, lower my bag to my side, and try to remove the sternness from my tone. Anastasia trusts me, but she also told me I can be scary—not toward her, but scary in general.

That's the last thing I want my Ana to feel toward me, but if it's to protect her, I won't only be scary—I'll blow the whole fucking world to smithereens.

I place a hand on her shoulder, stroking gently. "You know you can tell me anything, right?"

She nods twice.

"Then what aren't you telling me?"

Anastasia bites her lower lip again. "You won't be mad?"

Unlike most of the Vory who have a noticeable Russian

accent, she speaks English in a perfect American accent, probably because I've been teaching her since we were young.

"I will never be mad at you." I smile at her, which is possibly the warmest type of smile I can offer to anyone.

"Papa said…he said…"

"What?"

She gulps. "He said I need to get ready."

"Ready for what?"

"You know."

"Unless you tell me, I don't, Nastyusha." I use her Russian pet name since she responds better to that.

"F-for…marriage."

"For *what?*" I snap, and she flinches, her shoulders turning rigid under my touch. I internally curse myself for frightening her and take several seconds to calm down. "Did he mention who he's marrying you off to?"

She shakes her head once while staring at her flat shoes. "He just said I need to get ready. Does…does this mean I can't continue my studies?"

Her voice breaks with her last sentence. Few things affect me this deeply, and Anastasia is definitely at the top of the list. Seeing her in pain is like having one of my limbs cut off.

I raise her chin and she stares up at me with a wretched expression. There are no tears because she was brought up to be the perfect Vor's daughter from a young age.

For her, crying isn't a weakness like I consider it. In Anastasia's dictionary, tears aren't ladylike and shouldn't be shown in public.

The fact that she wants to express her sadness, but can't, digs the knife deeper into me.

I force a smile, stroking her hair back. "You don't need to get ready for anything. I'll talk to Granduncle, and none of this will happen."

Her expression lights up. "Really?"

"Have I ever made a promise and not kept it?"

A gentle spark invades her expression. "Never."

"Go study and don't worry about this. Since you have exams coming up, you don't need to come to the company."

"I want to."

Ana has been interning at V Corp for almost a year now. She followed computer engineering, which everyone thinks is useless in our line of work. I'm the only one who encouraged her because it's the thing she chose freely and without shackles. She's a numbers genius and it would've been a waste if she didn't put that talent to use.

"As you wish. Where's Granduncle?"

"He's in the dining room…but you might not want to go in there. Papa is having a meeting with the rest of the Vory."

"Of course he is, and let me guess—Mikhail is in there?"

"Umm…yes."

Why am I not surprised that Granduncle brought up the whole marriage thing when that pest was around?

"Go back to your studies, Ana. Don't let any of this get to you."

She hesitates, then blurts, "Be careful. You know they don't like you there."

"They will dislike me more after today."

"Rai…"

"Don't worry. I'll be careful," I say to please her even though I'm already plotting a war.

She steps forward and hugs me. "Stay safe, Rayenka."

Then she takes moderate steps up the stairs.

I've never liked my Russian pet name unless Anastasia says it. When I came to live with *Dedushka*, he insisted that my mother named me Rai and that it was in fact short for Raisa, a Russian name. He invented that whole story just so he could have a Russian pet name for me.

Since his death, only Anastasia ever calls me that anymore.

Oh, and *Granduncle* Sergei when he's not mad at me. Let's just say, he'll have no pet names for me today, because I'm fully prepared to ruin his meeting.

The one I wasn't invited to—again.

After *Dedushka's* death seven years ago, Ivan, Grandpa's nephew whom he raised as his own son, wanted power so badly he attempted to kill not only me but also his own uncle, Sergei.

I went through hell and back, working in the background and arranging meetings with the security group, the support group, and the four brigadiers who are the working arm of the Vory. I even went as far as recruiting the powerful *boyeviks*, whom the brigadiers' leaders trusted more than their own family.

Dedushka left me the black book that contains names of influential people the Vory deals with. He said whoever has that book is meant to rule. Needless to say, everyone in the brotherhood would've killed me before allowing a woman to reign over them.

It's not that I wanted to, but *Dedushka* entrusted me with the family name. My mission in life is to protect my family's honor. Just because I was born a woman, doesn't mean I'll let anyone stomp all over me.

But since I knew any resistance would get me, Ana, and Granduncle killed, I gave him the book. With that, Sergei Sokolov became the current *Pakhan*. The boss. The leader of the brotherhood.

At least on the surface.

Only he and I, along with our most loyal member of the elite group, know that Granduncle has lung cancer he's been fighting for months.

The moment the rest of the elite group know, it'll all be over. The *Pakhan* can't be weak. He can't lead the Vory if he can't stand up straight.

They will remove him and then it will be an all-out war

between the four brigadiers, the literal kings who bring money into the brotherhood. The leaders of the security and support group might join too. It will be wolves against wolves, and one thing is for certain—Anastasia and I will either be coerced to marry into their families or killed in the case of disobedience.

Considering my rebellious character, they'll definitely kill me.

There's no way in hell they'll kick me out of the brotherhood that prospered in *Dedushka*'s time. He started this legacy, and I will continue to uphold it.

While Granduncle has been ruling, I've risen up in V Corp's ranks. It's the legitimate front of the brotherhood and funnels a lot of money that takes care of most of the tax business.

I snatched the executive director's post from a greedy associate of the Vory a year ago. In such a short time, V Corp's net profit grew by fifty percent, and it will continue to in the future.

Granduncle is the CEO, but it's only in image. In reality, all the work falls on my shoulders.

I've never considered it a burden, though, since it's my way to claim my place at their table. Granduncle began to proudly invite me to the Vory's meetings due to the accomplishments I've been presenting to the brotherhood—but not all of them, apparently, since I wasn't invited to this one.

Inhaling deeply, I stand in front of the dining room. Its double doors are rimmed with golden ornamentation, and I use the intricate design as an opportunity to meditate.

Right on, war. Here I come.

"Miss Sokolov." The sound of my last name coming from my left stops me. I stare at Vladimir—or Vlad, as I like to call him.

He's part of the elite group, a *Sovietnik*, which is essentially the main coordinator between the *Pakhan* and the four brigadiers. He plays an important role that keeps the peace between the four brigadiers and makes sure they bring in profit to the Vory.

Vlad is the only member of the elite group that I trust—or more like I trust his loyalty. He was brought in by *Dedushka* and rose in rank to become who he is today.

Like me, he wants to keep *Dedushka*'s name in the ruling position.

"Morning, Vlad."

"It's either Vova or Vlodya, miss. Don't use American nicknames on me." He speaks with a Russian accent, but it's not as distinctive as everyone else in the brotherhood.

"I will use whatever I want."

He grunts a response. He does that a lot, grunting and releasing breaths as responses. He's brooding to a fault, and it especially shows when he expresses how much he really doesn't like the American half in me or how that half addresses him.

Vlad is generally a grumpy but intense person who barks orders at his soldiers with a tone that's only meant to be obeyed.

He also has the looks that go with his grumpy personality. I'm not short by any means, but he's so tall and broad that he blocks my vision whenever he stands in front of me. He dwarfs his suit's jacket, and his beard adds more to his intimidation factor.

"Now, move, Vlad. I have a meeting to attend."

His small pale eyes remain the same, but he steps between me and the door. "You were not invited."

"Still, I have something to say."

"I think it's better if you keep your words to yourself, miss."

"Guess what, Vlad? I don't care what you think."

"Miss."

"Vlad." I meet his impenetrable gaze with my own.

"You don't want to be inside."

"Why not?"

"The four kings are there."

"The more the merrier. They all need to hear this."

He grunts. "You cannot embarrass the Vor in front of them. It's a sign of weakness."

"I know that, and it's exactly why I try to not displease him in front of them, but if you think I will let them rot his mind while I stand by and say nothing, then you don't know Rai Sokolov."

"Rot his mind?"

"They want to have Anastasia. Granduncle told her to get ready for marriage, and do you know who's behind this? Those four fucking kings, that's who, because Granduncle wouldn't want to marry her off."

Vlad's expression doesn't change, but he says in a monotone tone, "No."

"What do you mean by no? I can't allow them to coerce Ana into marriage. She's fucking twenty, a kid who doesn't even understand the world yet and wants to continue studying. I will claw their eyes out before they put her into a wedding dress."

Vlad stares down at me with what seems like condescension mixed with bemusement. "I'm sure you will."

"You bet I will, so don't stand there telling me no."

"I meant no, as in Sergei won't force her into this."

"How would you know if neither you nor I are there, huh?"

"You are not allowed to weaken the boss, miss."

"Yeah, yeah." I throw a dismissive hand up at his stern tone. He reminds me of that fact every day.

He remains silent for a second, and I think he'll fight me tooth and nail on this, but then he asks in a contemplative tone, "How about you do it?"

"Do what?"

"Get married."

"Get *what?*"

"You're older—you can take a husband."

"Have you lost your mind?"

"This is, in fact, a perfectly sane solution. The only way to protect Anastasia and to continue ruling is to get married."

"You think I haven't thought about that? But any husband within the brotherhood will make me into his obedient tool. I would rather die first."

"What if you can make him *your* obedient tool?"

"What do you mean?"

"Don't take a husband to rule for you. Take a puppet you can rule through."

"And you think such a man exists in the brotherhood? Every last one of them is hungry for power."

"There are those who, like you, have other people ruling in the background on their behalf. You can just take that position."

Oh. I have heard stories about that, but I always thought they were myths.

"And how would I be sure such men exist?"

"They do. I've encountered a few, and that's how I came up with this plan."

"I like the way you think, Vlad."

He grunts and I smile. Even though he's a little rough around the edges—okay, a lot—Vlad has my best interests in mind. If we can find someone who fits the criteria, then this can solve Ana's problems and mine. I can push my puppet husband to the top and then, not only will I preserve my grandfather's legacy, I will also protect Anastasia from any barbaric wedding.

"Any candidates in mind?" I ask Vlad with a coy smile.

"I will look into it and bring you complete files."

I grab his chin with my thumb and forefinger. "Have I told you lately that you're the best?"

"More than enough." He pushes back, muttering under his breath, "Americans and their need to touch."

"I heard that, and I'm as much of a Russian as you are, Vlad."

His face remains the same. "If you go inside, it's to tell Sergei you're available for marriage."

I am.

Am I, though?

I release a deep breath as memories of sinister blue eyes invade my head. At times, they're the best part of a dream, and at others, they're the most horrifying thing in a nightmare, the one thing that jolts me awake in the middle of the night, sweating, shivering, and shaking.

No. I'm over that bastard.

He betrayed me first. Now, it's my turn.

THREE

Rai

I PUSH THE DINING ROOM DOOR OPEN AND GO INSIDE with my head held high just as *Dedushka* taught me.

It's easy to be intimidated by the leaders of the elite group. Most of them, Granduncle included, have served time in jail. While that's disgraceful in the outside world, it's a stamp of honor for any member of the Vory.

Granduncle Sergei sits at the head of the table. He's old, in his sixties. His once-blond hair is now completely white and washed by time. While cancer has made him look older, it didn't take his hair away, probably because of his stubbornness about refusing to undergo chemotherapy. I try not to glare at him now that I know he's trying to ship Anastasia off to one of these ruthless men who will eat her alive.

Vlad leaves my side and sits on Granduncle's right, which is his position as the *Sovietnik*. On his left sits Adrian, the *Obshchak*. He holds the same level of power as Vlad, but instead of coordinating between the brigadiers and the *Pakhan*, Adrian holds a more critical role that entails securing the brotherhood. He knows the right people to bribe and has a line of intelligence that rivals the CIA, probably because he has big connections within the Mossad itself.

Despite being in his mid-thirties, Adrian has been around since *Dedushka*'s time and played his role without fail. He keeps his cards close, and he's the most private out of the elite group. That's why I feel like I should always be wary of him.

The fact that he showed up at this meeting means it is important. Adrian rarely attends gatherings or invites anyone to his house, but he always got a free pass from *Dedushka* and Granduncle because of his crucial role. In short, no one wants to get on Adrian's bad side, because those who do? Yeah, no one knows where the heck they disappear to.

He's silent to a fault, too, and only speaks when he absolutely has to, which is when the boss addresses him. Adrian is loyal to the Vory, but that's the only thing he's loyal to. He wouldn't hesitate to crush me if we somehow ended up on different sides of a battle.

The four kings, aka the brigadiers, occupy the rest of the chairs: Damien, the old man Igor, Kirill, and the motherfucker Mikhail.

The latter glares at me and I glare back, unblinking. Despite being old himself, a bit younger than Sergei, he still stands tall and his blue eyes are piercing to a fault. I have no doubt he's the one who suggested marrying Anastasia off, probably to one of his sons, who are more loathsome than he is.

That asshole is in charge of the most despicable part of the Vory, the one I've been actively trying to eradicate: the prostitution ring.

He wants me gone because I boldly suggested in front of *Dedushka* that the brotherhood doesn't need the prostitution ring, that we're wasting effort on that part when we can secure better money from V Corp.

Mikhail has wanted me dead since then. He's the one who backed Ivan, my mom's cousin, to become *Pakhan* and kill me off. If he thinks I would ever forget about that, he must not know our last name at all.

"What are you doing here?" he snarls, as expected.

I ignore him, take Granduncle's hand, kiss his wrinkled knuckles, and lift it to my head. This is how all the members of the Vory greet their *Pakhan*. I might not have an official title or position, but I'm one of the pillars keeping this organization standing whether they like to admit it or not.

Behind every member of the elite stands their best *boyevik*, which is basically their senior soldier/bodyguard whom they trust with their lives. Usually, these leaders don't move without a horde of soldiers, but in a meeting with the *Pakhan*, only one is allowed out of respect to the boss.

My senior *boyevik*, Ruslan, follows after me and stands behind my chair as I sit beside Damien. The latter grins down at me in that snakelike way. I smile back and don't bother to hide that it's fake.

He's not only a slippery slope; he's also reckless as hell. Damien is the type of king who orders hits on other crime families within our territories if they've disrespected us in any way. He says it's to teach them to bow their heads when the brothers are around. His violent nature and unsatiated ambition have always kept him on my 'to be wary of' list.

Kirill clears his throat from his position opposite me. He has a physique similar to Vlad's, bulk-wise, but he's more calm like Adrian, probably due to the camouflage he excels at. His black-framed glasses make him appear sharp, smart, but they don't hide the intensity of his foxlike eyes. I smirk internally. I have something on that sucker, so now he can't open his mouth and agree with Mikhail's statement.

"Do you have something for us, Miss Sokolov?" Igor asks in his serene, but very noticeable Russian accent. He's also as old as Sergei but appears younger because he's healthy and still actually works out with his soldiers. Igor's brigade is the most closed off and family-like. They would go to war for him with their eyes blindfolded if they had to. After *Dedushka*'s death, he was one of those who helped me put Sergei in power, but he's also a traditionalist and sexist like the rest of them. He'd never bow down to a woman.

"Yes, Miss Sokolov. To what do we owe this pleasure?" Damien waggles his brows at me. Although both his parents are Russian, he is American born and bred, and therefore, he speaks without an accent most of the time.

They talk in English around me because they think I'm that 'American' who doesn't belong with them even though I have proven again and again that I'm as much Russian as they are.

"Yes," I say in Russian, looking at Granduncle. "I will report V Corp's numbers for the last trimester as well as projection for future net profit."

"You can do that in the company." Mikhail doesn't hide his aggression. "You have no place among the Vory, Rayka."

I grit my teeth at the disrespectful way he used a nickname, but I plaster a smile on instead.

Kill them with kindness, Rai. Don't weaken Sergei.

"I beg to differ, Mikhail." I reach into my bag and retrieve my report, then start listing the numbers. After I finish, I interlace my fingers on the table and stare at him with so much dispassion I feel my face turning stone cold. "Last I checked, your brothels don't bring in half what I do. Last I checked, a member's worth is measured by how much he or she brings into the organization. Maybe we should double-check who belongs in the Vory and who doesn't."

He stands up, his round frame nearly bouncing with the effort, and points a finger at me. "You little—"

"Sit down," Vlad orders. "Show respect to your *Pakhan*, Kozlov."

Mikhail mumbles an apology and begrudgingly sits while still giving me the death glare.

"It's good that you're here, Rai. We have some business to discuss." Sergei speaks for the first time since I came in. There's a huskiness to his voice due to the cancer, and soon enough, it'll be noticeable to everyone.

"I have business to discuss, too, *Dvoyurodnyy Ded*."

Kirill scoffs under his breath at the affectionate way I addressed Granduncle.

My attention turns to him. "You have a problem?"

"None at all, Miss Sokolov." He pauses, readjusting his glasses with his middle finger. "Yet."

The threat behind his gesture doesn't escape me, so I counter using his subtle way. Still keeping eye contact, I slide the cup of coffee in front of me then crush a piece of sugar inside before it melts. "Good to know."

His brows furrow, and his most loyal soldier, Aleksander, stiffens behind him, his hand going to his gun. He has feminine features and a smaller frame for a guard, but he's as merciless as his direct boss.

He won't do anything, though, because they both know that at the sign of any danger, I won't hesitate to bring Kirill and his whole brigade down.

Sergei clears his throat, and I smile, pretending to drink from my coffee in a leisurely manner. My granduncle doesn't want me to provoke anyone in the brotherhood, not even if they belittle me.

So I do it behind his back.

What he doesn't know won't hurt him.

Damien hits my shoulder with his, grinning like we're close friends and he wants in on the secret.

"Fun in paradise?" He reaches for the pack of cigarettes in

front of him and retrieves one. Instead of lighting it, he places the lighter a breath away from it.

"None of your business," I counter.

Kirill's secret is mine and mine alone. If anyone else knows, it undermines the reason behind holding something over his head.

Adrian watches me for a beat, which means he's also caught on to the fact that something is going on.

Vlad shakes his head at me, too, and Igor keeps watching Kirill and me from above his cup of tea. The only one who's huffing and puffing like a damsel in distress is Mikhail. He's too focused on not wanting me at this table and didn't notice anything. The idiot.

His *boyevik* isn't stupid, though. While he stands like a board at his back, he's hearing and watching everything so he can report it all back to his boss later.

"We're here because there's a looming threat from the Irish." Sergei speaks in Russian, using a moderate tone. "Adrian's men have gathered intel that indicates they intend to attack the territories we rule with the Italians."

"Those fucking Irish." Mikhail snarls like the big bad wolf he thinks he is.

Vlad leans on the table, interlacing his fingers. "Rolan has always come strong against us, ever since he became the head of the Irish after his brother's death. He tried before but has never gotten so close. This time he seems to be going all in, even bringing in some of his allies from the small eastern European organized crime families."

"We wouldn't have had a problem with them if it weren't for your irrational attack, Damien," Igor says in a low and accusatory tone.

Damien raises his hands in the air, expression incredulous. "I was protecting my fucking soldiers, thank you very much."

"You were protecting your foolish pride," Kirill mutters.

"You always put us in war," Igor accuses.

"What's better than war when it's well deserved?" Damien lights his cigarette, takes a drag, and blows a cloud of smoke in the air. "It's not my fault you're too old to handle it anymore. How about letting your son inherit it if you've become such a bore?"

"It's called being cautious."

Damien yawns. "Which is another word for boring. You should try excitement sometimes."

"You should stop making us enemies we don't need," Kirill shoots back.

"Oh, fuck you. Rolan would've hit us anyway since his brother, sister-in-law and nephew were killed due to one of our attacks during Nikolai's times. It happened decades ago, but he's still after revenge."

"So you decided to give him the opening on a golden platter?" Igor snarls.

"I was only being a good sport and started the war before they could. You should thank me."

"Or punch you," Kirill says.

He and Igor gang up on Damien, and they get into an endless argument in intense Russian. Mikhail interrupts only to talk about how much money Damien's brigade is wasting, but he forgets to mention that even with the recurring attacks, Damien still brings in more than he ever will.

Sergei, Vlad, and I watch silently. Adrian, on the other hand, sips from his coffee, not even pretending to pay attention to them. It's like this is the last place he would rather be.

I agree with him on that front. While I don't like being left out, this war of testosterone always gets on my nerves, mainly because nothing useful comes out of it.

"Enough." Sergei finally puts an end to it, and they all fall silent. "It doesn't matter whose fault it is, because the fact remains that we're under threat."

"And our Italian allies aren't in much of a hurry to help," Vlad adds.

"*Blyad*," Mikhail curses. "Didn't they always hate the Irish? Besides, We have a deal."

Vlad pauses before his monotone voice fills the space. "They said the deal doesn't stand when we bring this on ourselves."

All eyes turn to Damien, who raises his hands in the air with feigned innocence. "Not my fault we didn't strengthen our relationship with the Italians before this. Hey, Adrian, aren't they your friends?"

The latter finishes sipping his coffee. "Why should my friends clean up your mess?"

"Come on. Do this for the brotherhood."

"I can ask around, but they probably won't grant enough manpower to ward off the Irish."

"How about the Triads? The Japanese?" Igor suggests. "They owe us a favor or two."

Kirill scratches his chin. "This isn't their war, so even if they offer help, it will be minimal."

"We will take what we can get," Damien says cheerfully, like he didn't land us all in this clusterfuck.

Vlad glares at him before he speaks to the group. "The Italians are still our biggest allies. If we don't have them all in, we might lose territories."

"Then we should force them in," I say.

"Who asked for your opinion, *Rayka*? Aren't you better off dressing dolls or something?" Mikhail smiles at me, and both Kirill and Damien snicker.

"I stopped dressing my dolls the day I outranked you in income, *Mikel*," I say with a smile. Since he keeps using the disrespectful version of my name, I use a wrong name for him, one that's even more diminutive.

Vlad's lips twitch, but he doesn't go as far as to smile. Damien nudges my shoulder, smiling wide.

Note to self: Don't sit next to Damien in the future.

"How should we force them?" Vlad asks me, bringing us back to the subject.

I place two pieces of sugar on the rim of the coffee cup, one more close to the edge than the other. "This one is us, because the Irish are targeting the brotherhood. The Italians are here." I motion at the other piece that's a bit behind. "If we're going down, we might as well bring them with us so they take this seriously."

"And how do you suggest we do that, little miss genius?" Mikhail asks.

"We can't make the Italians our enemies." Igor says this to me, but looks over to Adrian since he's the one who handles most of our outside PR.

"We will bring them in, not make enemies with them." I push the first piece of sugar. "If the Irish attack the Italians, even indirectly…" I pause for dramatic effect then jostle the cup causing the second piece of sugar to fall with a small plopping sound. "They will have no choice but to defend their territories and their honor."

"Do you suggest we betray our biggest allies?" Kirill stares at me as if I murdered a member of his family.

"I'm suggesting we don't take the hit when the Irish attack. If we lure them to the Italian territories, the chess pieces will take care of themselves. We can go and help after the damage is done."

"That way, we can reinforce our relationship with the Italians while dragging them into war with us," Vlad explains.

"Exactly." I push my coffee away because there's no way in hell I'll drink it now that it has so much sugar in it.

Igor, Adrian, and Damien remain silent, but Mikhail clears his throat and Kirill makes a face. They know I'm right and my plan is the best we have, but their male egos don't like the fact that a woman outsmarted them.

"Igor." Sergei speaks, and everyone at the table pays attention—including Adrian. "Work on getting as much manpower as possible from the Triads and the Japanese. Kirill and Mikhail, protect the territories, including the shared ones. We never know where they will hit next. Adrian, keep negotiating with the Italians."

For a second, I think he completely disregarded my plan. After all, he still wants Adrian to play nice with the Italians.

But then, my granduncle fixes his eyes on Vlad. "Use our spy in the Irish territories to figure out where they're going to hit next, and then, lure the Italians."

"Yes, Vor," the men say, and I sit up straighter in my chair. This is the first time Sergei has ever taken my suggestion seriously. Ever since I proved my worth in V Corp by snatching one deal after another, Sergei doesn't see me as Nikolai Sokolov's spoiled granddaughter whom he shouldn't have allowed into the brotherhood's meetings.

Damien raises a hand like an attention-seeking kid in class. "Umm, hello? What about me?"

"You stay put and protect your territory." Sergei looks at him with his light green eyes. He might have always come second compared to *Dedushka*, but Sergei has a wise quality to him that he gained over the years he stood by my grandfather's side. He knows what he's doing, and he's never allowed his sickness to get in the way of leading the brotherhood.

"Come on, *Pakhan*, I can do something," Damien argues.

"And make it worse," Igor mutters.

Damien clicks his tongue at him. He has no such thing as respect for the seniors in the Vory. He has his way and his crazy super weird vision, and it seems that's the only thing he needs.

"If you lose one of your territories, it would be cut off from your brigade, Orlov," Sergei addresses Damien by his last name. "Am I making myself clear?"

"Crystal," Damien mutters.

"Rai." My granduncle's attention turns to me.

"Yes?"

"You will funnel the necessary finances to any brigade that has a shortage."

"I will only do that after I see their numbers."

"You won't see my fucking numbers." Mikhail is the first to protest.

I smile sweetly at him. "Then you won't get a single dime from V Corp."

"You don't own V Corp."

"And neither do you. I will not be giving away money like candy. I need the accountability report to know everyone's needs, and I expect everyone to return the funds as soon as you're bringing in profit again. V Corp is not your one-way bank."

"And if we don't?" Kirill raises a brow.

"Simple. The difference will be cut off from your company shares. You're not the only shareholders in V Corp I need to worry about. The money isn't yours to confiscate any time and without repercussions."

"*Pakhan?*" Igor cuts Mikhail off before he can most likely curse me.

"You will all provide V Corp with numbers so every brigade is treated equally," Sergei says. "We will talk about returning the funds at a later date."

I stare at Granduncle, but he already issued his order and he won't go back on it. The asshole Mikhail smiles at me like a petty child with issues.

I'm fuming on the inside, but I keep my uptight position on the outside.

"Now that we agree on that, we will move to the next topic." Sergei clears his throat to get everyone's attention. "I served the brotherhood with my life, sweat, and blood, just like you. But as everyone knows, I'm getting old. There will be a time where I will have to step down as *Pakhan*."

I swallow as the weight of his words falls on me. Is this why everyone is here, Adrian included? Sergei isn't possibly planning to tell them about his cancer, right?

"I have decided that the future *Pakhan* will be a member of the elite group. I will consider everyone carefully for the next few months, and when it's time to choose someone, it will be one of you."

They straighten in their seats, the greed for power filling some of their eyes. The fire burning inside me threatens to spill like a volcano ready to eradicate anything in its path.

I can't believe Sergei is giving away the family legacy to these wolves so easily.

"However, I want my daughter married into one of your families. Consider it a blessing in advance."

Mikhail moves in his seat, ready to suggest his asshole sons, but I cut him off. "No."

Vlad shakes his head at me, probably at the tone I used.

"What do you mean by 'no'?" Sergei's voice has an edge to it that declares his word is the first and last. I might be his grandniece, but family knows better than to defy him in front of the members of the brotherhood.

"No, Anastasia isn't ready to get married yet." I smooth my tone. "She knows nothing about becoming a wife."

"And whose fault is that?" Igor mutters. "You've been sheltering her like she's a stray kitten."

That's because she needs sheltering in this world, but I don't say that since it'll most definitely be used against me. I can't allow myself any loopholes, even if it's Ana.

"You want the Sokolov name to live on, right?" I gulp. "I will do it."

"Color me surprised! I thought you'd be a spinster for life." Damien pauses dramatically, then mimics a claw with his hand. "Marry me, tigress."

"In your dreams, asshole."

"You will really get married?" Sergei asks in an unsure tone.

"Yes, but I get to choose."

My granduncle motions ahead. "Then choose."

"Poor motherfucker," Kirill mutters under his breath.

"Careful, or I might choose you," I taunt, even though that will never happen. This table is full of alpha assholes who will either lock me up or make me go crazy or both.

"Spare us the suspense and choose." Damien rubs his hands together. "Here's a hint. Me."

"I said, not you." My gaze roams until it lands on Kirill. He pauses, probably thinking I will go on with my threat. "Not Kirill either, for *reasons*. He can't handle me."

He fixes his glasses and flips me off discreetly. I ignore him and continue on.

"Not Vlad. He's like my brother. Obviously not Adrian, because he's already married—unless we can move to a country that allows a second wife?"

His expression remains the same. "I'm flattered, but I'm going to decline the offer, Miss Sokolov."

"Pity." I pretend to be bummed.

"That leaves Mikhail and Igor's sons," Sergei says.

I meet Mikhail's gaze with a smile. "You have two sons, right?"

"I do."

"Last I checked, they were boys."

"They grew up. My eldest is thirty."

"Age doesn't mean maturity. They're still boys. I wonder where they got that from."

"Rai." It's Sergei who reprimands me. "That clearly eliminates Mikhail's offspring, which leaves you with Igor's. We will go with the eldest, Alexei."

"Wait—no." My eyes widen despite myself. Alexei is even worse than Igor, and he's someone I'm definitely more wary of than his father. I can't marry him. He's a traditionalist and strict to a fucking fault.

He'll smother me before I know it.

Maybe I should've picked one of Mikhail's idiot sons after all, but that would mean having the asshole as a father-in-law. No thanks. He hates me enough without family relations.

Dammit. How did I get myself cornered with Alexei? *Think, Rai, think.* I need to get myself out of this.

"Alexei isn't my eldest, *Pakhan*." Igor's calm voice cuts into my thoughts. "I have finally found my long-lost eldest son who we thought we lost in a car crash. In fact, I meant to introduce him to you today. He's waiting outside."

"Congratulations, Igor," Sergei says without his usual note of firmness.

The others follow suit, and he thanks them one by one, even though his expression remains the same.

"Let him in," my granduncle orders after they finish.

Igor motions at his guard. He nods once, then goes out of the room.

Long-lost son? I've heard stories about how Igor lost his firstborn thirty years ago during one of his trips to Europe. *Dedushka* told me it changed the man forever. There was an Igor before losing his son and another one after. I didn't know there was a chance his firstborn was still alive. Does this mean he knows nothing of the brotherhood?

This is my chance to latch onto him and use him as a puppet, as per my plan with Vlad. I stare at the latter, and we share a moment of understanding. I soon cut off eye contact because Adrian and Kirill are watching us.

I smile so big I feel the strain in my cheeks. "Igor's eldest it is, *Dvoyurodnyy Ded*."

"I'm honored," Igor says, more to Sergei than to me.

The door opens and in comes Igor's guard, followed by his boss's son.

My smile falls when the *boyevik* takes his place behind his leader, revealing the newcomer.

Blood drains from my face and my smile falters as I stare into the eyes I never thought I would ever see again.

But here he is.

Igor's son, the husband I just willingly chose, is none other than the one who stabbed my heart then walked all over it.

Kyle fucking Hunter.

FOUR

Kyle

I STAND IN FRONT OF THE PEOPLE WHOM I ONCE belonged to, the people who opened their doors for me when I was twenty-six because Nikolai, the previous Pakhan, took a special liking to me.

Now it's different.

Now, the tension rolls in the air like a whip ready to split my back open.

Most of these men used to like me because, well, I was the most efficient hitman in the Bratva. None of their soldiers could come close to my skills. I did all their dirty work and sniped down people they needed taken care of.

While I was in their good graces before, the fact that I left for years doesn't sit well with any of them. No one is allowed to leave the brotherhood—at least, not alive. The only resignation is death.

My gaze trails from the head of the table, Sergei—Nikolai's

youngest brother—to his elite group, who are all watching me peculiarly, all except for Daddy dearest, Igor, since he already knows about this.

Oh, and her.

I tilt my head to the side to get a better view of my little mafia princess. She's actually sitting with the inner circle. That's progress she must be proud of.

Rai is not so little anymore, though. Her face has aged and lost the few remains of innocence she used to hold on to in her grandfather's time. Now, she appears like a cold, white statue with her light blonde hair and fair skin.

Her face's contours are sharp, but it appears that way due to her makeup. It's like she's in disguise. Her lips are painted a nude color, and her eyeliner is like a preview of witch makeup for Halloween. Her posture is straight, flat, almost like she can't move or control her limbs.

She's nothing like the Rai who used to run all over the place and bug Nikolai so he would come out with her to the garden, or the Rai who used to pester Vladimir and me so we would teach her how to shoot.

It's like the girl inside was taken away and this frigid woman was put in on her behalf.

Her eyes widen when they meet mine, though. It's the only reaction she shows in her mute state, and it's the only one I need.

There's always been something mystical about Rai's eyes. They're blue, but not quite. There are situations where they darken like the sea in the middle of the storm, and there are times where they lighten to a clear summer sky. Then, there are instances like now where they're caught in the middle, not sure if they want to wreak havoc or simply let it go.

Slowly, the widening disappears and the blue of her eyes turns pitch-black. I smile to myself. Of course, Rai wouldn't choose to let go. She's the epitome of determination and infuriating stubbornness.

Her Russian half always gets the better of her. It doesn't matter that she spent the first twelve years of her life with her American father. The moment she joined her grandfather, she shed away the person from the past and completely embraced this lifestyle.

"What are you doing here?" It's Damien who asks first, with subtle aggression. "You escaped the Bratva when you knew the punishment." He stands up and points a gun at my chest. "If you came to your death with your own feet, I'm happy to grant you your wish."

Igor stands up and slides in front of me, blocking Damien's gun. My 'father' is old and has a bad knee that bothers him in the winters and when it rains—as he used to complain to Nikolai—but he's tall and broad with a white beard that he keeps trimmed. Igor might not be the most famous king— mainly because Damien is an attention whore—but he has the charisma and the critical mind that has kept him in a position of power for decades.

He's the best at not only picking his battles, but also at winning them. In a way, he's the best ally to have in the Bratva. The others are elusive as fuck.

"Kyle is my son. You are not allowed to touch him."

"Just because he's your son, doesn't mean he's exempt from the rules." It's Rai who speaks in her detached, cold tone. "Betraying the brotherhood is punishable by death."

Well, is that an *ouch* moment, or what? Even though I expected this reaction from all of them, for some reason, I never thought Rai would voice her thoughts concerning me this directly.

"If you hurt a hair on his head," Igor says to Damien, "I hope you're ready for an internal war."

"There will be no internal war," Sergei chimes in.

"You heard him," I whisper to Damien. "So how about you sit the fuck down?"

He glares at me, his finger pressing on the trigger. Honestly? He's so bloody unpredictable he might actually shoot me right here and now. Anything with the word 'war' in it is fun and games to Damien instead of a threat. He gets off on the high more than anyone else in this room.

Aside from me, of course.

"Sit down, Damien," Sergei orders.

Damien complies, begrudgingly hiding his gun away, because if he keeps it out, it's disrespectful to the *Pakhan*.

Igor remains by my side, as if he suspects one of the others will stand and repeat Damien's show.

My gaze slides to Rai, who's glaring at me with malice so deep, as if I murdered her family and ate their remains.

Anger is good. Anger will keep her on her toes around me, which is exactly what she needs to do.

"Kyle," Sergei calls my name.

I face him with a smile. "Yes, *Pakhan*."

"I'm not your *Pakhan*."

"Yet?" I grin.

His grim expression remains the same. "You have one chance to explain yourself. Use it well."

"Hmm, where do we start?" I pretend to be deep in thought. "When Nikolai brought me in, I was always an independent hitman, you know. I do clean hits, then go away until it's time for the next job. It was freelance work. Technically, I didn't belong to the Vory, and *technically*, I didn't leave it."

Damien curses me in Russian under his breath, and I pretend I don't understand. "English, please. My Russian is bad as hell."

"Where have you been?" Sergei asks.

"We looked a long time for you," Kirill declares with his almost perfect American accent. He and Mikhail don't want to get on Igor's bad side; that's why they've kept their mouths shut this entire time. It's the bastard Damien who doesn't give a fuck about anyone.

"I went on a discovery journey," I say in a serene tone.

"A discovery journey?" Rai mutters through gritted teeth. "Are you making fun of us?"

"I really did go through it, Princess." I wrap an arm around Igor's shoulder. "I was looking for my family. Who knew he was exactly where I left them? It was such a coincidence that I was with the Bratva before I knew who my family was. I guess I take after my father unknowingly."

"I'm curious," Kirill muses. "How did you end up in England when you were young?"

"Ah, that. I lost my memories from childhood and was adopted by my assassin friends." I motion at Adrian. "He knows my background; he's the one who did a check on me before Nikolai recruited me."

Adrian takes a sip of his drink. "He was an orphan who was brought up by reputable hitmen."

I grin, snapping my fingers. "Exactly. But I always wanted to find my real family."

"It took you thirty years to do that?" Damien questions.

"You would be surprised how long it takes to track down an accident that happened decades ago, especially since I didn't have much info to go on and was busy with killing and stuff. Seven years ago, I decided to dedicate my time to finding my family. That's why I left."

"And you spent seven years searching for your family?" Rai shoots back.

"It's a long, tiresome journey. Do you want a play-by-play account?"

She ignores me and takes a sip of her coffee then grimaces and slides it away on the table.

Damien grabs another cigarette and shoves it in his mouth before he speaks. "I say he can't be accepted back in."

"I also say he can't be part of the brotherhood anymore." She agrees with him, and my jaw tightens underneath the welcoming smile. "This is not a child's playground where he can waltz in and leave as he wishes. Vlad?"

Vladimir, who has been silent, watching the scene with Adrian, releases a breath. "Kyle was given the title of a Vor by the previous *Pakhan*. We can't simply get rid of him as if he never existed."

"Vlad!" Rai hisses, but he lets out a grunt in response.

"Yeah, Vor." I point a thumb at myself. "That's me, remember?"

"Let's vote," Sergei finally says. "Those who want Kyle punished and exiled, raise your hand."

Damien and Rai do so at the same time. I smile on the outside, but the need to shake her the fuck up grips me out of nowhere. Since when is she on that arsehole's side?

She keeps glaring at Vladimir, probably so he will follow her lead, but he doesn't.

"Now, those in favor of Kyle returning to the brotherhood, raise your hand," Sergei says in his calm, very Russian-accented speech.

Igor raises his hand first, then Kirill and Mikhail follow. Vlad and Adrian are next. Those two are the smartest. They know my skills are more important than the brotherhood's laws.

Sergei raises his hand last, crushing Rai and Damien by six to two. When they all drop their hands, he says, "Welcome back to the Vory, Kyle. If you leave this time, you'll be punished."

I make a cross sign and grin. "I'll serve the brotherhood until death does us part, cross my heart and hope to die."

Rai stands up, her face reddening underneath the thick layers of makeup. "If you'll excuse me."

"Wait." Sergei stops her before she takes a step. "You agreed to marry Igor's eldest son, and he is here now."

Jackpot.

"You agreed to marry me?" I pretend to be surprised. "I thought it was going to be Anastasia."

"Rai volunteered to get married on Anastasia's behalf," Igor explains.

As I thought she would. When I got Igor to plant the seed in Sergei's head about marrying Anastasia off, I figured it'd somehow come down to this. It doesn't take a genius to know Rai would sacrifice herself for the girl she's been sheltering ever since they were kids.

"I..." She trails off, probably wanting to backpedal, but she realizes the highest principle in the brotherhood is to keep your word. The moment you lose that, no one will respect you.

"Have you changed your mind?" I push.

"No." She meets my gaze with her lethal one. "I'm a Sokolov, and we keep our word."

Sergei nods in agreement with a hint of pride at his grand-niece. "It's settled then. Bring me the dowry, Igor."

"Will do, *Pakhan*."

Rai looks like she's about to throw up, but she kisses Sergei's knuckles and leaves, the sound of her heels loud and confident in the silence of the room.

I smile as the door closes behind her. The second part of the plan is done. Time to move to the third.

I grin at Sergei. "If you'll excuse me, I need a word with my fiancée."

FIVE

Rai

M Y HEARTBEAT IS ABOUT TO EXPLODE INTO HOT lava as I march down the hall.

Ruslan tells me he'll get the car ready and I give a nod as he leaves before me. I remind myself to greet the staff back when I pass them by so I don't seem like an arrogant bitch. I don't mind being that way with the members of the brotherhood, but the staff is another story.

Both Dad and *Dedushka* taught me to respect those beneath me and to burn those against me.

I stop at the corner to catch my ragged breaths. My chest rises and falls so hard, almost like I'm coming out from a run.

Only, the scene I witnessed inside was worse than a run. It was a whole nightmarish marathon.

My legs shake no matter how much I try to force them to remain steady. It's like they're done holding me up for the day.

The gold-rimmed pillar turns blurry, and I quickly wipe the evidence of frustration from my eyes.

It's done. It's over.

To be part of the brotherhood means to always keep your word. I can't get out of this marriage, even if I want to.

It's already cemented and ready to be sealed.

Why does it feel like there's something breaking and resurrecting in my heart at the same time? It shouldn't be this way. I should be plotting a heinous murder scene where Kyle will be the victim. Maybe then, this raging fire inside me would finally ebb. Not only that, but I would also manage to save myself from this marriage.

A presence appears at my back, his warmth and faint clean scent mixed with mint enveloping me from the tip of my head to my toes. Before I can turn around, his hot breaths tease the lobe of my ear as he whispers in a low seductive British accent, "You voted for punishment. Is that your kink, Princess?"

I swing around and raise my hand at the same time, ready to smack him. But he holds my wrist prisoner before I can touch him.

It might have been seven years since he left, but there's nothing in this world that can make me forget what it feels like to be this close to Kyle.

He should be around thirty-five now, but he's no different than the twenty-eight-year-old man I used to know once upon a time. The hitman who joked around with everyone but still retreated to the shadows when necessary. The assassin who killed with no remorse and taught me to never hesitate.

He's taller than me, but he's not too broad like Vlad or Kirill. His body, while muscular, is lean, fit, and agile, allowing him to move silently like a panther. It's impossible to hear his movements unless he makes himself noticeable.

His black suit pants are tight against his strong thighs and complement his long legs. He's wearing a white shirt but no tie. He never wore those, not even at official occasions or banquets organized by the brotherhood. It's like he was born to be a rebel and takes great pride in it.

Kyle's face is all sharp edges and straight lines like he's a model in some magazine. His eyes, though? They might appear cobalt blue, but they're muted, unfeeling, almost like they're colorless. They're one of the reasons why it took me so long to trust him before. It always felt like a fortress was hidden behind the façade and he never let his true self out—or maybe his true self is the person who kills people without blinking.

He holds my wrist in his hand, stroking the pulse point ever so softly. "Violent as usual, I see."

I yank my wrist away. "Murderous, too, in case you want to try."

"You're so cruel, Princess." He drawls in that accent that makes everything sound seductive. This asshole shouldn't be allowed such a beautiful accent.

"Stop calling me that. I'm not a spoiled little princess anymore."

"Mmm. I see you snatched your place within the elite group—I'm proud of you."

My breath catches in my throat like a rusty knife ready to cut. Undecipherable emotions attempt to flood me all at once, but I block them out. "I don't need you to be proud of me."

"Doesn't make me any less proud."

He needs to stop saying the words I foolishly waited a long time to hear after *Dedushka*'s death. Why is he, of all people, is speaking them?

He's a traitor. He's nothing.

"So, marriage, huh?" He grins. "Is this going to be fun, or what?"

"No."

"No?"

"You didn't agree to this in front of Sergei yet. You can go back in there and tell them you don't want to marry me."

He leans close so his presence towers over me, confiscating any type of personal space I could have. "But I do want to marry you."

"Why the hell would you?"

"Hmm." He grabs my chin between his thumb and forefinger and slightly tilts my head back. The touch is barely-there, but it feels so intimate, as if he's forging a path into my deepest, darkest parts. "For your beautiful eyes."

He takes another step forward so his front nearly grazes mine. The feeling of being completely taken by something overwhelms me. It's like losing control of my actions, emotions, and everything in between.

I can't lose control. That's the only thing that's keeping me high enough so no one can reach inside me, let alone touch me.

Kyle can't come back after seven years and shake my control just like that. So I push him away, panting.

"I hate you." I tell him the words I've kept quenching for freaking years. "I would never marry you if it were up to me."

Kyle lets his hands fall to his sides. "Would you have married Damien? Or how about Vlad?"

"Gladly. Anyone but you."

He smirks, but instead of taunting, it appears downright sinister, almost as if he's bottling something else behind the gesture. "Unfortunately, you're stuck with me."

"Not if you tell Sergei no."

"Why would I?"

"Are you fucking serious?" I yell.

"Keep your voice down." He advances toward me again, this time flattening his hands on either side of my face, caging me against the wall. "And yes, I'm dead serious. I will make you my wife."

"In your dreams."

"Fine with me. But will it be fine with you?"

"What are you talking about?"

"If it's not you, Anastasia will do. I heard she grew up into a fine young lady."

"Don't you dare, Kyle."

"It's easy. You already took her place in front of the others, so you might as well continue."

"You will keep your filthy hands far away from Ana."

"Filthy hands, huh?" He wraps a hand around my throat, his long fingers closing firmly, but not tightly, around my neck. I can still breathe, but each intake is torturous, as if I'm borrowing air from my life essence.

The familiarity of the gesture keeps me pinned in place, almost like he hit a button of sorts and I couldn't move even if I wanted to. There has always been something special about his hands. His fingers appear long and masculine, like a gentleman's, but in reality, they're the same fingers that've pulled countless triggers without hesitation.

A killer's hands, and a very heartless one at that.

His head lowers so his hot lips meet my ear. "You didn't think they were filthy when they taught you how to kill."

"Let me go." I meant to snap, to yell, but my voice comes out low and almost wounded.

"Then I guess these filthy hands will be all over Ana."

"Not if I kill you first." I glare at his unfeeling, expressionless eyes.

"You think you can kill me? That's grand coming from you."

"You think I can't?"

"Not unless you're ready to be brought down with me. You know me, Princess, I give back as much as I take."

"So do I."

"Really? How so?"

"You think I don't know you're playing a game right now?"

He smirks, and this time, it's mischievous. "What type of game?"

"A power game. You left the Vory for a reason and came back for a reason."

"What type of reason?"

"I don't know yet, but I will find out."

"Until then, I will marry Ana."

"No way in hell."

His face turns blank as he tightens his hold on my neck as if to drive the point home. "Then do us all a favor and stop being fucking stubborn."

I meet his unfeeling eyes with my grudge-filled ones. I try not to be angry because anger makes me do stupid things. Anger drives me out of my element and gives my opponent the upper hand.

I'm cornered into this no matter how much I try to get away from it. I have no doubt that Kyle will move on to Anastasia if I refuse him. His purpose isn't me; it's the power he can get by finding a way into the Sokolov family, and until he achieves his goal, he won't stop. Ever.

So instead of fighting him head-on in a losing battle, I choose to retreat to reform my line.

"Fine. Let me go."

"Does this mean you agree?"

"Yes," I manage through gritted teeth.

He releases me, but doesn't step back as he whispers, "For better or worse."

"Fuck you."

He chuckles, the sound echoing around us like a sonata. I try not to get caught up in how handsome he looks when he laughs, when his angular features ease and he appears every bit the model on the cover of a GQ magazine.

After his fit ends, Kyle reaches out a hand and traces a finger over my bottom lip. "I will take good care of you, Princess."

The joke's on him.

I'll forget about whatever foolishness I felt for him in the past, because that? It was a big fat lie. Instead, I'm going to get under Kyle Hunter's skin so deep, exploit his power, and then use it against him.

When the hurricane hits him out of nowhere, he'll understand why storms are named after women.

SIX

Kyle

I STARE AT RAI'S BACK AS SHE LEAVES THE HOUSE. HER steps are confident and wide, with a gentle sway of her hips I'm sure she doesn't even notice having.

Beneath the ice-cold exterior, there's a feminine side she crushed and burned before it was able to blossom.

But it's not completely dead. Not even close.

My lips twitch at the prospect of thrusting myself into her life and exploiting those hidden parts of her, the ones kept under lock and key.

My gaze follows her all the way to the entrance even though one of her most loyal soldiers, Katia, meets her and accompanies her outside.

And yes, only Rai would specifically choose a woman as one of her closest guards. She always did things differently while flipping the world her middle finger.

I'll be the exception in that world.

She thinks she can go to war with me, but what she doesn't know is that the war already started a long time ago. Her cards were already dealt, and all she can do is play her role as previously planned.

It would be a shame to see her princess eyes shed tears, but what's victory without sacrifices, huh?

Still...I rub my thumb against my forefinger, relishing the feel of her skin against mine. She's so soft, like untarnished silk, and according to the red marks that remained on her neck after I released her, she might bruise easily, too. No idea why that fact excites me, but it does. It could be my depraved nature, or the simple fact that I always liked breaking things, ruining them, then watching them shatter in the wake of their destruction.

People become raw in that state and show their truest, most hidden tendencies.

Rai will join the list as my latest acquisition. Sure, it won't be easy considering the way she stabbed me with those darkened eyes as if that's her favorite sport.

My dick strains against my trousers as I recall the feel of her pulse beneath my hand when I held her throat. Rai might act like she's all that, but in that very moment, her breathing hitched and I saw a hint of her muted desires.

Desires I would be more than happy to explore.

I place a hand in the pocket of my pants and turn around, silently heading back to the dining room. I stop at the corner when I spot the four kings and Vladimir leaving along with their guards.

That only leaves Sergei and Adrian inside, which means juicy business.

I wait until the front of the room is empty then I approach slowly. I don't eavesdrop like an idiot in front of the room. That will give me away to any of the guards stationed nearby.

Instead, I stand in front of the hall mirror, retrieve my

in-ear piece, plug it deep inside so it's not noticeable, and then tap it. I got this gadget from my friend's most talented hackers. The guards who sweep daily for bugs can't for the life of them find it because it doesn't really exist. It appears like a normal lamp wire.

There's a small rustle from the other side before the voices filter in.

"What's so urgent that needed all the others gone?" Sergei asks in Russian, voice low and tone perturbed.

"You're the only one I trust with this information, *Pakhan*, especially considering the current circumstances." Adrian, who's usually so silent you forget his voice, continues in the same language. "Someone is stealing from the brotherhood."

"What?" Sergei hisses. "Who has the balls to steal from us when they know the penalty is death? Is it one of our own?"

"I'm not sure yet. I still need to run background checks so I know the exact numbers. What I'm certain about is that a sum has been strategically transferred from V Corp to multiple accounts abroad for the last year. At first, I chalked it up to something unimportant, but in total, it's close to one hundred thousand dollars."

"Is it not related to the money laundering?"

"No. That is separate."

"What do you suggest we do?" Sergei throws the ball completely into Adrian's court, which isn't so surprising considering he's responsible for the Bratva's security. Not only that, he's also the genius mastermind of this brotherhood. The reason why they always slip through the authorities' hands isn't because of the four kings' ruthlessness; it's because of Adrian's brains and strategic thinking. He usually finds the right influential men who will give them immunity.

He predicts solutions to events that haven't happened yet, and that's why he's the best ally I currently have. However, that doesn't change the fact that he will turn into my worst enemy in the future. As much as he keeps away from the limelight, Adrian's loyal to this fucking brotherhood to a fault.

"Let Rai collect all the brigades' financial reports and then send me a copy," he says to Sergei. "I will be able to figure out if it's from the inside."

"You got it."

"I will also need V Corp's numbers."

"Are you suspecting Rai?" Sergei's voice hardens, taking offense on behalf of his grandniece.

"I suspect everyone, *Pakhan*. Family is not exempt from this. If my suspicions are correct, I—"

I cut off the feed on my own when I feel a presence watching me from the corner, then I pretend to button my shirt in front of the mirror, whistling joyfully.

"What are you doing here?" Vladimir stands in front of me, trying to intimidate me with his tall and broad frame.

Poor Vladimir doesn't know that I could stab him in the throat in a heartbeat and he wouldn't have a chance.

But that would be unnecessary violence, especially at a time like this.

So I grin at him. "What does it look like I'm doing? Looking at how handsome I am while waiting for my father."

"Igor left."

"Oh, he did? I didn't know that since, you know, I was talking to Rai."

He steps in and grabs me by the collar of my shirt. "Hurt a hair on her head and I will rip your heart out."

I push him away, still smiling. "I see you're still loyal to the Sokolovs—nice. But you don't have to threaten me. I intend to cooperate with her."

He narrows his ghostly eyes. "Cooperate how?"

It's my turn to get in his face. "It's a husband-and-wife matter. Stay out of it."

I don't know why I say that. Since I'm on a mission to be

everyone's favorite, I don't want to provoke Vladimir. However, the way she was always close to him—and apparently, still is—pisses me off to no end.

Ask me why it pisses me off. Go ahead.

The answer is, I have no fucking clue, which is even more infuriating.

I step past Vladimir to leave when he says, "She's not your wife yet."

Stopping, I meet his flat gaze with mine. "She will be."

I feel the words instead of just saying them, because there's no doubt in my mind that she will be my wife. It's not even completely because of the plan.

Rai will fall to her knees in front of me.

Just like everyone else will.

SEVEN

Rai

CONCENTRATION ESCAPES ME FOR THE REST OF THE day at work. I can't get my mind to focus no matter how much I try. I even go as far as taking breaks to meditate, but that doesn't work either.

So I sit in my office, head lying back on the top of my leather chair as I stare at the library across from me.

Despite having the worst college experience, where I had to attend most classes online, I got my degree in business management. I didn't need *Dedushka*'s last name to accomplish that. I did it on my own and with my own effort.

It took me so much to come this far, and yet I'm still expected to take a husband. Either that or Anastasia will pay the price. Either that or this position will eventually be snatched away from me.

I'm not a fool. I know I only rank so high because Granduncle is in power. The moment he's gone, I'll be kicked out or demoted, and I can't do anything about it because of my damn gender.

My phone vibrates, and I retrieve it. An automatic smile paints my lips when I see the name flashing on the video call. She's exactly what I need under the circumstances.

I straighten and answer with a smile. The exact replica of my face greets me. Well, almost exact. My identical twin sister has her hair loose to her shoulders, and she has pink lipstick on like the girly girl she is.

"Hey, Rei."

"Hi, Rai! Look who wants to say hello to his aunty." The screen shakes a little before she steadies it again, holding a tiny human on her lap.

He has his mom's light hair, but his eyes are a deep forest green like his father's.

Reina smiles at him. "Say hi, Gareth."

My heart squeezes at the way she named him after Dad. It's like he gets to live another life after his sudden and heartbreaking death.

"Hi, Aunty." He grins, showing his baby teeth, and makes a kissing sound. "Miss you!"

"Hear the boy?" Reina scowls at the camera. "It's been exactly six weeks since we last saw you."

"You're counting?"

"Damn right I'm counting. You're my only family, Rai."

"No, I'm not. You have Asher and Gareth. Also, Asher's father treats you like his daughter."

"None of them are my twin sister."

"You know I can't meet you often, Rei. It's for you and your family's security."

They're already using Anastasia against me, and while I can't send her away because of who her father is, I can at least save Reina.

No one but Granduncle and Vlad knows she exists. Wait,

no—Kyle helped me in saving her from Ivan's coup seven years ago, and therefore, he's well aware of her.

Shit. That's one more reason to keep Reina as far away as possible.

I was feeling safe concerning her because Sergei would never hurt *Dedushka*'s other granddaughter, but Kyle is another story. He won't hesitate to use every weapon in his arsenal.

"I know." She releases a breath, stroking Gareth's hair as he runs a car toy along her thigh. "Sometimes I wish I took your place."

"Don't say that. We both ended up where we should've."

"Did we, though? Maybe it would've been different if I were the one who went to Grandpa's side."

Mom and Dad separated when we were born because *Dedushka* didn't approve of her union with an American, even though he was a rich businessman.

Our parents decided to split my twin sister and me. Dad took me, and my birth name was Reina Ellis. Mom took my sister, whose birth name was Rai Sokolov.

While I was raised in a safe and loving entourage with Dad, Mom and my sister were on the run from *Dedushka* and his men their entire lives.

Mom didn't want her to live the sheltered mafia princess life she had to endure. When we were twelve, Mom came and took me from school so we could leave the country. *Dedushka* was getting closer to catching her, and she didn't feel like Dad could keep me safe.

That was the first time I met my mother and the second half of me—my sister.

We spent the most excruciating month on the run, but it was the most exciting, too. I got to know Reina—Rai then—and my mom, whom I'd constantly asked Dad about.

But then, they found us. They weren't only *Dedushka*'s

men, though. Ivan was also there, and he planned to eradicate every last Sokolov offspring so he could rule.

My sister and I were running, but we heard the gunshot that took Mom away. Ivan disguised it as suicide, but I know he killed my mom.

Back then, I gave my sister my name and told her to go to Dad and live my life with him. Then I stepped in front of Ivan and Mikhail and told them, "I'm Rai Sokolov."

Despite being scared of what they could've possibly done to me, I never lowered my head or cut off eye contact. Dad taught me to never act like I'm wrong when I'm right.

That was the day my sister and I swapped places. Ever since then, I became Rai Sokolov and she is Reina Ellis—well, Reina Carson now.

Ivan wanted to kill me as he did with Mom, but a younger Mikhail snatched me from his hands and told him that the *Pakhan* wanted me alive. Needless to say, Mikhail must regret saving me every day now.

Dedushka and I didn't always get along. If anything, I yelled and screamed and scratched his beard for how he sent his men to kill my mom. He said that he only wanted to bring her home, and that he never wished for his only daughter to die. It took me months to believe how genuine he was, and I wanted to tell him that Ivan was the one who killed Mom, but I didn't, because I had no evidence and a practical man like my grandfather only believed in evidence. Besides, Ivan would've sold me in the black market before I could endanger his position at the time.

A while later, my grandfather sat in front of him and told me the words that snapped me into focus. "The only way to protect yourself, your sister, and your father is to become powerful."

Since then, I realized that I needed to take advantage of his power. Over time, I saw how rightful Nikolai Sokolov actually was, and how much my mother's death ate at his soul. He often said that he regretted not being the safety she needed and that I was his second chance.

Just like that, my life became different—especially from that of my twin sister.

When I keep my distance from her, like now, she often says stupid things, like maybe she should've kept her name. My poor sister doesn't know that she would be eaten alive in my world. She wouldn't be able to live her event-free life with her hotshot lawyer husband.

I sit upright. "Yeah, different, as in you would be dead, Reina."

"Are you telling me you're not heading there yourself?" Her voice catches, eyes filling with tears. "I'm worried about you."

"Don't be. I can take care of myself."

"What if something happens and you can't? Who will take care of you then?"

"I have my man and woman. You met them."

"Ruslan and Katia are your guards, not your family."

"Hey, they are. Don't go insulting my right and left hands."

She scoffs. "I don't know if I should laugh or be sad that you consider your guards your family."

"It's because they're loyal, Rei."

She shakes her head. Right then, Gareth jumps from her lap and runs toward the door where his father comes in.

Asher scoops him in his arms and tickles his tummy, making him break out in uncontrollable giggles.

Reina's husband is tall and handsome with dark hair and a broad build that he's maintained since playing football in high school. He's wearing a beige suit that gives him an approachable yet firm edge.

The camera moves a little when Asher lowers his head and captures Reina's mouth in a kiss. It's not only a peck or a mere brush of lips against lips. He goes all the way in, making her moan as she pushes away from him, cheeks flaming. "I'm talking to Rai, Ash."

Asher grins at the camera, his green eyes twinkling. "Hey, Rai."

"Hey, Asher," I say in a tone that suggests I wasn't the least bit affected by their PDA, but sometimes, it gets to me in ways I can't explain.

All I'm sure about is that I need to protect the scene in front of me, Reina and her happy family. At least one of us needs to have that. One of us needs to love with all her heart as Dad taught us to.

Reina struggled for years to find her happy ending, and it's my mission to make sure it continues.

There's a knock on the door before Vlad waltzes in with both Ruslan and Katia. Right—I called this meeting.

"Listen, I've got to go," I say, then hang up before Reina can say anything. Now that Asher is around, she won't be too focused on bugging me about paying them a visit.

I join the other three in the sitting area across from my desk. Ruslan remains standing because he's too into that ridiculous rule about respecting hierarchy. It's not necessarily about me, but it's about Vlad. He would never, and I mean ever, sit in his presence.

Katia heads to the cabinet to fix us drinks. She's a fit, tall woman with dark brown hair she keeps gathered in a ponytail.

Her high cheekbones and freckled cheeks give her a distinctive look that can be adorable if only she loses the serious expression. She and Ruslan are cut from the same cloth.

"You don't have to make drinks," I tell her.

"Let me, miss."

I shake my head as I flop opposite Vlad. The reason I trust those two with my life isn't that they're some guards *Dedushka* picked for me. No.

Ruslan has been with me since Grandpa's time, but only

because I handpicked him from the fighting rings myself. He was only twenty then, two years older than me, and won all his fights. I used to go with *Dedushka* to watch the underground fights and always kept an eye on 'The Machine', as they called him. In one of the matches, he had a head injury and was about to be taken out by his trainer like a dog. However, I stepped in and punched that trainer in the face, telling him if he didn't respect his fighters, he didn't deserve to be part of the brotherhood. *Dedushka* agreed. The trainer was out. Ruslan retired and asked *Dedushka* if he could become my guard.

Katia came after Grandpa's death. She was smuggled in from Russia in a dirty container with drugs in her ass and was destined to become a whore in Mikhail's brothels.

Since I was making it my mission to intercept Mikhail's shipments and free as many women as I could, Katia happened to be one of those whom I was able to help out.

In order to save her from Mikhail's rotten hands, I kept her close. Then I accidentally saw her training in kung fu and found out she has a black belt. She was sold to the mafia for a debt her dead father couldn't pay.

Since then, these two have been the pillars I lean on, aside from Vlad when he's not grunting, like right now.

"Now, what?" I ask.

"You're really going to marry Kyle?"

I try my hardest to remain calm, even though everything inside revolts at the mention of his name.

Now that he's back, it's even worse.

If I'm being honest with myself, the reason I haven't been able to work properly today isn't only because of the marriage proposal. It's mainly the way he invaded my space, touched me, and wrapped his hand around my throat as if he had every right to. Those long, lean fingers—

"Rai."

"What?" I force myself out of my haze at Vlad's strong

voice. He rarely calls me by my given name, and when he does, it's serious.

"I was asking if you're going to marry the bastard."

"I don't have a choice. Either I do it or he'll go after Ana."

Vlad sucks in a breath but refrains from commenting. He's the type who doesn't like to meddle in others' business unless he's ordered to. "He's not a tool you can play with as we planned."

"I know that more than anyone. *Dedushka* put him as my guard at one point, remember?"

"Yes, I do. I also remember that you told me not to say his name again after he disappeared."

"I'd still rather we didn't talk about him."

"That doesn't make him disappear."

"I can pretend to."

"I don't know what happened back then that you hold a grudge against him, but it's different now that he's Igor's son."

"Do you really believe that he's Igor's son?"

"You don't?"

"I don't know. It just feels fishy that he's coming all in, to the extent of claiming familial ties. Why now, of all times?"

"If anyone can find out, it's you."

"Oh, you bet I will. He thinks he'll get the all-access card by marrying me, but he doesn't know that he'll be poisoned in the process."

"Keep your cards close."

"You don't have to remind the snake to be poisonous, my dear Vlad."

"My name is not Vlad."

"Whatever."

He grunts out a response. "The *Pakhan* ordered me to get you all the financial reports from the four brigades."

"Hello, Mikhail's trouble." I stare over my shoulder at Ruslan. "How much do you bet we will find something fishy in there?"

"A hundred," he says in his somewhat sophisticated accent.

"That's so little," I tease him.

"Five hundred." Katia places a tray of coffee in front of us and steps back to stand beside Ruslan.

I grin. "Now we're talking. I will call you on that."

Vlad takes a sip of his coffee. "You need to submit V Corp's reports too."

"To who?"

"To everyone. Sergei wants everything to be out in the open with this one."

"Why now?"

"Adrian might have something to do with it. He stayed with him last."

I lean my elbow on my knee and tap my chin with my forefinger. "You think he's plotting something behind our backs?"

"Most likely. Remember, he only pushed Sergei up when he knew Ivan was dead and couldn't be *Pakhan*. You need to be extra careful with that one."

"Why? Did you hear something?"

He pauses with his cup halfway to his mouth. "Maybe."

"What is it?"

"My spies tell me he had a meeting with Igor and Kyle prior to coming to today's meeting."

"Motherfucker." I ball my hands into fists. If Kyle has Adrian by his side, I'm most definitely screwed. "If you knew that, why the hell did you vote for him to stay? Why did everyone? I just don't understand why *Dedushka* favored him so much, and now even Sergei does."

"Simple. He's efficient. You can't deny that during the times he was with us, no one dared to come near the brotherhood. They knew they would be sniped in their sleep by him."

"He's still a killer."

"We all are."

"We kill for necessity, to protect our honor and our own.

He kills for sport and profit. People like him who follow no codes of honor and have no loyalty are the most untrustworthy."

"No one trusts him. We're all just using his skills."

I pause at Vlad's words, the meaning behind them sitting badly with me for some reason.

"Do you know why I'm a shadow, Princess? It's because no one notices when I'm gone."

I shake Kyle's words away, refusing to allow them weight.

They do remain in my head, though.

They grow and magnify until they're the only thing I can think of, because I did notice when he was gone.

I did more than notice.

It ripped me apart from the inside out, and I'm still not sure if the wound will ever heal.

Now, I have to marry him and dig the knife deeper with my own hands.

EIGHT

Rai

TODAY IS MY WEDDING DAY.

It might as well be my funeral.

I don't know why it feels like something inside me is struggling for breath, smothering in nothingness and slowly dying. Maybe it's been dead for a long time, but I'm only noticing it now.

During my entire life, I've never been the type who dreamed about fairy tales and weddings. I preferred stories about monsters and demons. I thought they were more realistic than the cheesy Prince Charming ones.

Reina believed in her white knight and her fairy tale. She secretly loved Asher since they were children, and those feelings only got stronger as they grew up. She painted her own fairy tale and didn't stop until it finally came to its happy ending.

Well, the process wasn't exactly fairytale-ish, but the result is what matters. They've been happily married for many years and even had little Gareth.

Me? I always thought that type of life was not meant for me.

But even with my lack of belief in such things, I never thought I would get married this way, like cattle for the best buyer.

I shake my head as I stare at my console mirror. I'm wearing a simple white dress that falls to my feet. Lace is buttoned to my neck in the back and the front and covers my arms.

My hair is gathered into a neat twist at the back of my head. My makeup is thick, as usual, but I opted for red lipstick, because the devil needs to look pretty to lure in her prey.

If it were up to me, I would've changed the color of the dress to black, but that would reflect badly on Granduncle and the brotherhood in general, so I smothered that urge and went with this look.

The face that greets me is calm, serene, almost like this is in fact my wedding day.

It isn't. Today is the day I take the next step toward my goal.

There's a knock on the door, and I clear my throat. "Come in."

Sergei walks inside, his steps moderate as he tries not to put too much pressure on his stamina. His white hair is neat and well-styled, and he's dressed in the tux he reserves for special occasions. I don't know if I should be flattered or sad that he thinks this is a special occasion for me.

I stand up and kiss his knuckles. He places his other hand at the top of my hair, stroking gently before letting go. "Nikolai would've been proud of you."

My throat closes at *Dedushka's* name. Today is the worst occasion to mention him or how much I miss him or how much I wish he was standing by my side.

I bottle up my emotions and say, "If he were here, neither Anastasia nor I would have to be compromised."

Sergei sighs, and the sound comes out a bit scratchy, like he finds it difficult to breathe. "It would've eventually happened. Neither Nikolai nor I could protect you for life."

"But you could at least protect Anastasia. You had her at forty—doesn't she mean anything to you?"

"She means the world to me, but she was born into the brotherhood and she will follow the brotherhood's rules." He pauses. "As will you."

"Yeah, yeah, because a woman can't go so far." I try to keep the mockery out of my voice.

"Who said she can't?"

"You and everyone else here. That's what I've been told since I was a little girl."

"That's because we wanted to protect you."

"I don't need protection. People need protection from me."

"They sure do, you troublemaker." He smiles a little and a fit of coughing takes over him. It rises up in volume and intensity until he topples over. I rush to my console, snatch tissues, and place them in his hands. He coughs blood into them, the white color turning red.

My heart lodges in my throat as his fit continues.

"*Ded...*" I call him by the term I only ever used to address *Dedushka.* "Breathe, breathe..."

His coughing comes to an end, slowly but not elegantly. The tissues are soaked with blood as he waves a hand and throws them in the bin. He retrieves clean ones to wipe his mouth. When I try to help, he raises a hand, stopping me in place.

Even old and sick, Granduncle is still a Sokolov and the *Pakhan.* He doesn't like anyone, including his family, to see his weakness.

"Are you okay?" I ask tentatively. "Should you see the doctor?"

"Doctors are useless." He approaches me slowly, then places both hands on my shoulders, making me stare up at him. When he speaks, his voice is a bit breathy. "Those who say women can't go far in this world are afraid of what the likes of you can do. That's why you have to be careful and smart, because your enemies are more than you can count or see. Don't look at this marriage as misery, look at it as an opportunity to stay in a position of power, even from the background. That's the only way you can protect yourself and everyone you love."

His words strike a deep chord inside me, not only because of his advice, but mainly because of the fact that he believes in me. He believes in what I'm capable of despite everything that's thrown in my direction.

I know Granduncle wouldn't dangle a ripe fruit in front of me. Not only would that put his position in danger and weaken him, it would also put me in a horrible spot. As it seems, I don't like to find my fruit easily. I prefer to hunt for it.

"Thank you, *Ded*." I kiss his knuckles again, and he taps my head as a show of acceptance before he offers me his elbow.

I tap under my ample dress, making sure my gun is well strapped to my thigh.

"Ready?" he asks.

No, but I don't say that, because I have to be ready. Pain, whether physical or emotional, is only a phase. That's what Mom used to tell Reina and me.

"Ready." I place my gloved hand in the crook of his arm and let him lead me out of my room.

The wedding is taking place in an orthodox church because…well, traditions, and then the reception will be held at the main brotherhood compound where we will live.

Kyle readily agreed to live with us instead of me having to move to Igor's, which is fishy as hell. Usually, men are so eager to mark the women as their property, and that includes having a wife in his own home.

Kyle is being weird, but since I have no evidence to back up my suspicions, and would rather stay with Sergei and Ana, I've remained silent about it.

It's been exactly a week since he returned from the unknown, and this whole time, all he's done is insert himself back in the brotherhood as if he never left, as if he didn't cut a wound open and never allowed it to heal.

Aside from that first day where he cornered me, we've only met twice, both times over Sergei's breakfast table with the other leaders to talk about strategizing and the Irish threat.

Kyle hardly looked in my direction or acknowledged me, not even when I ganged up on him with Damien.

It's not that I wanted him to, but we were to be married in such a short time. Couldn't he, I don't know, talk about it or something? Because if he were waiting for me to broach the subject, he'd be waiting for too long.

Sure, I could've delayed the wedding, but what's the point of delaying the inevitable? Besides, Sergei wanted this to happen sooner rather than later because of the threat to all our lives.

The preparations were made for critical security measures. I wanted a small and unimportant event, but Sergei said that would be a disgrace to our family name.

He went all out and invited all the big heads from all our mafia, political, and business allies.

The air is suffocated by the endless number of guards who came to protect their bosses. Needless to say, our own men are checking everyone and everything with hawk eyes. Sergei made specific instructions that he wants everything to go perfectly today and that no mistakes are allowed.

Even Ruslan and Katia are standing diagonally to the aisle, half-camouflaged by the decorative flowers. I shake my head internally. As if anything can hide Ruslan's frame.

Traditional classic Russian music plays as Sergei walks me

down the aisle. The large space grows silent. Some women look back to stare at me. I recognize a few faces from the Camorra families, the Triads, the Yakuza, and even the Bratva's business associates.

They didn't come for me, though. They came for Sergei and the power he represents. Their presence means nothing to me. If Reina were here, it would be a different story. Maybe I would be less hesitant about what's to come.

It's for the best this way. At least she's safe and I can protect her from afar. There was no way in hell I would bring my identical twin into the midst of all these dangerous people who wouldn't hesitate to hurt her in order to get to me.

The attendees' faces soon become blurry as I focus ahead, my expression calm, serene even.

We pass by Kirill, who smirks, probably thinking I'm suffering right now. I ignore him, because even though that might be the case, *Dedushka* taught me to never show my pain to the outside world.

"If they think you're strong, no one will dare to attack you."

His words are my mantra and the reason why I'm able to do this. After all, no one can win if the war hasn't started.

Damien sits beside Kirill since they're the only two who are still single in the elite group, aside from Vlad. Damien stares at me without expression, now silent, after he openly expressed that he doesn't think this marriage is a good idea. His jacket is wrinkled over his untucked shirt, as if he's just rolled out of bed to be here.

Igor, Mikhail, and Adrian sit with them, too. The first two are accompanied by their wives while their sons sit behind them, but Adrian's is absent. Vlad is backstage since he's responsible for the security of the event.

Anastasia settles beside Adrian, on the far right, smiling joyfully at me. I told her I wanted this, and because she believes everything I say, she actually thinks this is a happy event.

That makes one of us.

At least I have Ana here, since Reina was out.

The music comes to a halt as I stand at the altar in front of the priest. He's dressed in traditional Russian religious clothes with a hat that has a golden cross on top.

Murmurs break out in the crowd when it's clear that the groom isn't here yet. We're supposed to come out at the same time because I said I didn't like the whole bit of him waiting for me.

My lips tremble and a wave of different emotions hit me all at once: rage, hatred, betrayal, and—most of all—sadness.

He can't possibly wound my pride for the second time in a row.

This can't be happening.

And yet, as I stare at the crowd, the reality creeps in on me slowly and without notice.

Ruslan meets my eyes and shakes his head. He was the one who told me he saw Kyle around earlier.

Then where the hell is he now?

As Kirill snickers and Damien smiles, the realization of what's currently happening slaps me straight in the face.

Kyle abandoned me. Again.

Only this time, he's done it at the altar and in front of the world.

NINE

Kyle

I LIE ON MY STOMACH AND STARE THROUGH THE LENS of my rifle.

As much as Vladimir was Nazi about the security, he couldn't tighten it enough to eliminate the invisible soldiers on the roofs—especially the faraway locations.

Besides, the church is so low that all the surrounding buildings could and would be used as a sniper nest.

This is Brooklyn, after all; the tall architecture is a sure way to carry out missions.

I narrow my lens's focus to the altar, where a beautiful woman stands beside Sergei. I zoom in until she's in full view.

White looks good on her, majestic, almost like she's some screwed-up type of angel who came down to torture humans.

Rai's expression is far from angelic, though. Even though she's still hiding behind countless layers of makeup, she can't camouflage the twisting of her lips or the reddening of her delicate neck that's begging for my fingers around it.

She's become an expert at bottling her rage, but not enough to fool me. After all, I was with her every step of the way when she was trying to get rid of her hotheaded personality—or to at least keep it under wraps. The truth of the matter is, there's no way in hell she could've become docile and obedient, at least not in this lifetime.

Rai was born to conquer and crush anyone who defies her or poses a threat to her family. She never once stopped or hesitated, her gender be damned.

That woman is more tenacious than most of the men I've met.

And because of that, she's dangerous to my mission.

It would be so easy to pull the trigger and erase her from my path. What is she anyway, aside from an insignificant pawn who will cause more trouble than it's worth?

My finger won't move. It can't.

I don't know when this state began, whether it was after I saw her again or if it were there seven years ago. All I know is that I can't pull the fucking trigger on Rai Sokolov, even though she's my worst enemy.

I direct the rifle at the building opposite of the church where the other crime organizations' guards are stationed. Who knew my wedding would be a vipers' den for New York's most notorious criminal faces? It's not only the Italians, Chinese, and Japanese; there are also the Armenians and the Ukrainians. While most are classical allies of the Bratva, they're not closely tied to Sergei's reigning period. They could marry among each other to strengthen their relationships, but most clans are too traditionalist to give their daughters to outsiders.

Lucky for me, Sergei absolutely wouldn't.

Bloodlust runs in my veins as I aim my rifle at three guards standing at the back of the building. My muscles tighten, but

THRONE OF POWER | 79

my body remains inert, calm, almost like I'm sleeping with my eyes open.

The cloudy sky is my only limit.

There's no wind, no disturbances. There's only the need for chaos.

I pull the trigger, hitting the first guard in the forehead. The moment the other two turn to him, raising their guns, it's already too late. I hit one in the heart and the other in the hollow of his neck.

The three of them fall over each other without a sound or a fuss. Clean. Fast. Efficient.

First part of the mission is complete.

Still on my stomach, I glide backward, hide the rifle in its case, and then I remove the bricks I dug out a week ago when I decided on this location. Next, I hide the weapon between the rocks.

Once finished, I crawl to the entrance and only stand when I know no one on top of the other buildings will see me.

I zip up my hoodie, wearing my mask and my sunglasses, as I take the stairs three at a time.

"Target one eliminated." I speak to my second sniper through the intercom attached to my ear. "Take care of both Kai and Lazlo."

"Got it," he replies in his bored tone. I brought him with me from England, and I'm not sure if that's the brightest decision I have ever made.

But, the fact remains, Flame is the one who taught me how to snipe in the first place. It goes without saying that if anyone can take care of this, it's him. I still don't like that he's deep into my business, though. While we belonged to the same organization, he serves himself and himself alone.

"And don't touch a hair on the head of Rai," I add.

"Pussy-whipped already?"

"Fuck you."

"Not really my thing. But now that we're chatting, are you going to tell me why you want to hit Kai and Lazlo, of all people?"

"Because Kai is the equivalent of Adrian for the Japanese, and Lazlo is the equivalent of Sergei for the Luciano family."

"You're killing their brains—smart."

"I know that."

"Always the arrogant one, Kyle. Guess your dishonorable discharge from the group didn't change anything about you."

I ignore the jab at the past and say, "Get to your position."

Flame may have a more senior rank than me, but as he said, I don't belong to that group anymore—thus, I have no obligation to respect the hierarchy.

I click the button and exit the building as silently as I came in. Since it's still new, the cameras aren't fully working yet, so I can slip into their blind spots more easily than if I would've chosen another building.

After I sneak to the back entrance, I get rid of the mask, the glasses, the fake mustache, and the hoodie, remaining in my black tux. Then I throw them in the rubbish can.

I run two streets up to find my Porsche. As soon as I'm inside, I kick my sports shoes away and put on my leather ones. I stare at my face in the rearview mirror.

I look ready for a wedding.

It takes me a minute to reach the church. I spot Vladimir at the front, expression grim, knuckles white. His tension doesn't lessen when he sees me. If anything, his rage rushes to the surface like an active volcano.

Holding out a small box, I step out of my car and throw the spare keys to one of the guards. I always have another one on me in the case of an emergency.

Vladimir is in my face in a fraction of a second. "Where the fuck have you been?"

I shake the box in front of him. "Getting the rings. I almost forgot about them."

He narrows his eyes on me but says nothing, so I push past him and head inside, pretending to be flustered that I'm late.

Sergei's and Igor's faces ease at my presence. If I hadn't shown up, it wouldn't only have been an insult to Rai, but also to the entire brotherhood. I might have been forgiven before, but if I abandoned Sergei's grandniece at the altar, he'd chop my head off with his own hands—or he'd probably let Rai do it.

There's no forgiving disgrace.

While the church calms down upon my entry, Damien, the fucker who needs a bullet in his skull, glares at me, obviously displeased that I showed up.

He must've been waiting, biding his time, planning to take Rai away, but he doesn't know who he's up against. He has no idea that I'll be his worst nightmare.

Rai's expression doesn't change, neither in relief nor in apprehension, but that spark doesn't leave her eyes. My future wife looks ready to rip me a new one. I smile at the thought of what I'm going to do to her tonight.

After the show I prepared, she'll have nowhere to go but to me.

Only to me.

As I walk toward her, I can't help but notice how her simple white dress molds to her tits at the top. The décolletage, although partly camouflaged by lace, hints at enough cleavage to leave me salivating for more. The cloth hugs her curves and falls to her feet. It's simple, elegant, like everything about her.

Who knew someone who looks so much like an angel could harbor a devil inside? And I'm very glad to make its acquaintance. After all, I've been raised among devils since I was five.

Some would argue I became one myself, but I digress.

When I reach Rai, she huffs under her breath and turns away from me. It's Sergei who places her hand in mine.

"Take care of her," he tells me in a low tone only I can hear.

I'll do more than take care of her, old man. I'll ruin your entire empire through her.

"It'll be a miracle if he takes care of himself," she mutters under her breath.

Sergei clears his throat, kisses her head, and then offers her his hand. She kisses it, then I'm forced to do the same to show respect and blah fucking blah.

As soon as he leaves our side, Rai faces the priest, her expression closed, but there's something she can't control—her eyes. They're darkening and glimmering with the promise of a battle brewing in the distance.

I lean over to whisper in her ear, "What's made my beautiful wife mad?"

She elbows me with the strength of a warrior. Fuck, it's hard enough that she nearly knocks the air out of my lungs. "Your existence."

"You wound me, Princess," I joke.

"You deserve more than a wound." She meets my eyes for the first time today, and I don't like what I see there. It's not about the anger she wears as armor, or the frustration that accompanies her inability to inflict violence. It's everything else, from the slight tremble in her chin to the tears shining in her eyes. No matter how much she tries to chalk those up to anger, they're not. Far from it.

"You weren't planning on showing up, so why did you? Are you taking pity on me?"

I wrap an arm around her waist, pulling her close to my side. I spent a long time away from this woman, so long it's become blasphemy to put even more distance between us. "I came because you're becoming my wife." She tries to pull away, but I keep her pinned in place as I smile at the old priest. "Please proceed."

He clears his throat and speaks in English, but with the signature Russian accent. "We're gathered here today for the holy union between Kyle Hunter and Rai Sokolov."

He goes on and on about the importance of marriage and God and his lovely angels and everything in between. His words filter in through my ears but never really register. My entire attention is on Rai, who's concentrating way too hard on the priest's nonsense.

Her brows draw together when she's in focus mode and her lips part a little, revealing the slight teardrop at the top lip.

She can look so delicate and soft—breakable, even—that is until she speaks or takes action. That's when people know they have a feisty, take-no-nonsense type of person on their hands, the kind it's almost impossible to win against because they were trained to never lose. Either they win or they destroy.

"What are you looking at?" she snaps through gritted teeth without cutting off her concentration on the priest.

"You, Princess."

"Focus."

"I will do the focusing thing later when we consummate our marriage."

"Kyle!" she hisses.

"What? You're the one who's tempting me."

"You'll be far from tempted when I kick you in the balls."

"Kinky—I love it." I lower my voice. "Does this mean I get to use toys?"

"Toys to choke the life out of you, maybe."

"I had other types in mind. You know, the ones that make you scream for more." The priest clears his throat, and I motion at him to continue. "Never mind us, Father. We're laying the grounds for our future 'holy' union."

He gives us a weird glance as if thinking there's nothing holy about this union. He wouldn't be wrong, but I also don't believe in holy things, per se, so it doesn't apply to me.

After he finishes his monologue, the priest faces me with his version of the Russian vows. "Do you, Kyle Hunter, take Rai Sokolov as your wedded wife to be with you always, in wealth and in poverty, in disease and in health, in happiness and in grief, from this day until death do you part?"

"I do." The words come out a lot easier than I expected, even though I'm staring at her expressionless face. I think it's the last bit. I like it.

Till death do us part.

Yes. I definitely like it.

He turns to her. "Do you, Rai Sokolov, take Kyle Hunter as your wedded husband to be with you always, in wealth and in poverty, in disease and in health, in happiness and in grief, from this day until death do you part?"

Silence.

Long silence.

Seconds tick by, but they feel like years as she stares at me, and just then, her blank expression cracks, showing a hint of the girl I knew seven years ago. While she doesn't show vulnerability, she's showing something, a wound, or another emotion I can't put my finger on.

Then, I see her free spirit—the one that refuses to be tied down by anyone or anything.

Fuck. She's going to run.

"Rai?" the priest calls.

Her expression closes again, and I expect her to bolt right then and there, like in some runaway bride film. Unlike those sappy things, though, I'm ready to follow her to the ends of the earth and kidnap the fuck out of her if need be.

"I do." She says the words as if they weigh on her.

The priest and the crowd release a collective breath. I continue watching her tells, not sure if it's a ploy or if she'll change her mind any second.

No idea why, but it feels like I can't be relieved as of yet.

The priest asks us to exchange rings. I take Rai's hand in mine and stroke the back slowly, sensually, almost like I'm seeing it for the first time.

I might as well be. I don't remember her hands being this soft. They're too fair, her veins semi-transparent. I slide the ring on her finger as slowly as possible, then smirk up at her.

She goes immediately on the defensive. "What?"

"If you're going to hit my balls with these hands, I'm game."

It's fast, almost unnoticeable, but her cheeks heat as she pulls her hand away and forcibly takes mine.

Holding in a smile, I lean in and murmur against the shell of her ear. "It's the other hand."

"I know that," she blurts then switches to my left one.

Fuck me. Who knew I would ever get to see Rai's flustered side and enjoy it this much?

She slides the ring on, then pauses in the middle of her task, her expression freezing. I expect her to back down now, but she's staring at my hand.

I follow her field of vision, and that's when I see what she does. Blood is smeared on the side of my ring finger. It's not dried either. *Fuck.* It must've been from when I physically subdued some of the guards before I went to the building's roof. I was careful enough to not stab anyone in order to stay clean, so how did the blood end up here?

Rai raises a questioning gaze, but I grab her hand and slide my ring all the way on.

"By the power granted to me by the church, I now pronounce you husband and wife," the priest says. "You may kiss the bride."

Rai attempts to give me her cheek, but I wrap an arm around her waist and slam my lips to hers. She protests at first, but the moment I move my mouth against her own, she remains as still as a board.

I dart my tongue out and lick her upper lip, then feast on her lower one. She tastes like addiction and bad decisions, and yet I would still come back for a hit every day.

Rai places a hand on my chest, letting out a protest, but I

use the chance to plunge my tongue inside her mouth. Her arguments turn into a moan when I twirl my tongue against hers.

Her eyes widen at the sounds coming from her, and I wish I could freeze this moment in time so I could revisit it every day.

Who knew we would have our first kiss here?

I don't release her, not even when murmurs break out among the crowd, or when the priest keeps clearing his throat like he has a bad cough.

Fuck them.

The only person who matters in this room is in my arms, hot, bothered, and fucking mine. Now, I need to keep my promise about the consummation part.

The church's glass breaks and screams fill the space.

I freeze for a fraction of a second.

Well, fuck.

I was too lost in my new bride and I momentarily forgot about the mission. That's a first.

I begrudgingly release Rai's lips and grab her arm, pulling her behind me as everyone brings out their weapons.

Let the chaos begin.

TEN

Rai

SCREAMS FILL THE AIR.

Soon after, an influx of different languages mix and rise in volume until almost none of them are intelligible.

Women squeal as leaders bark orders at their guards. Guns rise high in the air, and the sound of outside gunshots gets everyone's attention.

It takes a second for the rest of the Vory and me to realize who could be behind this.

The Irish.

Everyone is taking refuge, including the crime family leaders and their companions.

Kyle is dragging me toward where the priest has disappeared to. I twist my hand free from his, lift my dress, and run in the direction of Sergei and Anastasia. There's no way in hell I'm leaving my family to die while I save my own neck.

Ruslan and Katia are by my side in a second, their expressions alert and their guns in hand.

I find Granduncle covering Anastasia while Igor, Mikhail, and Kirill surround them in a circle, their guns held taut in their arms. They at least have the loyalty to protect the boss.

Damien is running straight outside, pushing people out of his way and checking his gun's magazine on the way. His men follow after him like a storm ready to erupt.

Adrian, on the other hand, is standing with the Italians. His gun, although drawn, is hanging limply by his side as if he knows he won't get the chance to use it.

I'm about to yell at him for not coming to protect Sergei, but the view of blood stops me. Lazlo, the leader of the Lucianos and one of the most important heads of the Camorra, has been shot.

I don't have time to focus on that as I grab Sergei by the shoulder. Anastasia gets to her feet as well, expression fearful and skin pale, but she's not crying like she used to do when we were young.

"Come on," I urge. "Let's get you out of here, *Ded*."

"Like fuck you're taking him away," Mikhail snarls in my face, looking ready to direct his weapon at me.

"The outside isn't safe yet," Igor says, agreeing. "We can't get the boss out before Damien or Vladimir return."

"I'm not taking him away." I motion to where the priest went. "Old churches have hiding places." I throw a glance behind me, thinking Kyle disappeared, but a deep part of me, an irrational one, holds on to the hope that he didn't.

"They do." His voice comes swift and calm from beside me as he checks his gun. "Follow me."

Mikhail grunts but complies when our guards and we form a circle around Sergei, Anastasia, and Mikhail's and Igor's wives, each person facing a different angle as we move in unity toward the hideout.

Kyle attempts to push me inside, but I lift my dress, re-trieve my gun from the holster attached to my thigh, and jut my chin at him. He shakes his head but quits trying to push me.

We take a few turns, following his lead, and then descend old, narrow stairs that only accommodate two people at a time. The commotion from outside slowly withers away as we go down slowly.

When we reach a secluded room in the basement, Sergei is panting. His face has paled, and I know it's because he's holding in his cough. If he has a fit and blood comes out in front of the others, it'll be bad.

We find the priest praying silently in a corner. I help sit Sergei down in a chair beside him without making it so no-ticeable. Anastasia joins him, holding on to his arm like it's a lifeline.

Mikhail's wife is trembling noticeably. Igor's wife, Stella, however, seems completely in control of the situation. She stands beside her and holds her hand, whispering what I as-sume are soothing words. Stella has always seemed like a tough cookie who, although she shouldn't belong in the Bratva world, has managed to fully adapt to Igor's lifestyle.

Her husband is talking to his guards in clipped Russian, but I catch the brief moments he steals glances at her, as if making sure she's safe and sound. Stella nods discreetly at him, and even though no words are spoken, it's like a whole chain of communication has just happened between them.

It's admirable to witness their connection firsthand. *Dedushka* always said Igor was the luckiest in his generation, but now I fully understand what that means. *Dedushka*, Sergei, and many others lost their wives, whether to illness or assassi-nation, but Igor protected his with his life.

The sound of gunshots echoes above us, getting closer by the second, as if coming from inside the church.

"Stay here," Kyle says. "Kirill and I will go see what's going on."

They're not one step toward the door when they notice me joining them. Aleksander remains by his boss's side, expression alert.

Kyle stops in his tracks and faces me. "What do you think you're doing?"

"I'm going too."

"No, you're not."

"Yes, I am. The bastards don't get to shoot at my family at my own wedding and expect me to stay in hiding."

"I will take care of it," he mutters.

"It'll be easier if I'm around."

"Fuck, Rai." He grabs my shoulder and whispers against my ear, "You're in your damn wedding dress."

I lift it up and tie it so it's no longer skimming the floor. "I can run in a dress."

"Rai..." The warning in his tone doesn't escape me, but I keep holding eye contact, refusing to budge.

"If you're done flirting..." Kirill rolls his eyes from under his glasses.

I step out first, and Ruslan and Katia stand on either side of me.

"Stay and protect Granduncle," I tell both of them, not waiting for their reply.

They don't like being left out of the action, especially when I'm in the midst of it, but their role beside Sergei is more important.

I take the route back to where we came from. Kyle and Kirill follow after, covering for me and each other.

By the time we reach the church, it's empty, except for the Italians who are protecting their injured man.

Adrian isn't where we left him.

Excessive gunshots are coming from outside. Considering

the randomness of the shots, I can't exactly pinpoint their source.

"Let's separate." Kirill lifts his glasses up his nose. "I'll take the back. Kyle, the front. Rai, stay here."

He and Aleksander leave before either of us can agree.

"I'll take the front," I tell Kyle. "You stay here."

"Funny."

"I'm not joking. You have better aim than me and would be able to take down any target from the inside."

"No."

"Then I'm coming with you." I don't wait for him to agree because I know he won't. Keeping my back to the wall and away from the windows, I creep to the entrance.

Kyle, though? He breezes through the door in the midst of the raining bullets.

I have no clue if he's that brave or has no value for his life—or both. My heart nearly jumps out as the gunshots continue and he throws himself right in the middle.

He finds some of Igor's men, motions something at them, and jumps over the fence toward the parking lot. Where the hell is he going?

I shake my head as I click the bullets into the chamber of my gun and slowly slip out. A few stray gunshots echo around me, and I fire two of my own. Four to go.

Kyle is the one who taught me to count my bullets, especially when I have no ammunition left. He said there's nothing more stupid than dying by your own mistake. It's ironic how his words stayed with me, particularily during dire situations.

I sneak behind our men toward where Kyle headed, making sure Vlad doesn't see me. If he does, he'll forcefully grab me and send me back beside Sergei.

The gunshots continue going at a sporadic speed. I hide behind the walls, holding my breath every time I move from one surface to the next.

Cars, mostly German, fill the parking lot, but there's no sign of Kyle. I use the vehicles as camouflage while I try to track down where he went.

He always does this thing where he fucking disappears into thin air until it's almost impossible to find him. And then, when someone does find him, he's already finished several people and comes back all covered in blood as if it's a normal occurrence.

We might all be killers, but the difference between Kyle and me is that I only kill when I absolutely have to, mostly in self-defense or to protect my family. He's the type of unfeeling psycho who does it as a pastime. Not only that, he also doesn't take backup. A lone wolf through and through.

I lift my head over a BMW to study my surroundings, but I come face to face with the opening of a gun.

Fuck.

"Throw your gun behind you," the man who holds the weapon says in an indecipherable accent, but I don't have to guess at his origins. His Asian eyes and thick hair give him up as either Chinese or Japanese.

"I'm Rai Sokolov, Sergei Sokolov's grandniece."

"Gun on the ground or it will be your brains."

Shit.

I slowly let go of my gun, making sure to throw it far enough and on its back so it doesn't go off.

He motions at me with his weapon. "Put your hands behind your head and come out."

I follow his instructions so I'm standing in the open in front of him. "Don't you know who I am? You're making a grave mistake."

"Maybe you made it, Miss Sokolov." The suave voice coming from my right takes me by surprise, especially since I recognize it well.

The man with the gun bows his head in respect—to his boss.

Kai Takeda.

He stands a few feet away from me, taller than his guard, but leaner and with the aura of an undercover assassin. He lost his jacket somewhere, since I recall him wearing it at the beginning of the ceremony, and is now only wearing a black shirt and pants. His eyes are Asian like his guard's, but darker and more mysterious. His hair is thick, ink-colored, styled back, and falling to his nape. His face is also stronger than most of his countrymen, and he has a quiet beauty to him that fits his role.

Kai is the brains of the Yakuza here, and a very dangerous person at that. However, the fact remains, he's one of our allies and a ruthless investor in V Corp.

I drop my hands to either side of me. "What are you doing, Kai?"

He pauses for a beat before he speaks quietly in a flawless American accent. "I should ask you that."

"What are you talking about?"

"I must admit, I hadn't thought you capable of carrying out a hit at your own wedding, but it's a mistake I will not repeat again."

"A hit?"

He motions at his side, and that's when I make out the blood oozing out of his shirt. Since the cloth is black, I didn't notice it before. "Either your sniper missed, or perhaps…you asked him to do it on purpose? What is your message, Miss Sokolov? Do you think you can threaten me?"

His guard's posture tightens more at his boss's words, and his grip on the gun turns deadly. I have no doubt he'll shoot any second now.

The thought of dying like this cripples me, but I hold on to logic, because Kai only respects that.

"We have no sniper."

"Yes, you do."

"The only sniper we use in the brotherhood was standing with me at the altar."

"It could've been a different sniper, one for hire."

"And you think I would hire them at my wedding to terrorize my family?"

"At first, I didn't believe it, but it's becoming more plausible by the second."

A shadow appears behind Kai and points a gun at the back of his head. My breathing hitches at the view of Kyle's face. He's grounded, his grip on the gun steady, almost like he's not holding a deadly weapon. "Tell your guard to drop his gun."

Kai's expression remains the same as if his life isn't on the line. "Not before Miss Sokolov confesses."

"Then your guard will be collecting your corpse."

"And you will be collecting your wife's."

"I didn't do it." I meet Kai's neutral black eyes. "I would never put my family in jeopardy and you know that."

"You could sacrifice a member for the greater good."

"We don't believe in that in the brotherhood. We're one for all and all for one."

"There was a sniper," Kai insists. "Do you deny that?"

"No." I saw the window break myself. Even a toddler would know there was a sniper at the scene.

"Who do you think it is?"

"The Irish," I say confidently. "They're after the Italians and us. Lazlo and Sergei were their targets. Either you were caught in the crossfire by pure accident or they're also bringing you in because you're our ally."

Kai motions at his guard with two fingers, and he lowers the gun. Kyle doesn't disappear from behind him, probably because Kai can order his henchman to shoot me at any second.

"What option do you think it is?" Kai asks me. "Was it an accident or intentional?"

"Intentional." I don't even hesitate. "You wouldn't have been that lucky if it were an accident."

His lips twitch as he approaches me, not attempting to stop the blood oozing from his side. Sure, it's not a lot, but it's still a wound.

"I will pay a visit to V Corp."

"Not Sergei?" I ask, bemused.

"Not Sergei." He motions at my waist, and I follow his gaze to find blood on my front and on my wrists. I must've caught it during my sneaking journey. "Congratulations on the wedding."

He reaches a hand out, probably to shake mine, but Kyle steps between us, blocking my vision of Kai. "You don't get to touch her after you threatened to kill her. Piss off."

"Fair enough." I don't see Kai's face, but I can hear the smile in his tone. "Until we meet again."

The guard bows his head in a show of respect and follows Kai. The moment they disappear, Kyle turns around so abruptly I flinch backward.

I've never seen this expression on his face. His eyes are fierce and the mask he usually wears is completely gone, allowing me a peek at the real man inside. And what I see in there? Well, it's more complicated than anyone can decipher.

"What *the fuck* are you doing here?"

It takes me a second to try to wrench myself out of his magnetic hold. "I told you I was coming with you."

"And I told you to stay put."

"Just because we're married, *barely*, doesn't give you the right to dictate my actions."

"Bloody hell, Rai." He kicks the car, causing its alarm to go off. "What if he shot you, huh? Would your stubbornness have saved you?"

"He wouldn't have. Kai is our ally."

"What if he decided he's no longer an ally? What if he killed you to send a message to Sergei?"

"He wouldn't do that."

"What if he did?"

"I would've gotten myself out of it."

"You can't get yourself out of death. The moment the bullet is in, it's in—do you understand?"

I don't know if he's still talking about this situation or something entirely different, but I nod anyway. Even I realize we're at different skill levels and this could've really ended badly for me.

He wraps a hand behind my back, and I yelp as he holds me in his arms bridal style.

I grab his shirt with my fingers for balance. "What are you doing?"

"Consummating our marriage, Princess. It's long overdue."

ELEVEN

Rai

DID HE JUST SAY HE'S GOING TO CONSUMMATE OUR marriage?

Yup, I think he did.

I'm stunned into a long silence at his words, my limbs staying still and my hold on his shirt loosening.

For some reason, my chest rises and falls heavily, and it has nothing to do with the adrenaline rush from earlier.

I stare at his face as he carries me, like, *really* stare at him—at the sharp lines of his jaw, his straight nose with the slight crookedness that makes him imperfect in so many ways, the man who became my husband because I agreed to it.

At that moment when the priest asked me to be his wife till death do us part, the past crashed into me and all I wanted to do was to run and never return.

My heart still bleeds from back then, and I didn't trust that I could let it exsanguinate this time. Because now? Now, I have a feeling he will hurt me irrevocably if I let him.

By the time I shake myself out of my reverie, he's reached his car and has opened the passenger door.

I squirm in his hold, needing to put as much distance between us as possible. "Let me go."

"No."

"I have to go back to check on Sergei and Ana."

"They're fine. The Irish who showed up were taken care of by Vladimir and the others."

"Still—"

He holds the back of my neck with his rough, strong hand, forcing me to stop squirming. His face is mere breaths away as his hard eyes peer into mine. "Quit worrying about everyone else on your wedding day."

"This is not a real wedding." I meant for my voice to be hard, but it's almost a whisper.

"Yes, it is. You said 'I do' in front of God and all his holy subjects."

"You don't believe in holy things."

He smirks. "You remember. Were you that obsessed with me?"

I huff, turning away from him, but his hold on my neck keeps me pinned in place. "Don't flatter yourself. I only remember things that will be of use."

"You remember my teachings, too."

"I do not," I snap, chest going back to its heavy rise and fall. "That's not the point."

"Then what is?" His voice drops in range. "Oh, is it the part about how I don't believe in holy things?"

"Yes."

"You do. That's what counts."

"Who says I do?"

"You believe in anything the brotherhood believes in. A Bratva princess, through and through."

I hit his chest with a closed fist. He lets me, then feigns a dramatic wince. "Kinky this early in the evening? I'm going to have my hands full with you tonight, aren't I?"

"Not if you want to keep your dick where it belongs."

He chuckles, the laugh lines around his eyes turning them lighter, shinier. "Oh, it will stay where it belongs and maybe I'll use it to shut that stubborn mouth for once." He strokes his fingers across my skin, eliciting zap-like sensations from the bottom of my stomach. "You won't have much to say when your lips are wrapped around my dick, will you?"

A shudder goes through my entire body at his explicit words, and I blurt something out to camouflage my reaction. "Maybe when you're in a coffin."

"It's a bad omen to imagine being a widow when you're a bride, Princess." He aligns his mouth with my ear until his hot breaths are the only thing I feel on my skin. "It might come true sooner than you think."

I pull away, his words hitting me like an electric shock. "W-what do you mean?"

He places me on my feet only so he can nudge me into the passenger seat. I don't protest, because all I can think about are his words. What does he mean I'll become a widow sooner than I think?

Kyle climbs into the driver's seat, and I fully face him. "What did you say just now?"

His whole body leans over in my direction, and my nostrils are assaulted by his distinctive clean smell as he straps the seatbelt over me. His mouth is a few inches away from mine when he pauses and expands the palm of his hand on my stomach where there's a stain of blood.

"Our life together started with blood," he says in a calm tone. "How do you expect it to end?"

I swallow the clog that lodges in my throat without warning. "Didn't you tell me we choose our own destiny?"

"I lied. It's always decided beforehand. Every action we

take only throws us back to the path we were always meant to follow."

It takes me a second, but I see it: the determination in his eyes. It's not the normal type like the kind I have when I stare in the mirror every morning. It's blacker, fiercer, and with the intention of reaching his end goal even if it means burning everyone—himself included.

What happened to you during these past years, Kyle?

I hate myself for thinking that question, for even voicing it in my head when I promised myself I'd never get caught in his maze again.

"Why did you marry me?" I murmur the question I've meant to ask for the past week.

"Because I wanted to."

"That's not an answer."

"It is the only answer you'll need. I married you because I wanted to. You're my wife now, and nothing and no one will change that fact. Not even you."

"You better be ready for the hell I'll bring to your life, then."

"Oh, I'm more than ready." He kisses my forehead and I freeze, not expecting the soft, intimate gesture. His lips linger for a second as if he's savoring the moment and the newness of it. Kyle has never kissed me on the forehead before, not that I would've let him, but now, he seems hell-bent on doing whatever he wishes.

He pulls back before I can protest, but the imprint of his lips remains on my skin, burning like wildfire.

Kyle reaches to the back seat and brings out a half-full bottle of Jack Daniels, takes a sip, and then offers it to me. "To the hell you'll bring, Princess."

"I'll drink to that." I snatch the bottle from his fingers and down a generous gulp. Kyle smiles, giving me his side profile as he drives out of the parking lot.

We don't go past the others, so I don't catch a glimpse of the guards or Vlad. The sounds of the gunshots have disappeared, though, so that should mean the attack has ended.

If it weren't for the brute next to me, I would be escorting Sergei and Ana safely back to the house.

I catch myself watching his face again and his smile. It appears genuine, happy even, but it's all a part of the façade he puts on so well. I can count on one hand the number of times he's actually smiled from his heart.

His lips move, but not his eyes, as if they're not part of the same face.

"I know I'm attractive and you can't help staring, but rein it in until we're not in public, Princess."

"I don't know what you're talking about." I take another sip from the bottle, letting the burning liquid slide down my throat.

"I love it when you play innocent. It weirdly suits you."

"Shut up." I down a larger gulp this time, wincing at the aftertaste.

"Liquid courage." He winks. "Nice."

"Who said it's liquid courage? Maybe I want to finish the bottle so I can shove it up your ass."

"Kinky again. I didn't know you thought of me sexually so much, but take it easy on the drinking—I know you're a lightweight."

"*Were*. Past tense. I'm no longer a lightweight."

He raises a brow, briefly shifting his focus from the road to me. "Really now?"

"I can finish the bottle." I swallow the largest gulp I've ever had, trying not to wince at the burn and the strong aftertaste.

"If you say so."

I jut my chin out at him, continuing my mission. While he drives through Brooklyn's streets, I consider the bottle of Jack Daniels my current war and drink one sip after another.

Kyle watches me peculiarly every now and then before focusing back on the road.

By the time the car stops, I've finished. I dangle the empty bottle in front of his face. "It is dooone," I slur, then giggle at the end.

I slap a hand over my mouth to kill the sound.

Well, damn. I'm drunk.

I'm the type who more or less loses their inhibitions when drunk. That's why I don't allow myself to reach this stage. One time, I went to Kirill's club and gotten so drunk that I couldn't even go home. It was one of those nights it got too much and I needed something to make me forget. What I didn't count on was what I witnessed in Kirill's club that night.

One of the only times, drinking was worth it. This situation is entirely different, though.

My head is swimming in the clouds, and my skin is too hot, like someone threw me straight into summer.

Kyle shakes his head. "Told you you're a lightweight."

"Am not, you asshole." I shake the empty bottle in his face again. "I finished it all, thank you very much."

Kyle climbs out, and I squint at the unfamiliar place he brought me to. Tall trees surround us from everywhere. There's a cottage-like house on my right, and water glints in the distance.

Wait…is that a lake?

My door opens, and Kyle undoes my seatbelt.

"What is this place?" I throw my finger in the air. "It's not home."

"We'll spend the night here. It's safer," he says ever so casually.

"Noooo. I wanna go home and make sure Sergei and Ana are fiiiine."

"They are."

"Hooow do you know?" My slur rises in pitch.

He sighs as he retrieves his phone and shows me a text

conversation between him and Igor. Kyle taps the last line to bring my attention to it.

Igor: The *Pakhan* and Anastasia are now safely in the main house.

"Happy now?"

"No. I still want to go home. Taaake me."

"We will go in the morning." He gently pulls me out by the arm, and I shudder.

It's the alcohol. Definitely the alcohol.

Once outside, I pull my arm free of his. "I can waaalk on my own." The moment I take the first step, I stumble and fall back against a hard chest. I giggle and murmur, "Oops."

"You were saying?" He raises an eyebrow, his gaze meeting mine even though my back is to his chest. I don't know if it's the liquor or the dusk's sun, but his eyes appear shinier, as if he's genuinely concerned or something.

I turn around, still clutching the empty bottle, and place my chin on his chest to stare up at him closely. His scent envelops me in a cocoon and it feels so peaceful and…right?

No. It's wrong. The alcohol is messing with my head.

"I hate you," I murmur.

"I know."

"No, you don't know how much I *reaaaaally* hate you."

"Why don't you tell me?"

"I hate your face."

"You're in the minority on that, Princess."

"I hate your accent."

"Still in the minority."

"I hate your cheeky attitude when you don't mean it."

He strokes a strand of hair behind my ear, and my eyes flutter closed. "So you love it when I mean it?"

"Screw you, Kyle," I say without opening my eyes.

"Let's get you inside and we'll work on that." He carries me again, and this time, I don't protest as my arms wrap around his neck. I lay my head on his chest, and I begin to fall asleep. I faintly register a lock opening, but his steps are as silent and agile as usual. I don't even feel the distance.

But then, he places me on something soft. My eyes flutter open and I find myself in a cozy room. The bed on which I'm lying is in the middle. Soft light comes from the two lamps on the nightstands. There's a large window in the front with transparent curtains pulled.

This place is hot, or maybe I am. A few clips are missing from my hair so I yank at the others, letting my hair loose then kick my heels away. *Sigh*. Much better. I sit up and reach a hand to the zipper of my dress, pulling it down, but it gets stuck at the middle. I groan as I release my grip.

I stare ahead in search of a solution. Kyle removes his jacket and bowtie and places them on a chair opposite the bed, then rolls the sleeves of his shirt to his elbows. I'm momentarily transfixed by the scene, not only the meticulous way he does it, but also the ring on his finger—the one I put there, even though he had blood on his hand. We did start with blood, and there's no way to change that now.

"Kyyyyyle."

"Yes, Princess?"

"Open it."

"Open what?"

"My dress. It's hoooot."

"Are you going to take a shower?"

"Not now."

He stalks toward me with slow steps and sits beside me, then grabs me by the shoulder and turns me around. I giggle and squirm at the feel of his skin on mine.

"Stay still," he reprimands.

"Okaaay, okaaay."

"If I'd known you'd be this adorable, I would've gotten you drunk before."

"No one gets me drunk but me, and don't call me adorable."

"I'll call you whatever I wish, *wife*." His voice drops in range as he drags the zipper down my back, but instead of letting me go, his finger traces my spine.

A full-body shiver takes hold of me as his digits continue stroking my skin, up and down, up and down, like he can't get enough.

"A snake tattoo," he whispers. "Interesting."

"It's a viper."

"A viper—even more interesting choice. When did you get it?"

"When you weren't around." I push away from him and shove my dress down my shoulders, then kick it down to my feet, remaining in my black cotton bra and panties.

I motion at myself. "Black means staaay the fuck away."

He wets his lower lip with his tongue, and I follow the motion with my eyes as if I'm starved and it's the most delicious meal on earth. "Says who?"

"Says me. Black is like a funeral."

"The joke's on you. I love black." He grabs me by the wrist and I squeal as I end up on my back on the bed. He crawls atop me and imprisons both my wrists above my head. "And so do you."

TWELVE

Kyle

I EXPECT RAI TO KICK ME IN THE BALLS LIKE SHE promised she would. I'm already prepared to catch her knee.

But that's sober Rai.

Drunk Rai stares at me with sadness so deep its sharp edge points at my chest.

I have no idea why I allowed her to get drunk in the first place, knowing full well she becomes even more unpredictable—and free—when on the liquor. She lost some of her shackles on the way here, and I'm seeing a glimpse of the carefree girl she was when Nikolai was alive, the girl who couldn't care less about the traditional binds or what the world thinks of her.

"Why do you know I like black?" she murmurs, not attempting to release her wrists from underneath my hold.

"You think I forgot just because I left?"

"You should. That's how it's supposed to be," she pants, slamming her eyes shut hard before she opens them again. This time, moisture coats her lower lids.

I wipe a finger under her eyes, taking her tears for my own. Everything that's hers will be mine now, whether it's her tears or her anger, or even her hotheaded stubbornness.

The moment I saw Kai's henchman hold a gun to her forehead, I nearly killed them both then and there. For a second, I forgot about my mission and the fact that, for my plan to work, Kai and Lazlo need to be only injured, not gone. It wouldn't do me any good to eliminate the two strongest heads whose organizations wouldn't hesitate to seek revenge as a result.

However, at that moment, I wanted Kai's vacant eyes, and I wanted them even more when he tried to touch her. It took godlike patience to hold on to my end goal and only threaten the bastard.

"I never forgot anything about you, Princess." And it wasn't by fucking choice. Rai has always been something I can never erase from my head, no matter how much I try to.

It's like having an unreachable itch and not knowing where exactly it is located.

She closes her hands into fists, and she would probably hit me if they were free. "Liar. Asshole."

"I'm fine with that, but do you know what I'm not fine with?" My voice gains an edge as I wrap my free hand around her throat. "You putting yourself in danger or running straight to it like you did today. Repeat that again and I'll punish you."

"You...you can't punish me." I don't miss the way her drunken voice lowers at the word punish.

"Oh, I very much can and I will if you keep having such little regard for your fucking safety. Also..." I tighten my hold around her neck, not hard enough to cut off her oxygen, but firm enough to keep her attention on me. "You don't let other men near you. You don't touch them, act friendly around them, or talk to them more than necessary."

"Or what?" she asks coyly. "You're going to puuuunish me?"

"I will."

"Hooow?"

"I have my methods."

"Why don't you show me?"

"Show you?"

"Yup." She giggles then whispers as if she doesn't want anyone else to hear. "*Punish me.*"

Fuck me.

My dick strains against my trousers with the need to rip off her flimsy underwear and fuck her into the mattress so hard she'll remember me on her for days. I'll mark her fair skin so it's full of my bites and evidence of who she belongs to.

The only thing that stops me from doing so is her drunken state. I might be immoral, but I'm no rapist. Knowing her episodes, she'll have little to no recollection of this in the morning, and I will not be integrated into her mind as the one who fucked her when she was wasted.

Besides, I want her completely in the act with me, and I sure as fuck want her to remember me come morning. After all, it's no fun when she doesn't scream.

"Why aren't you doing it?" She bucks against the bed, but a squeeze of my hand around her throat keeps her in place. She groans, her cheeks heating with the effort. "You did it earlier."

"When?"

"At the wedding."

"No, I didn't."

"Yes, you did. Like this." She lifts her head, and I give her a bit of leeway to see what she'll do. Rai seals her lips to mine. It's brief, almost like a peck, before she attempts to fall back. I let her, but I don't allow her lips to leave mine.

Fuck it. I feast on her as I did at the altar, licking and nibbling. She keeps her lips closed for a fraction of a second before she opens up with a moan, letting me eat her whole.

Her eyes roll back as I kiss her hard and rough. I don't stop to allow either of us any breath. I don't stop when she whimpers, her body going slack underneath me.

I kiss her like this is our first and last time, like I've been deprived of it for life, and I probably have. Why the fuck wasn't I kissing this woman before?

It takes all my self-restraint to wrench my mouth from hers. She's panting, staring at me with heavy-lidded eyes that are asking for trouble, something I'm more than willing to provide.

I release her neck so I can latch onto the delicate skin of her throat.

Rai's back arches off the bed as small, needy noises leave her lips. It's the first time I've heard her arousal, and fuck if that isn't a bloody turn-on.

I ravage her faster, licking then biting down, causing her to gasp and moan at the same time, as if she doesn't know which one fits the situation. Despite her stony external image, her skin tastes like fucking honey.

Her scent, something like roses and citrus mixed with alcohol, intoxicates me, and I become drunk on her. Not the liquor—*her*.

Her taste and scent hit me straight in the head, and the animal in me rears up, demanding to play.

I bite and suck on her skin, imagining how it would feel if I owned every last inch of her body here and now.

"K-Kyle..." Her moan hits me in the head, too, like a double shot. Then she does something sober Rai would never do. She glides her stomach up and down my dick, grinding against me slowly, seductively even.

Holy. Fuck. I might come here and now like a bloody teenager.

She doesn't stop her up and down motion, keeping a steady rhythm. "A-are you going to punish me, Kyle?"

"Yes, I will," I rasp against her throat.

"Now?" The uncertainty in her voice gives me pause.

After one last lick to her neck, I begrudgingly release her skin and pull away from her, causing her to stop the grinding.

I was too close to taking an irrevocable step.

Rai blinks up at me, her half-naked body still splayed in front of me, tempting me to fuck it and her to the point of no return.

I pull the sheets from underneath her and cover her to the chin.

"What about my punishment?" She doesn't hide the disappointment in her tone.

"Not in the mood."

"Fuuuuck youuu." She forces her eyes shut and a tear slides down her cheek.

Soon after, her breaths even out and she lets out a deep, pained sigh. I wipe her tear and pull her to my side as I lie on my back.

My lips find her forehead and she whimpers softly, her leg wrapping over mine.

"I'll take a raincheck on punishing and owning you, Princess."

Because when that happens, there'll be no going back.

THIRTEEN

Rai

L IGHT ASSAULTS MY EYES AND THEY FLUTTER OPEN as I grimace.

Someone turn the lights off.

"Katia…" I groan when a stabbing pain lodges at the back of my head. "Katy, get in here."

She usually appears at my side in a fraction of a second. What is wrong today? And why is my head on the verge of explosion?

"I didn't know you swung in that direction."

The strong voice coming from my right gives me pause. It's close. Too close, as if…

Oh God.

I slowly stare up, and sure enough, my head is lying on a strong bicep. Kyle's.

"What the hell are you doing in my room?" My voice strains with the force I exert to get past my headache.

"You are in my room, Princess." He lifts my hand, making me see the diamond ring around my finger and the band around his.

The rings. The marriage. The attack. Everything slams back into me all at once, causing my head to swing. *Oh shit. Fuck.* I got drunk in Kyle's company on our wedding night. What the hell was I thinking?

Closing my eyes, I try to recall what I did last night, but the only thing I can comprehend is a splitting headache. I lift the sheet to stare at my body and find myself in my underwear. That should be a good sign, right?

I sit up, disentangling myself from Kyle's embrace. His head-turning scent is still all around me, though. I don't think there's a way to get rid of the traces he leaves on me anymore.

Licking my drying lips, I try speaking in my no-nonsense tone. "What happened last night?"

Kyle leans sideways on his elbow so he's watching me closely like I'm his next target. Hell, I might as well be.

He's only in a shirt and pants. I loosely remember him removing his jacket and pulling the cuffs over his strong, veiny arms before he touched me and…what? Why can't I remember the following events?

"What do you think happened?"

"I don't know. That's why I'm asking."

He raises a brow. "What do couples do on their wedding night?"

"D-did you…?" I hate the stutter in my voice, hate how unsure and confused I sound.

"What do you think?"

I don't feel any soreness between my legs, so he couldn't have, right? Unless he did other things to me? Whose brilliant idea was it that I should get drunk? Oh yeah—mine. *Idiot.*

"You didn't," I say, more to myself than to him, but I don't cut off eye contact. I want him to look me right in the eye when he tells me.

"I didn't because you were drunk." He grabs the hem of the sheet before I can properly be relieved, and yanks it off my body. "But you're not now."

"Kyle!" I mean to scold him, but his name comes out as a surprised squeal instead.

"What? I was promised that I'd get to punish you today."

I hold the sheet to my chest as he tries to remove it again. Our warring gazes meet over the cloth. "I made no such promise."

"Drunk Rai did, and I take her word for granted."

"You're lying. I would never *ever* make such a promise." *Right?*

"Your exact words were…" His voice lowers, mimicking mine. "*Are you going to punish me, Kyle? Now?*"

"Shut up. I didn't say that." I couldn't have. But on the other hand, considering all the things I keep bottled inside, I could have let go of my inhibitions after the shitload of Jack Daniels. Note to self: never drink again, especially when with Kyle.

He runs the tip of his fingers over my cheek. "Why are you blushing then? Are you playing the amnesia game to get out of wanting me last night? You rubbed your pussy all over my dick, urging me to 'punish' you, and when I didn't, you were so disappointed you went to sleep with a pout."

I can actually feel the flames igniting all over my face at his crude words, at the suggestion of what could've happened. A flashback of that exact moment hits me straight in the head.

Are you going to punish me, Kyle? Now?

My voice…that was me.

My headache is forgotten as my eyes widen. Kyle's right—I nearly begged the bastard for it.

Drunk me and sober me are not friends anymore.

My lips part, but nothing comes out. What am I supposed to say anyway? That I didn't mean those words? He would never believe me. Hell, I wouldn't believe me either right now.

Lost for words, I pull the sheet with me and stumble out of bed. I trip on my dirty dress that's lying on the floor, but I catch myself at the last second and fly in the direction of the only other door available in the room. Thankfully, it is a bathroom.

I lock it from the inside and press my back against the door, screwing my eyes shut and breathing harshly as if I just ended a workout.

You will not get drunk again, Rai. Never again.

A knock sounds on the door, startling me from my thoughts.

"Open up."

"Go away."

"You don't get to lock yourself away from me. It's part of the rules you have to follow now that you're my wife."

"You don't get to tell me what to do. It's part of the rules you have to follow now that you're my husband."

I expect him to shoot something back in reply since he doesn't like to let me have the last word, but nothing comes. *Hmph.* He learned his place.

The bathroom isn't as small as I thought it would be from the size of the room. It's simple with gray tiles, a black sink, a toilet, and a shower stall large enough to fit three people.

Someone likes black. Like me.

Kyle never told me if this place is rented or if he owns it. Since he disappeared for the past seven years, I'm betting on the first option.

I let the sheet slide to the floor then unclasp my bra and slide my panties down my legs so they join the pile.

Something in the mirror catches my attention, and it's not only my tangled loose hair that's framing my face, making it look younger, prettier, in a docile way like Reina's. It's the violet mark on the hollow of my neck that's angry against my fair skin, almost like someone tried to rip a piece of flesh out.

Did...did the bastard leave a hickey on me?

THRONE OF POWER | 121

I reach my fingers to it, touching gently as if expecting it to disappear if I press any harder. While it doesn't hurt, the mark is visible evidence of last night, of when he touched me and I… touched him.

I did touch him. There was a moment where I didn't want to stop.

Forcing my mind to shut that thought down, I break eye contact with the hickey and head to the stall. After testing the water on my fingertips, I step under the hot stream.

The mark tingles with the water, and I find myself tilting my head as if wanting it to sting more.

My breasts feel heavy, and when I look down at myself, my nipples are slowly peaking. My stomach clenches as if demanding something. What, I don't know.

It's the water. It's only the water.

I close my eyes, leaning my head against the wall to distract myself from whatever is happening in my body. I try thinking about what I will do today to distract my mind: check on home, V Corp's report, talk to Vlad about the attack and—

A hot body appears at my back and a hand wraps around my throat from behind. I gasp on water, eyes shooting open, but I don't attempt to move.

I can't.

It's like my muscles are locked together and I'm unable to take a single step.

"I'll barge through any door you lock, so you might as well save your energy next time."

He pushes his hips forward, and my chest heaves at the feel of something very hard and ready at the crack of my ass.

"Now, about that punishment…how should I start?" He parts my ass cheeks, and I get on my tiptoes as he slides the length of his cock against my back hole. "Here?"

"S-stop it." My voice is low, insincere, even to myself.

"Why? Are you scared of the pain? Don't worry, I'll prep

you so you can take my dick up your virgin arse like a good little princess."

His dirty words are supposed to make me buck and fight him, claw at his chest and hit him in the face, but my entire body is held hostage in his grip. My nipples tighten to the point of pain, and this time, it sure as hell isn't because of the water.

"But we will start here." He parts my legs, and they open of their own volition like they were always meant to.

I don't know why I allow him to do this to me, to treat me this way like it's his God-given right, but somewhere deep inside me, I think I always longed for the moment Kyle would take from me as savagely as his real self is.

Because the actual person behind the smiles and swift kills? That person isn't visible to anyone but me, and right now all I want to do is dig my fingernails into that version, provoke it, and let it out in all its full glory.

Reina always told me I'm drawn to danger, and maybe she's right because I'm salivating for the danger that is Kyle Hunter, despite how much I hate him.

He runs the crown of his cock against my folds, causing friction so deep my legs shake.

He stops at my entrance and I tense.

"You don't have a condom."

"And that's a problem because...?" He nibbles on my earlobe.

"Because you've been dipping in God knows where and I'm not ready to catch an STD."

"That mouth of yours was more compliant when you were drunk." He continues his up and down motion, turning me hazy. Forget about being drunk—he's erasing all my thoughts right now. The only thing I can focus on is the stimulation against my sensitive folds and the unrelieved ache deep inside me.

He squeezes his hand around my throat at the same time

as he replaces his dick with two fingers, plunging them into me. I gasp on water, a moan tearing from my throat and echoing in the air.

Holy. Shit.

"This is only the preparation for your punishment." He speaks against my ear, nibbling on the shell and the earlobe. "This cunt will belong to me."

He thrusts in and out of me, and I close my eyes in mortification at the sound my arousal is making.

"Hear that? That's how much you crave what I do to you. It doesn't matter whether you're drunk or sober."

Can't he shut up? The more he speaks with that raspy British accent, the more I'm sensitive and burning for his ministrations.

His dick continues the delicious friction at the crack of my ass, syncing it with his rhythm at my pussy. "This arse will be mine, too."

I don't know if it's because of the double assault or because it's him, Kyle, the only one I haven't been able to kick out of my fortress, but the overstimulation turns me boneless. It's like all my nerve endings are about to explode at the same time.

The merciless hold of his hand around my throat adds to the unbearable stimulation.

His thumb teases my clit as he quickens his rhythm, plunging in and out of me like he's a man on a mission to destroy me.

And he does.

"Ahhh…Kyle!" I whimper as the orgasm hits me with a wrecking force. My body falls slack in his hold as my legs tremble so intensely they can't keep me standing.

It's Kyle's strong body that does. He holds me against the wall and removes his fingers, but not his dick.

I gasp as he thrusts his length between my legs, almost like he's going inside. With his hold on my neck, I strain to look back at him for the first time since he ambushed me.

His sinfully beautiful face appears right out of a photo-shoot as water glues his dark hair to his temples and forms rivulets down his neck and chest. I'm temporarily distracted by the hard ridges of his muscles and the ink that peeks out from over his abdomen.

Since he's fully covering my back with his chest, I don't get a full view of his tattoos. That little disturbance brings me back to the reason I turned around. "W-what are you doing?"

"I won't fuck you," he grunts as his pace picks up.

"Then what..."

I trail off when he jerks his hips forward, and the sensation nearly brings me to orgasm again. He thrusts between my thighs and against my core once, twice, before he groans, his chest tensing on my back. His cum covers my inner thighs before it's soon washed away by the stream.

"Fuck! Bleeding hell," he curses in a strained tone, and even though I'm barely holding on by a thread, I recognize that he just spoke in a different accent than his usual one.

It still sounds British, but it's not English, more like... Irish? Northern Irish?

That's the first time I've heard him speak in such an accent, and for some reason, it doesn't feel like he did it on purpose, more as if it came out on its own.

"What did you just...ooh..." My words end on a moan when his lips latch onto the hollow skin of my nape.

Holy. Hell.

Is that spot supposed to feel this good?

Kyle sucks on my skin while he rides his orgasm, and I remain still, as if any movement will ruin this moment. He releases my throat and holds my hair in a fist on the side to give him better access to my neck.

His other hand holds me possessively by the hip as his teeth nibble on the same mark he left yesterday. The sting starts at my throat but ends straight between my legs.

"K-Kyle…"

"What, Princess? You want more?"

I don't speak, not wanting to admit the effect he has on me. Because, yes, I do want more. It doesn't matter that I just came or that everything seems too much.

"Say it." He pulls on my hair.

"Say what?"

"Say you want every deranged fucking thing I do to you. Say you like being at my mercy when it's only the two of us."

I clamp my lips shut, refusing to acknowledge how true his words are.

"Are you or are you not going to say it?" He nibbles harder on the sensitive spot, making me wince and whimper at the same time.

Why does he get to make me feel all these polar opposite emotions all at once?

He tugs on my hair so that I'm staring back at his eyes. They appear icy, even though they're heated. He's a fucking paradox, I swear.

"Say the words, Rai. Admit. It." He enunciates the last words.

I meet his gaze with my defiant one, refusing to budge. He must see the determination on my face because he narrows his eyes. "I'm going to make you scream it."

"Never," I mutter.

He releases me and I stumble from the loss of his weight, my body suddenly feeling empty and barren. I turn to face him, but he's already stepping out of the shower.

Kyle stares at me over his shoulder and roams his hungry eyes over my naked form like he's engraving it to memory.

It takes everything in me not to fidget. I never thought being naked would make me this exposed in front of him, and yet the stupid self-consciousness won't disappear.

"Come out. We need to go." And with that, he completely steps out.

I get a full view of his fit back with the broad shoulders.

A dagger tattoo is inked in the middle, dripping blood into a pool underneath it. It's both beautiful and gruesome and so much Kyle.

The killer whose origins are unknown to all, along with the identity of who taught him to be a perfect killing machine.

The only time I allowed myself curiosity and asked him, he disappeared for seven fucking years.

I shake my head and focus on washing my hair even though my body still tingles from the orgasm he wrenched out of me.

After I'm done, I wrap a towel around my torso and another one around my hair.

While I've always prided myself on not being intimidated by men, Kyle obviously screwed that over like every other rule in my playbook.

I find him standing in front of the window, the morning light forming a halo around him.

He's dressed in black pants and a white shirt. His fingers glide over the cuffs, buttoning them with firm movements. Those same fingers were inside me not too long ago and—

I try not to focus on him and busy myself by picking my dress up off the floor. He turns around that instant, and I freeze as if I'm a kid caught stealing from a jar.

"Don't put that back on. It's dirty and bloodied."

"Do you suggest I go out in a towel, genius?"

"My wife wouldn't go anywhere in a fucking towel."

I want to curse him for the possessive way he speaks, but my insides liquefy at the way he said 'my wife'.

Stay down, insides.

He opens a closet that I thought was filled with sheets and brings out a plain black shirt and sweatpants. "Wear these."

I release the cloth and step in front of him. They're a few sizes too big, but they're better than a bloodied dress.

He holds the clothes out of reach at the last second. "Not so fast."

I give him a bemused stare. "What?"

He grabs me by the waist and tugs so he's sitting on the bed and I'm right between his legs.

I have no clue what's happening until he throws the clothes behind him and opens the nightstand, producing a small gadget. "Punishment first, Princess."

FOURTEEN

Rai

I STARE BLANKLY AT THE THING IN KYLE'S HAND. I didn't see it wrong the first time.

It *is* a sex toy.

The shape is weird, long at one end and short at the other. I've always been content with my own fingers and never really used vibrators, so I have no clue what that is.

All I know is that there's no way in hell that gadget is coming anywhere near me.

"You're out of your damn mind if you think I will let you use that *thing* on me." I try to push Kyle away, but he effortlessly keeps me trapped between his legs, using his firm grip around my waist.

"It's the punishment you asked for, though it's not really a punishment since it will bring you pleasure."

"You honestly thought I would let you punish me? *Me?* Rai Sokolov?"

His lips tilt at the corner as strokes his finger along my side, and although his skin is separated from mine by the towel, it's almost like he's caressing me directly. It's gentle but feels callous, savage, and with the intent to stimulate the deepest, darkest parts of me. It doesn't help that I'm still terrifyingly sensitive after that orgasm.

"You do like punishment. You just don't like to admit it. If I reached under this towel, I think I would find the evidence of how truly affected you are by the word 'punishment.'"

Air stops moving in and out of my lungs, and I feel the asphyxiation as I tense. What if he actually checks under the towel? The last thing I want right now is to get caught in Kyle's orbit after I've hardly left it.

But did I really leave if he keeps dragging me back in? If he effortlessly provokes parts of me I didn't even realize existed?

"Don't," I say in my stern tone.

"Don't what?"

"Don't *touch* me."

"Are you that scared of your body betraying you?"

"I just don't want your filthy hands on me."

His jaw ticks as his hold tightens around my waist to the point of inflicting pain. In a fraction of a second, his mood goes from semi-light to full-on severe. "You came like a slut by these filthy hands, Princess. So how about you drop the high-and-mighty attitude?"

"You agreed to marry me, flaws and all, so you kind of have to accept me the way I am."

"As do you—filthy hands and all."

We stare at each other for mere fractions of a second that seem like years and decades. I didn't mean it as a jab against his origins. It's a defense mechanism of mine so I can create distance between us—though it's an epic fail thus far.

In so little time, Kyle managed to get so close to parts of

me I've been diligently hiding from the world, and that's dangerous. Actually, it's more than dangerous. It can destroy what I've been building for long, painful years.

"You're not putting that toy inside me." I stare him square in the face. "You can't force me."

He pauses for a second as if contemplating if he should do just that, but then he speaks with a calm that takes me aback. "Let's make a bargain, since you love those so much."

"What type of bargain?"

"You'll wear any toy I want you to wear in exchange for information about where the Irish are going to strike next."

I narrow my eyes. "How would you know that?"

"I have a spy."

"The brotherhood's spy?"

"No, *mine*. A colleague of sorts."

"Vlad has his spy, too. He will find out."

"His spy isn't as highly ranked as mine."

"How highly ranked are we talking about?"

"High enough that he can rearrange things so the Irish hit exactly where the Bratva want them to. Remember your recent plan about luring in the Italians to take the fall?"

"You're supposed to do that without resorting to bargaining with me. You're part of the Vory now, and it's your duty to help."

"Not if it doesn't benefit me."

"I will tell Sergei."

"And I will just deny it. Do you have evidence of my spy's existence?"

Ugh. The infuriating asshole. He hit me on the arm that hurts the most. There's no way I'll let go of such a golden opportunity, and Kyle knows that more than anyone.

"What's it going to be? My offer expires in about…three, two—"

"Fine!" I heave out. "Just get it over with."

He grins like the Cheshire Cat. "Glad to do business with you."

"I'm sure you are," I mutter under my breath. He tugs on the towel, but I plant a hand on it. "You don't need to remove it."

"That's up to me to decide, and I say it needs to be gone." With a swift twist of his hand, he yanks the towel free, letting it pool around my feet. I'm standing completely naked in front of him, again.

My nipples harden, and I tell myself it's because of the air. Just the air.

I breathe through my nostrils, then my mouth. Slowly.

In.

Out.

He won't affect me if I don't allow him to. All I have to do is pretend all this means nothing.

Kyle glides his fingers over my folds in what seems to be a gentle stroke, but there's nothing remotely gentle about Kyle. He might appear like an elegant gentleman, but he's all rough edges and power simmering under the surface, waiting to be unleashed on the world.

His fingers tease at my entrance, close enough to thrust inside, but he never gets on with it. "I thought about prepping you, but you're already wet."

I purse my lips together to not get caught up in the feel of his fingers near my entrance.

"Look at your cunt inviting my filthy hand in." He smirks up at me, and now I'm sure his touch is meant to antagonize me.

"Do it, already," I manage, barely holding the moan inside.

"Patience." Still teasing my entrance, he slides the toy's head over my wet folds. I stand on my tiptoes at the sensation. While it's not entirely the same, it's similar to what he did with his cock earlier, and now I can't chase away the image of when he was wrenching that orgasm out of me like a relentless savage.

My nails dig into his shoulders because I feel as if I will somehow lose my balance any second.

Kyle slides the toy to my entrance where it meets his fingers, then runs it back up to my clit. I let out a whimper, and he watches me with a heated gleam that is too intimate and ferocious like a villain's kiss.

"Aren't you going—" My words cut off when he thrusts the head inside me in one go.

I topple over, using his shoulders for balance.

Holy. Shit.

I think I'm going to come or throw up. Or both.

"You're too tight, aren't you?" he muses. "If you can't take this toy, how are you going to take my dick?"

It's bigger than this? Sure, I felt his bulge earlier, but I never really got a close look at his cock.

The question must be written all over my face because Kyle smirks in that sadistic way. "When I get inside you, I'll make you scream with both pleasure and pain. In the meantime, I want you to walk with this dildo inside you and imagine it's me."

"You can't control my imagination."

"I just did." He fusses with something until the small part of the vibrator is tucked between my folds.

It's not entirely uncomfortable, but it's still odd, like something I've never imagined before, let alone wondered about trying.

"You like it, Mrs. Hunter."

"I'm not Mrs. Hunter. I told you I won't be changing my last name." I'm a Sokolov and I will remain a Sokolov until the end of my days.

"Doesn't matter. You're already Mrs. Hunter in my head."

"That doesn't mean anything."

"It does to me." He picks up the clothes and hands them to me. "Now, get dressed."

"Wait—you expect me to go out with this thing inside me?"

"Of course. What did you think?"

"I thought you'd play with it here."

"That's not fun."

"I'm not going outside with it."

"Yes, you will. You will wear it to meals and meetings and even to V Corp. Every time you move, you'll remember I'm with you every step of the way."

"You're sick."

"Thanks."

"It wasn't a compliment."

"I take it as one. Now, are you going to keep your word?"

He knows exactly which buttons to push to have me comply with his stupid-ass games. I snatch the clothes from his hand but make sure to tell him, "I hate you."

Kyle stands up abruptly, startling me when he steals a brief kiss. "But you'll love my games, Princess."

FIFTEEN

Rai

I TRY NOT TO WALK FUNNY INTO THE HOUSE, BUT THE thing Kyle shoved in me shifts with every step I take, creating friction I want to consider uncomfortable when it's anything but.

We stopped at the mall because there was no way in hell I was allowing anyone to see me with a makeup-less face and in baggy, unflattering clothes.

I'm now dressed in a simple dark gray dress, my hair is pulled up, and my makeup is flawless. I had to buy a set of pearls because even heavy foundation didn't completely conceal the hickey on my neck, which has now turned dark blue.

Kyle gave me a disapproving glance when I came out to meet him. What right does he have to look at me that way after the unbearable sensation he's causing me with the toy right now?

"Something bothering you, Princess?" A low voice whispers

at my ear, and it takes everything in me to not swing around and hit him across the face just to erase that smug tone. He's having so much fun tormenting me.

"Stay away from me."

"No can do. We got married yesterday, remember?"

How could I forget? My lips still tingle from the possessive way he kissed me in front of the world as if that has always been his purpose in life, as if claiming me in front of everyone has been his mission, his fate, and his driving force.

"Being married doesn't mean anything." I try to speak casually in a hopeless attempt to kill the chain of thoughts forming in my head.

"Just because you refuse to admit it, doesn't mean it has no meaning. You'll get used to it, though."

He speaks with so much arrogance, as if he knows the future and is taunting me with it.

I swing around, causing us both to halt. "Don't think you're something because Igor somehow decided to make you his son. You'll always be the stray dog *Dedushka* took in and turned into somebody."

His expression doesn't change, but he shoves a hand in his pocket as if stopping it from acting on something. "Careful, Mrs. Hunter. The more you insult me, the more I will drag you down by the throat."

I point a finger at his chest. "I'm not scared of you."

He grabs my hand in place, and when I try to escape, he keeps it imprisoned in a hold so tight it's impossible to break. His face lowers so it's a few inches from mine. The meticulous mask he wears so well falters a little, and I get a glimpse of his true self.

His eyes are…empty. Desolate.

Dedushka used to tell me there's nothing more frightening than a man who has nothing to lose.

And now, I'm staring right at the soul of one.

"You should be," he says with a chilling calm that stabs straight to my bones. "You really, *really* should be."

We remain like that for what seems like hours, just gazing at each other as his words sink in.

Even a long time ago, Kyle always managed to confiscate my attention and cage it behind metal bars. Seven years later, he still has that effect on me, and what's worse is that he's coming off stronger, harsher, as if it's his final strike.

A clearing of a throat cuts off the connection. I blink once as Kyle's immaculate mask snaps into place and he loosens his hold on my hand.

I step back as if I've been shocked, heart hammering at a strange pace.

It takes me a few seconds to refocus on Sergei coming down the stairs, accompanied by Anastasia. She's grinning from ear to ear as her gaze goes from me to Kyle and back again. That girl has always been a hopeless romantic.

Schooling my features, I join them and take Ana's hands in mine. "Are you guys all right?"

"We're fine." She smiles like an idiot. "Tell me about *you*."

"There's nothing to tell." I direct my focus to Sergei. "What were our casualties? Did we lose any men? What happened after the attack ended?"

"One question at a time, Rayenka." Sergei calls me by the nickname he would never use in front of the other men because that would mean he was showing favoritism toward me.

"Tell me."

"Join me." He motions his head at Kyle. "You too."

Anastasia kisses his cheek then tiptoes over and whispers in my ear, "You'll tell me all about the fun you had last night, okay?"

I push her away teasingly, and she giggles as she heads back up the stairs.

One of the guards opens the dining room door for Sergei, and the three of us go inside.

We're greeted by a heated argument between the four kings in Russian. Adrian and Vlad are nowhere to be found. It's not a surprise in the case of Adrian since attending meetings isn't a habit he maintains, but Vlad's absence is concerning.

"Where's Vlad?" I ask Sergei.

"He's taking care of the police procedures so that nothing falls back on us," he tells me, speaking low enough so the others don't hear. "The attack caused quite the commotion."

"It's all because of your reckless behavior," Igor accuses Damien.

"Me?" Damien laughs. "Sure thing, Igor, let's blame your lack of competence on me, shall we?"

"You fucked up, Orlov." Kirill throws his own accusation. "You threw us into a war we do not need."

"Stop being a pussy, Kirill. This is not rainbows and fucking unicorns. This is the Bratva."

"One of my men died," Kirill snarls. "Are you going to go to his mother and deliver the news?"

"No, but I will give her his fucking medallion of honor, because he died for his brothers."

"Two of my men were injured, too," Mikhail says, sipping from his glass of vodka. In fact, all the men aside from Igor have glasses of liquor in front of them. If they're drinking alcohol first thing in the morning, then shit is hitting the fan.

"Oh, shut the fuck up, old man." Damien rolls his eyes. "Your men need retraining."

"Are you saying my men are incompetent, Orlov?" Mikhail's face reddens with exertion.

"Exactly. Did dealing with pussy turn you into one?"

"You fucking—" Mikhail stands up, probably to punch Damien, but Sergei's presence makes them fall silent.

He slowly lowers himself into his seat, his expression neutral.

I attempt to sit beside Damien, but Kyle cuts in before me and snatches the seat so I'm forced to take Igor's side.

"Blaming each other won't bring any results," Sergei says as an indirect reply to the quarrel we witnessed. "We're brothers and we help our own when they're in need."

Grumbles and clearings of throats fill the room as Damien gives the other three a smug look.

"Lazlo and Kai were shot yesterday," Igor says. "That could bring the Italians and the Japanese closer or throw them apart."

"We need to test the waters with both," I say.

Mikhail clicks his tongue. "Shouldn't you be on a honeymoon or something?"

I smile. "And leave you to screw things up?"

Damien snickers under his breath, and I give him an appreciative glance.

"Test the waters?" Sergei asks.

"Kai thought we were the ones behind it, so if we prove we aren't, he'll bring the Japanese's full arsenal."

"So will the Italians," Kirill chips in. "Especially since they know about the Irish threat."

"We should send highly ranked people to both camps," Igor repeats my suggestion from earlier.

"I will meet with Kai," I say. "He seemed open to dialogue yes…terday."

My voice catches at the end when something moves inside me. The toy—it's vibrating.

Holy. Hell.

There's no noise, but the stimulation is definitely there.

My eyes widen, flying to Kyle across the table. He sits with one of his hands clutching a drink while the other is hidden under the table, no doubt causing this.

My panties feel soaked in mere seconds, and any squirming I do only causes the friction to increase.

"Are you okay?" Igor asks with genuine concern, obviously

noticing the fidgeting. *Please don't tell me my face is flushed or something.*

"I-I'm fine," I manage to mutter.

I try meeting Kyle's gaze, but he pretends to be overly interested in Sergei. His sharp features are relaxed, nonchalant even, as he speaks. "Kai appeared convinced. I suggest Kirill makes sure of that since he has better relations with the Yakuza than anyone here."

"I can check," Kirill complies.

I try to focus on him and not the humming inside me, but it's almost impossible with the stimulation. It's like I'm back in the shower with Kyle's fingers inside me, and—

No. Get out of my head.

"In the meantime, allow me to visit the Italians," Kyle tells Sergei. "Since it was my wedding, I can apologize to the Don and get an idea of what they're thinking."

"An apology goes a long way with the Italians," Igor says.

"Exactly." Kyle grins at his father then his gaze slides to me, slowly, unhurriedly, before his lips pull up in a smirk.

Stop it, I mouth, gripping the edge of the table for balance.

His smirk widens before he masks it and pretends like he's not torturing me in a room full of men.

"Take Adrian with you," Sergei says, and Kyle nods.

"I'm going too," I speak quietly, holding in a moan.

"No, you're not," Kyle says.

"Yes, I am. It was *our* wedding. They'll be more open if it's both of us."

"Or more closed off because you're a woman," Mikhail asserts.

"Adrian and I will be enough." Kyle meets my gaze as the vibration intensifies.

My fingers tremble, and it takes all my self-restraint to not moan or whimper or release any embarrassing sounds. I haven't been stimulated like this in my entire life, and the fact that I can't relieve it is turning me delirious.

"Rai," Sergei calls my name, and it scarcely filters through the buzz in my ears. "Are you unwell?"

"Are you?" Kyle reaches my side in two seconds and touches my forehead like a doting husband. I want to knee him in the balls, but I can't shift my focus from the humming inside me.

I clamp my lips shut as a trail of sweat falls over my temple. I can't even speak because if I open my mouth, the only thing that will come out right now is a shameful needy sound.

"My apologies, *Pakhan*. It appears I exhausted her last night."

I can feel my nerves constricting and the color draining from my face as his words fall on the room like doom.

Sergei and Igor clear their throats. Damien and Kirill snicker, and Mikhail appears like he wants both our heads on the table in front of him.

I can't believe he just said that.

He didn't, right? Please tell me what I heard was a figment of my imagination.

"I'll take her to rest." Kyle carries me in his arms with effortless ease. I couldn't resist even if I wanted to because the thing is still vibrating and my legs are Jell-O.

But at the same time, I hate how familiar this position in his arms has become, almost like it was a given.

Before we get out, the vibration increases. I release a squeal and then hide my face in his shoulder, muffling the sound as the toy thrums against my clit.

I bite on his shirt hard as the wave hits me out of nowhere.

Well, hell.

I think I just came.

SIXTEEN

Rai

I MUFFLE MY SCREAM WITH THE CLOTH OF KYLE'S SHIRT as he casually walks me out of the room. I barely register the murmurs from inside, Kyle's sure and confident excuses, and finally, the guard closing the door after we exit.

That didn't just happen.

I didn't orgasm in front of my granduncle and the leaders of the brotherhood.

Just when I'm contemplating the best way to get rid of Kyle's body, the humming intensifies between my legs.

"Stop it…" I trail off at the moan in my voice. The arousal in it is like nothing I've ever heard before.

"Stop what?" He comes to a slow halt at the foot of the stairs and murmurs against my ear, "Bringing you pleasure?"

The heat of his breath and the slight stubble of his jaw against the shell of my ear awakens a different type of friction that starts at my auditory sense and shoots between my legs.

No, this isn't happening again. Not again.

I wiggle so he'll let me down, but he only heightens the intensity level at my clit.

"Holy shit…" I exhale, sinking my nails into his shirt.

"Does it feel good?" He smirks.

"Fuck you," I manage to mutter.

"Not yet, but I can keep you satisfied with my toys in the meantime." He licks the lobe of my ear, sliding his tongue over it, flicking and biting as if he's feasting on my tongue. "I didn't expect you to be this sensitive. I can't wait to see the look on your face when my dick is plunged deep inside your tight cunt."

I can't help the whimper that spills free from between my clenched teeth. I tell myself it's only because of the toy's stimulation, but his words add more fuel to the fire.

He says them with sure certainty, as if they're meant to happen. For him, the question is when, not if, and for some reason, my chest flips at the promise, at the explosive pleasure I now know is waiting for me in the future.

"You're going to come one more time, aren't you?" he muses, releasing my earlobe just so he can show me the way he licks his lips.

I try to ignore the view as I shake my head frantically. I'll be damned if I let him get a hold on me again.

"Yes, you will. Are you picturing me inside you, taking my dick like a good little princess while I thrust into you hard and fast and rough?"

My thighs clench at the image he's painted in my head. I couldn't get rid of it even if I tried. It's so crude, so explicit, and yet my body responds to it in ways I never thought were possible.

"Rai?"

I gasp inaudibly at Vlad's voice coming from behind us. He can't see me like this. No one can. This is a sure way to destroy the image I've spent years building and sacrificing for.

And yet, I can't, for the life of me, stop the storm that's brewing in the distance. I can feel the air inside me changing, heating, prepping for the impact that will sweep me over and never let me go.

"Is everything all right?" Vlad's voice gets nearer, which means he's approaching us and won't let this go.

He, of all people, knows I never allow anyone to carry me unless I'm ill or injured or something. Why has it become easy to let Kyle manhandle me this way? But I couldn't put a halt to it even if I wanted to. My legs would fail me and my weakness would be visible for Vlad to see.

"Tell him to piss off," Kyle murmurs.

"Shut up," I hiss.

"Then maybe I should drop you right here and now so he can see how much of a slut his little mafia princess actually is." His voice darkens with every word.

"K-Kyle…" My eyes widen as I shake my head. "D-don't…"

"Add a please."

"Please go fuck yourself," I mutter.

"Not the right attitude when you need me." He starts to release his hands from around me as the thing inside me increases its vibrations.

Shit. I'm going to orgasm.

I claw at his shirt with my nails so he doesn't release me. "Don't! Please, *please.*"

"Perfect. Now tell your knight in shining armor to—as I said earlier—piss. Off."

"I-I'm fine, Vlad." My voice trembles and I bite my lower lip to stop any other sounds from escaping.

"You don't sound fine." Vlad stops in my peripheral vision, and I hide in Kyle's shirt. I would rather die than let Vlad see my face right now—a face even I wouldn't recognize.

"She's just a little unwell," Kyle speaks in the welcoming tone that usually gets him what he wants. "I'll take her to our room."

Our room? When the hell did it become *our* room?

"Let me look at her." Vlad steps in front of us.

"Why the fuck would you look at my wife?" All Kyle's nonchalance vanishes. "She's not the Rai you had free access to. She's now bound to me, married to me, and took vows to be with me so keep your fucking eyes and hands off her."

There's a grunt from Vlad, but he steps aside. No one gets between a husband and his wife in the brotherhood. No one, not even the *Pakhan* himself. The relationship is even more sacred than the one we have among each other.

That's why even Vlad doesn't push it.

"I'm really f-fine, Vlad," I repeat to reassure him without lifting my head.

By the time Kyle finally ascends the stairs, I can't keep on trapping the violent sensation brewing inside me.

I tighten my hold around Kyle's neck as I let the orgasm hit me. While the stimulation is mostly between my legs, my whole body clenches and I shake uncontrollably in Kyle's hold.

"That's it," he whispers. "Show me that abandonment face. Your real freedom."

I lift my head to stare at his expression because, for some reason, it feels like he's shed his mask.

Katia and Ruslan's silhouettes in front of my room put a halt to my curiosity. They rush toward us—or me, to be more specific.

I hide my face in Kyle's shirt so they don't witness me like this. They will see me as weak, and weak people don't survive in the Vory.

"Rai feels a bit unwell. I will put her to bed," Kyle offers on my behalf, and I'm so thankful for it, even if he's the reason I'm like this in the first place.

"Should we take her to the hospital?" Katia asks.

"I'll bring the car." Ruslan starts to leave.

"There's no need." Kyle motions at them. "You should go downstairs. She will call if she needs you."

They appear hesitant, but after a small nod from me, they comply and head to the stairs.

He pushes the door to my room open, and I take a peek to make sure no one is inside. Sure enough, it's empty.

My bedroom is simple. There's a queen-sized bed, a console, and two doors aligned symmetrically. One leads to the bathroom, the other to my walk-in closet.

The balcony's door is closed, as always. *Dedushka* taught me to be wary of snipers since I was little. That's why every window in this house is made of bulletproof glass. It cost a fortune to set up, but when you live a dangerous life like ours, nothing can be taken for granted.

Dedushka shouldn't have brought this killer who's carrying me in his arms after he taught me to be cautious of them. It shouldn't work that way.

Kyle places me on my feet to lock the door. I push away from him and brace myself against the wall for balance because, even now, the thing is still vibrating inside me, demanding more orgasms.

Holding on to the wall with a sweaty, trembling hand, I reach under my dress and close my eyes in mortification when the evidence of my arousal soaks my fingers.

"Stop."

The commanding word makes me pause, my eyes slowly fluttering open. I've never been one to bow down in front of authority, but the way Kyle uses it always stabs me in a secret part that confuses the hell out of me.

Kyle isn't hyper-authoritative like the men downstairs whom I've spent all my life with. I'm used to male reign and stopped being intimidated by it at a young age.

However, Kyle appears tame, approachable even, almost like he should be a doctor or some hot CEO instead of being in this line of work. While I know it's a deceptive façade, he's perfected it so well that when he shows his masculine, authoritative side, I have no choice but to stop and stare.

"If you remove it, our deal is null and void." He tips his chin in my direction. "The ball is in your court."

"You expect me to walk around with this thing inside me all day?" I hate how much my voice is trembling and how needy and out of control I sound.

"It should loosen you up a little, bring you down from your ivory tower."

"Kyle…" I meant to warn, but his name comes out like a whimper instead.

"We had a deal: you wear my toys, I get the Irish where you want. Are you going back on your world, Miss Sokolov?"

I hate when he calls me that. It feels so distant and strange after all the time we've known each other and everything we've been through. But who am I kidding? That time only meant something to me in the past. Now, it's nothing.

"At least make it stop," I say through gritted teeth.

"Say the word that will get you things from me."

"What word?"

"Beg me. Beg this filthy stray dog to relieve you of your misery."

"I'm Rai Sokolov. I beg no one."

"You did it in front of Vladimir. You can do it again. Don't worry, it will become a habit with time."

"I'm not going to beg you—ahhhh…" My words end on a moan when he increases the intensity of the vibrator until its sound can be heard. "Stop…ahhh…"

"I still have five more intensity levels to go, one for every minute you remain stubborn." He removes his hand from his pocket, revealing a small black remote. "Actually, let's take it up a notch and make that every second—starting now."

He clicks on the button, and I sag against the wall as the vibration intensifies to an unbearable level. My nipples tighten against the dress's built-in bra, and my legs shake.

"Kyle…"

"That's not begging. Try harder." He clicks again and I moan, my lips trembling in mortification as I feel my wetness soaking my panties and coating my inner thighs.

"Jesus…"

"Yeah, he's not going to help in this unholy union." He clicks again, and this time, I scream as the dildo gets deeper inside me. I'm no virgin, but the last time I was sexually active was a decade ago, so I might as well be.

"Two more to go…oh, wait. Turns out there are seven. I forgot it has special modes for naughty girls like you."

"Fine, you win, stop it."

"Not unless you beg and you make it convincing."

"Stop it…p-please…"

"What was that at the end? I didn't quite catch it."

"*Please.*"

"That's it." He clicks on a button and the vibration stops.

I slide to the floor, catching my breath and trying to stop the disappointed sensation that's settling at the pit of my stomach.

A shadow falls over me before his voice fills the air. "That wasn't so hard, now was it?"

I pull myself up to my feet, raise my hand and slap him across the face. The sound echoes in the silence surrounding us and my palm stings. "Don't you *ever* put me in a weak position in front of the men downstairs. I'm not only your wife, I'm V Corp's executive manager and an asset to the brotherhood. I didn't get this far for you to drag me down."

His jaw clenches, and instead of the anger I expected, a manic smirk tugs on his lips. "I'll play with you however I please."

"You will not break me, do you hear me?"

"You shouldn't tempt a predator with prey, Princess. That will only provoke my need to hunt."

"I'll get you back for this. You have my fucking word." I push past him to the bathroom to clean up.

"Don't remove the toy," he calls after me. "I'll know if you do."

I flip him off over my shoulder without looking at him.

A low chuckle follows me as I get inside and lock the door. Fuck Kyle's warnings about not doing just that.

I stare at my face in the mirror, and like this morning, I barely recognize the woman who greets me back. My cheeks are red, lips puffy, and my usually impeccable hair looks like a mess. The worst part? My insides are still tingling, demanding more of the torture I just endured at Kyle's hands.

In no time, he's turning me into a masochist who can't get enough of him and his ministrations.

What the hell is he doing to me?

Frustrated at myself, I yank a towel off the rack, wet it, and wipe between my thighs. I remove my ruined panties and throw them in the trash since they're not usable anymore. It takes me some time to make myself presentable again.

Kyle thought he could subdue me with this, but obviously he doesn't know the Rai he left behind while he disappeared to God knows where.

I exit the bathroom just as he opens the room's door. I catch a whiff of his last sentence: "...on my way. It's all going according to plan."

Or so he thinks.

Kyle won't feel the disaster until he's caught in the middle. As I promised, he'll pay for the whole shit show he inflicted upon me today.

SEVENTEEN

Kyle

I FIND ADRIAN IN HIS CAR DOWNSTAIRS.

He lifts his chin in greeting, and I do the same as I slide beside him.

We don't take off right away, though. He looks through the window and makes sure all his guards are in place. It isn't a surprise since he's known to be careful. It's his silent strategic nature that's allowed him to be one of the strongest pillars of the Vory, if not the deadliest.

"Where are your guards?" he asks.

"I don't need them."

His light grey eyes flicker a little. They're muted a dull cloudy sky, but at the same time, they're intense, hard, and merciless. It's strange how they add to his ruthless personality. He doesn't show it often, but when he does, it's game over.

His general appearance is different from the rest of the leaders. His jet-black hair and trimmed beard are always meticulous, and yet seem rebellious. He can pass as the least Russian-looking or the most, depending on whether he speaks in an American or a Russian accent. He uses that tactic a lot when he does his thing for the brotherhood.

"Underestimating your opponent is a sure way to be defeated before you even get started, Kyle." He uses the American accent.

"They can't reach my level."

"Arrogance is another way to lose."

"Stop the philosophical bullshit. I did get myself a guard after Igor insisted." I search the crowd for a bleached-haired brat. "There he is."

Adrian raises an eyebrow. "He looks like a kid."

"That's because he is one. Barely twenty, newly recruited orphan, school dropout. I'm teaching him the ways of the Bratva."

"How would you teach him something you don't believe in?"

"Hey." I pretend to be offended. "Just because I don't sing the Russian anthem doesn't mean I'm not part of this holy union."

"We don't sing the Russian anthem. Do you even know why the Bratva started?"

"Sure do—USSR and World War bollocks that I'm not interested in hearing about. What I am interested in, however, is your love story with the Italians. What made the overly distrustful Luciano family trust you so much? It can't be your non-existent charm."

"It could be something similar to why Rai married you."

"What do you mean?"

"Blackmail."

I smile even though I want to snarl.

"What?" He picks up on my change of mood. "She would've never married you of your own accord. Even Sergei knows that. Which brings me to the question: what will you do once she figures out who you are?"

"She won't."

"And if she does?"

"So what if she does?"

"She'll turn your life into hell."

I have no doubt she would do just that.

The image of Rai's defiant expression earlier comes to mind, the way she stared up at me even when she was suffering. The way she slapped me to prove a point. That woman is made of hard steel with incomparable tenacity. Nikolai developed the Russian endurance in her bones, and it fucking shows.

But if there's anyone who will melt that metal fortress and reach the person that's inside, it's going to be me.

The toys and the games are just the beginning, a preparation phase for what's really going to come.

I will start with her body and end with her fucking soul. The more she defies me, the more tempted I am to break her in.

Which is weird, considering that's not part of my mission. If anything, being tangled up in Rai Sokolov might compromise what I came back to do. And yet, whenever she looks at me with those challenging eyes, all I can think about is taking her up on it.

"Speaking of the princess," Adrian says, and my first knee-jerk reaction is to punch him in the throat. Only *I* am allowed to call her Princess.

I stare through the window, and sure enough, Rai marches toward us with sure, confident steps. Her makeup and hair are fixed, and she looks ready to take over the world.

I wouldn't be surprised if one day she does—when I'm out of the picture, of course.

She opens the door on my side and barges inside. When I don't slide in beside Adrian, she sits partly on my lap. It's a mere brush of clothes against clothes, but my dick jumps to life at her closeness, at the warmth of her skin under the dress, and at the fact that she's still wearing the toy I shoved inside her.

I inhale deep, and that only makes things worse since her scent infiltrates my nostrils. She smells like an exotic goddess out to destroy her peasants. It's not only about the intense perfume that makes her presence known, but also the way it mixes with her natural scent.

It takes me a few seconds to get my mind out of my dick.

"What do you think you're doing?" I don't contain my displeased tone.

Controlling our emotions is the first thing we were trained to do, and yet, all those years seem to vanish whenever this spitfire of a woman is around.

"You're paying a visit to the Lucianos, right?"

"Yes," Adrian says with a calm I sure as fuck don't feel.

She lifts her chin. "I'm coming, too."

"No, you're not." I try to push her out of the car, but she grabs my bicep, nails sinking into the cloth and my skin. It's like being scratched by a small kitten. The expression on her face is anything but, though. She's on a mission and won't stop until she accomplishes it.

That's one of the traits that never changed about her: determination mixed with fearlessness.

"You can't stop me. If you kick me out, I will follow you in my car."

"And do what?" I feign nonchalance. "Tell Lazlo you're sorry he got shot at our wedding?"

"Exactly."

"No. It will appear disrespectful if a woman is sent to visit him."

Her lips thin into a line, because she knows I'm right. The Italians are as traditional as the Russians, if not worse. They don't take well to women in leadership positions—at all. The only reason she's allowed in the Vory's inner circle is due to being Nikolai's granddaughter and her being smart enough to remain in the background while her granduncle rules. It doesn't mean she likes or accepts the sexist reality of the world she was thrown into, though. Rai has always been the type who swims against the current.

"It's not disrespectful since it was my wedding," she counters.

"*Our*," I correct her.

She glares at me but doesn't comment on that and says, "Point is, the Lucianos will appreciate the gesture."

"No, they won't, and you're not the one who will be faulted for this. Sergei will appear disrespectful for sending you."

"He didn't."

"They will assume he did."

"If we go together, it will be more respectful." She steals a glance at Adrian. "Right?"

Still not participating in the conversation and observing the show like a freak, he shakes his head once.

Rai's shoulders sag, expression falling. She knows she's been pushed into a corner and can't do anything about it.

For some reason, something inside me tightens at the look in her eyes, the frustration mixed with despair.

I don't want that look on her face. Ever. No idea why, but I just don't like it.

"Unless you ask to meet his wife?" I suggest.

Adrian raises a brow at me as if he knows exactly where my train of thought went and why the hell I'm saying this when I was so hell-bent on kicking her out.

"You mean, console her?" she asks.

"Something of the sorts, but it needs to look authentic and not out of pity."

"Then that's a good reason for me to go with you now."

"No."

"Why the hell not?"

"Because it wouldn't seem genuine." I pause, stroking her arm. She's as caught up by surprise as I am by the gesture, her huge eyes staring up at me. "Set up a brunch for women only and make her the guest of honor."

Her nose twitches as she winces before she quickly hides it. That's weirdly adorable. "I'm not good at female bonding."

"You're doing just fine with Anastasia and—"

She places her palm on my mouth, shutting me up, and shakes her head discreetly. Right. She doesn't want anyone in the Vory to know about the existence of her twin sister. I have my suspicions that Adrian has figured it out already, though.

I remove her hand but still hold it in my palm. I don't know when the fuck touching her became so familiar to the point of turning into an addiction. "Have Anastasia help you and you'll get through it."

She narrows her eyes on me in that suspicious way. I wouldn't blame her. All my actions have been red-alert-worthy.

"I don't trust you," she says point-blank.

"As you shouldn't. The moment you trust me, you start digging your own grave, Princess."

"Then how do you expect me to go along with this plan?"

"I don't have to tell you which is the best option. That brain of yours already works in overdrive, so listen to what it tells you."

She watches me for a second too long. I don't attempt to cut off eye contact. There's something addictive about a war of gazes with Rai—another thing that hasn't changed.

A clearing of a throat causes her to look away first.

"If you're done with your honeymoon..." Adrian trails off.

"Nah, the honeymoon starts tonight." I give Rai a suggestive glance.

"As if!" She hits me on the shoulder and opens the car's door.

"She's kinky," I whisper to Adrian.

She swings back toward me, glaring, and a red hue covers her cheeks. "I heard that, and I'm not."

"Well, one of us is."

Adrian's lips twitch, but he doesn't fully smile. Those are as rare as a passing unicorn over England's sun.

If possible, Rai's cheeks redden further, but she chooses to ignore me. "Can I count on Lia to come to the brunch?"

At the mention of his very sheltered wife, Adrian's demeanor changes even though his expression remains the same. There's a slight tightness in his muscles that a normal person wouldn't notice. The reason I do is that we were trained to read body language, especially that of an opponent before an attack. That's Adrian right now—he's ready to pounce.

Well, isn't that fucking interesting?

"You know her health isn't well these days," he tells Rai with a smile.

"Come on, it will be in the afternoon and I won't keep her for long." When he remains silent, she adds, "I insist. I'll text you the day and time." Before she slips out of the car, she pretends to be fixing the collar of my shirt, then leans in, her lips brushing against my ear. When she whispers, her stubborn voice makes my dick fucking hard. "This isn't over."

It sure as fuck isn't.

EIGHTEEN

Rai

"**A**BSOLUTELY NOTHING?" I STARE UP AT KATIA and Ruslan as we sit in my room's lounge area.

Or more like, I sit. My two guards still refuse to rest in my presence, not even when I order them to.

"I went as far as asking underground, miss," Ruslan says in his gruff voice. "And no one knows anything about Kyle Hunter prior to him joining the Bratva."

"Not even before *Dedushka's* time?"

He shakes his head.

"There's another thing," Katia chimes in, arms in front of her and legs apart as if she's on standby.

"What?"

"The last name Hunter could be a fake or forged."

Great. The man I took for my husband is the biggest mystery of all. When I asked my guards to look into him, I didn't expect a detailed report, but I thought I would at least know something about his past. It could be anything as long as I get to use it against him.

My blood still boils from the way I was kicked out of Adrian's car earlier. Kyle just came a few days ago, and now he gets to conduct important business on behalf of Sergei.

I figured out a long time ago that I'm living in an unfair world that depends on gender, but the sting is different this time. It feels like I lost more of my power to him, which will not happen again.

You can't let it happen again, I chide myself.

"Miss?"

I stare up at Katia. "Yes?"

"With all due respect, may I ask why you married someone we can't keep track of? We…" She shares a glance with Ruslan. "We are worried about you."

"We've never seen you unwell before," Ruslan adds.

They really shouldn't have said those words. Now the ice I've been cultivating and hardening in sharp blades is melting at their concerned expressions.

I've never seen loyalty as deep as I see it in these two. I have no doubt they'd run into the line of fire just to save me—not that I would ever let them. They mean so much more to me than mere guards. I meant what I told Reina the other day: they're family, and I protect my family even if I have to fight tooth and nail.

"You don't have to worry. I'm a Sokolov, and we always win. Besides, just because he keeps his past under wraps, doesn't mean it doesn't exist."

"What do you mean?" Katia asks.

"It means I have to dig harder with the man himself."

Ruslan shifts his attention to Katia then back to me. "He could lie."

"I won't be obvious about my digging, so he won't figure it out. First of all, I want to do a secret DNA test to know if his parental relationship with Igor is real. I'll get you Kyle's hair."

"Igor's won't be easy to obtain." Katia grimaces. "His security is like a fort."

"We can bribe one of the servants," Ruslan offers.

I shake my head. "They're not susceptible to bribery, and the whole thing might backfire in our faces. Igor won't stay still if he knows I'm spying on him, not to mention I'm already walking a fine line with him ever since I dug into his financials. I'll make up a reason to visit his wife."

"Yes, Stella likes you and kept asking about you at the wedding."

"Let's hope her opinion doesn't change after I do this." Because if she really turns out to be my mother-in-law, she'll probably know I'm not sincere toward her son.

During the rest of the evening, my guards and I continue our strategic planning for the brunch. If I want to have the Italians join, led by Lazlo's wife, I can't do it in our house. None of the Italians would send their wives to the Russians' compound. We may be allies, but it's jungle law, and no one completely trusts the other.

It needs to be a public place that's in a shared territory so that the Italians can feel like they have the same control as us and, therefore, will be safe.

Anastasia and Lia will have to join me so I feel more in my element with my people. It would've been perfect if Reina were here, too, but I would rather be shot in the chest than bring my twin sister into this world.

After my guards leave, I spend some time with Ana and tell her about the brunch, and she jumps up from excitement. Being sheltered her whole life makes her giddy at the slightest change of patterns.

Seeing her happy is contagious, and I go back to my room with a big smile on my face.

It immediately drops when I find Kyle sitting in the lounge area, his fingers moving over the keyboard of a laptop that's settled on the coffee table.

My stomach dips, and the toy that's still lodged deep inside me tingles, even though it's not moving. I hate these emotions, the familiarity, the intimacy I can't stop myself from feeling toward him.

So I go straight to the defensive. "What are you doing in my room?"

"*Our* room," he says without lifting his head. "We're married, *Mrs. Hunter*, remember? Or did you have too much to drink and need me to punish you again?"

I grab the nearest object, which happens to be a pillow, and throw it at him. He catches it over his head, his focus still on the laptop, but his lips tilt in a smirk as if he knows exactly which of my buttons to push.

Well, he's not the only one with surprises. But first… "I'm removing the toy."

"No."

"It's already night. You're not expecting me to wear it while I sleep, are you?"

"Whatever I plan is none of your concern. All you need to do is keep your part of the deal. Now, be a good little princess and stay silent while I have a conference call."

"With who?" I approach him slowly.

"The Lucianos' underboss and two of their capos. They want to discuss business with Adrian and me."

"I take it your visit to Lazlo went well?"

"Excellent, actually. He likes that I went personally, and he already dotes on Adrian, so it was as expected." He finally lifts his head to meet my eyes. "Do you now see how you would have ruined it by tagging along?"

I purse my lips, but it's not only because of the whole Lazlo thing. It's the fact that I can't stop staring at Kyle's face, at his gleaming eyes and sensual lips, his sharp features and the way a stray hair is falling haphazardly on his temple.

And now I'm ogling him. *Stop ogling him.*

"I'll stay and listen," I blurt to distract myself.

"Why?"

"Because this is Bratva business and I want to be in the know."

"And you don't trust me to do it alone." His declaration is strange, almost like he's anticipating a certain type of answer.

"Good. At least you know that."

His eyes fall back to the laptop, but he doesn't deny or confirm my demand. After a moment, he says, "If the Italians hear your voice, the deal will be null and void. They won't be able to trust us. Do you understand?"

The tone in his voice bothers me. It's mechanical, almost like he's dismissing me or pulling away from me.

I hate the sting that explodes in my chest. "Fine."

Kyle has no idea what will come to him in this exact conference call. I slip over to my closet and change into a short, dark red nightgown Ana bought for me as a wedding gift.

The lace that covers my breasts is see-through, so my nipples are visible if someone is close enough. The soft silk falls gently against my body but barely covers the crack of my ass.

I stand in front of the mirror and contemplate what I'm going to do. This looks like the last thing I would ever wear. Besides, seduction is my absolute weakness. Not only have I never tried it before, it also puts me in a vulnerable position.

At the same time, I know if I don't go for it, I won't have a chance to snatch back the power that was yanked away from me.

Tilting my head to the side, I run the tips of my fingers over the mauve hickey at the base of my throat. Needles of discomfort prick me when it stings. I wince even though my thighs clench at the same time.

"You can do this," I whisper to myself, then turn around and stride out of the closet with confidence I don't feel.

I recall how Reina walks when she wants to get Asher's

attention—not that she has to try hard since she always has his full focus. I sway my hips the slightest bit as I stand in front of the door.

"Our men will be stationed near the club downtown," someone says in an Italian accent.

"We will offer limited support on that side, but the number of soldiers is negotiable." Adrian's voice.

"I can get intel for this week." Kyle is still typing at a rapid-fire pace on his laptop, obviously multitasking while taking the call. "What are our main concerns?"

I try to think of the best way to get his attention without clearing my throat or making a noise. Just when I'm about to drop something from my console, Kyle lifts his head as if he knew I'd been standing there all along.

Our eyes clash and, for a second, I think he's seeing straight through me. Maybe he'll completely ignore me, causing my mission to fail before it even gets started.

But then, his hands stop typing on the keyboard and his lips part. It's the slightest bit, but it's all the reaction I need to walk toward him at a slow—and hopefully seductive—pace.

His attention remains on me as the Italians talk about some security problems in one of their clubs. Kyle follows my every movement as if he's expecting me to reach under my gown, retrieve a gun, and shoot him in the heart.

If I were able to do that, I would've done it seven years ago when he left without looking back.

I internally shake my head. This isn't about the past. This is about the present and my rightful power.

When I halt in front of him, Kyle's eyes heat as he measures me from top to bottom, stopping to pay extra attention to my visible breasts.

My nipples harden against the lace under his scrutiny, and it takes all of my self-control to not cross my arms over my chest.

When his eyes finally come back to my face, he gives me a questioning glance that silently asks, *What are you doing?*

Before my nerves get the better of me, I sink to my knees in front of him.

Time to snatch my power back.

NINETEEN

Kyle

RAI LOWERS HERSELF SO SHE'S KNEELING BETWEEN my open legs.

I'm barely paying attention to what the Italians are discussing with Adrian. All I can focus on is the woman in front of me in nothing but a provocative see-through nightgown.

My gaze slides back to the rosy nipples peeking through the red material. My mouth waters like a fucking horny teenager. All my urges culminate in the need to take those nipples in my mouth, suck on them, and bite down until she makes that startled, needy sound.

My chain of thoughts is interrupted when she reaches for my belt with sure yet slightly shaky hands.

I should stop her, take the laptop, and go to the balcony. Or, better yet, I could turn her toy on and torture her a bit for my own pleasure, but I'm frozen in place. My limbs don't move even when I order them to.

A deep part of me wants to see how far she'll take this and where exactly she wants to go. Rai's never initiated anything between us—sexual or not. She might appear like she's stronger than the world and a rebellious soul, but she's a traditionalist in the Russian way Nikolai brought her up.

Which will make exploring what she's truly capable of even more fun.

She undoes my belt faster than expected, then proceeds to undo the button and the zipper. Her brows are drawn in concentration as she sets out on her mission.

"Kyle will be able to get the information as soon as possible." The sound of my name coming from Adrian temporarily steals my focus.

"Yes," I say in a voice that's surprisingly calm, considering I'm hardening faster than a pubescent kid during his first time. "I only need detailed descriptions of the places you have in mind."

I stifle a groan as Rai takes my dick out of my boxer briefs in her small hands. All the blood rushes to my groin, and my thought process scatters into thin air. Thank fuck it's not a video conference, or my lust would be visible for everyone to see.

Rai gives me a coy smile as she crawls closer on her knees then licks her lower lip in a suggestive way. *Holy fuck.* Who knew there was this side to the uptight Rai? Or that she would willingly get on her knees for me?

She does a long lick, sliding her tongue from the base of my dick to the crown.

This time, I hit mute on the laptop and let out a grunt. She does it again and I grab my nape, bunching her hair around my fingers. "Are you going to fondle me for long, Princess?"

She moans, continuing her slow and unhurried licking. "Mmmm."

"If you don't do something in the next two seconds, I'm going to use that mouth."

"Kyle?"

My name coming from the laptop makes me hit unmute. She smiles against my skin, licking it up and down like it's a fucking lollipop. Her fingers fondle my balls with a finesse that matches the rhythm of her lips and tongue.

"I'll have the necessary measures in place," I manage to say even though I have no fucking clue what I just agreed to.

Rai might be on her knees between my legs, but she's holding me by the balls—literally and figuratively.

She takes me in her mouth, only for a second before she releases me with a pop, then goes back to licking and playing her bloody games with me.

"We need guards in front of the downtown club twenty-four-seven," one of the Italians says. If someone put a gun to my head and made me guess which one of the three we're talking with, I wouldn't for the life of me be able to pinpoint him.

"If we gather all our players in one place, it'll seem suspicious," I reply, then mute myself as my fingers slowly sneak into Rai's hair and I snatch away the pins keeping it pulled up in a bun.

Blonde, shiny strands cascade over her shoulders, but she doesn't stop her task.

"You're boring me." I pretend to yawn. "If you can't play the role, don't get on your knees."

Her eyes light up with that spark that usually means she's up to a challenge and will stop at nothing to win.

She slides me to the back of her throat, and even though I'm too big for her little mouth, she diligently tries to take in as much as possible. Thank fuck for the mute option because without it, the men on the other side would hear my groan that matches her moan simultaneously.

"Fuuuck." My head falls back against the sofa as she sucks me off vigorously, though not as noisily and experimentally as the vibe she gave off when she first walked into the room.

My blood boils at the thought of her doing this with another man before me. These lips belong to me. Rai belongs to me, and anyone who dares to challenge that fact will be shot dead in his fucking sleep.

It'd be the easiest kill I would ever have to make.

I stare down at her, still holding her hair hostage, as her head bobs up and down. Her movements aren't as fast as I prefer, but her determined expression and persistent moves make up for it.

"What time can you go to the club, Kyle?" Adrian asks me.

I unmute myself but keep my finger on the button as I manage to get out, "Nine a.m."

I mute myself again, but Rai releases my dick with a pop, licking her bottom lip, then slides her tongue to the upper one.

"Is your game over?" I breathe out.

"No." She runs her hand up and down my shaft. "I want you to fuck my mouth."

Bloody fucking hell.

I nearly come right then and there, but my dick can't pass up the invitation. I don't give her time to change her mind as I wrap my hand around her hair, grabbing it in a fist as I slam my cock to the back of her throat.

Her eyes water, which means her gag reflex has been triggered, but she doesn't try to fight me off, even though that's the most instinctive thing to do.

So I keep it there, confiscating her air and her damn character, which is a lot stronger than I gave her credit for.

Her face reddens and tears run down her cheeks, but she doesn't attempt to break eye contact. Her fingers latch onto my thighs, for support more than anything.

I pull out of her and she gasps, drool sliding down her chin and lips trembling.

"How many guards will you bring, Kyle?" Adrian asks.

I glide my dick along her lips, dampening them with pre-cum. "Open."

She does, her lips forming an O to take me in even though she's glaring up at me.

The knowledge that this spitfire of a woman is on her knees in front of me, allowing me to fuck her mouth, makes me harden even more, which should be impossible considering I was already about to spill all over her visible rosy nipples.

"Ten max," I manage in a semi-normal tone before I mute myself again and thrust until I reach the back of her throat.

Rai whimpers, her nails digging into my thighs so hard they nearly break through the cloth and the skin. I hold her head in place by her hair and ram in and out of her mouth. I keep my dick at the back for some time, grabbing her hair tightly to not allow her to move. Every time I do that, fresh tears spill down her cheeks and drool mars her translucent skin.

I don't stop, though. I do it over and over again, offering her the punishment she nearly begged for last night.

Unlike what she probably expected, I don't come fast. I hold it in, fucking her mouth as thoroughly as possible so when she gets on her knees again, she'll only think of this moment where she's staring up at me as if I'm holding her life between my two hands.

Which might as well be the case.

I keep her in place as my release hits me, tightening my balls and back muscles. I spill all over her tongue and lips.

"Swallow." I pull my dick away and grip her chin with my index finger, then close her mouth. "Don't waste a drop."

She does, gulping, but her eyes never leave mine. The fucking stubbornness this woman holds knows no limit. She's still on her knees in front of me, hair in disarray, tears, drool, and a streak of cum staining her face, but she looks at me as if she's the one who brought me to my knees.

Which might as well be the case.

She might have won this battle, but she'll never win the war.

One of the Italians addresses me again. I release her hair and unmute the microphone on my computer as I tuck myself in.

Rai rises to her feet and juts her chin in my direction before she heads to the bathroom.

I keep watching her retreating back and how the night-gown molds to her arse, revealing the line of her black panties with every gentle sway of her hips.

My dick rises back to life, turning semi-hard against the confines of my boxers. *Fuck.* It's become pussy-whipped in no bloody time.

I continue my conference call, faintly noticing that Rai heads straight to bed after she cleans up in the bathroom. She doesn't look in my direction or attempt to say anything.

By the time I'm finished, the only thought that's lodged in my mind is to join her.

I remove my trousers and shirt, remaining in my boxer briefs, and slip in behind her.

Her breaths are even, eyes closed.

Why did she fall asleep so fast? She didn't even ask about removing the toy.

Throwing the covers away, I reach between us and lift her nightgown to her waist then pull down her knickers.

I'm momentarily distracted by the gorgeous globes of her backside and grab one cheek in my hand. She moans, burying her head in the pillow.

"This arse will be mine," I murmur to her sleeping form. "Soon."

Getting to the task, I slowly part her legs and pull out the toy. While I love having a hold on her, it's not hygienic to keep it in all day and all night long.

She moans again, this time her finger teasing her nipple over the see-through fabric in a gentle rhythm. And now I'm hard.

Fuck.

Not that I can do anything about it with her fast asleep like this. I throw the toy on the carpet and attempt to wrap my arms around her. It would make my dick's situation worse, not better, but that's a detail I can live with.

Rai rolls around so her head is lying on my bicep and her hand rests on my arm. I take a moment to study her peaceful features. Her hair falls on my skin and her lips part the slightest bit. She looks so different when she's asleep—angelic, even.

If only she were as compliant when she's awake. But who am I kidding? This is the version of her that always grabbed me by the gut. There's nothing I would change about her personality—even if she can be infuriating.

I pull her into me so our heads are lying across from each other.

Leaving this woman behind will probably be the hardest part of my mission once I'm done.

TWENTY

Rai

I PUT ON MY PEARL EARRING AND TILT MY HEAD SO I CAN hold my phone over my shoulder.

Ruslan is briefing me about the security measures we spent two weeks putting in place for today's brunch. I made the calls and had Lazlo's wife, sister, and a few other Italian mafia leaders' women join in.

Even Sergei and Igor said it was a good plan. Kyle didn't mention that he plotted it and let me take all the credit—not that I needed him to. Still, as someone whose ideas are always credited to others—intentionally or unintentionally—it felt nice that he left the ball in my court this time.

Katia even said maybe he did it on purpose.

Who knows? All I'm sure about is that nothing will screw up this day.

"Get the car ready," I say after Ruslan finishes. "Anastasia and I will come down in a few."

My muscles are straining despite the long run I went on with Ruslan and Katia this morning. We often train together to keep in shape, but lately, even physical workouts aren't cutting it.

After I hang up, I finish putting on the other earring. My movements slow down when I catch Kyle's reflection in the mirror. He's standing right behind me, his chest separated from my back by a mere breath.

This is the dozenth time he's been able to sneak up on me, and I only see him when he intends it. What other surprises does he have in store for me that won't happen unless he allows them to?

He's dressed in a light blue shirt and dark gray pants. His hair is styled and he smells of his standard shower gel, only there's nothing standard about his scent. There's a special masculine musk that I'm only able to smell on him. Either he's too unique or I'm so attuned to him that I effortlessly recognize his natural scent.

"Shouldn't you be downstairs?" I pretend to fix the pearls around my neck.

"I'd rather drive my beautiful wife."

"I have Ruslan."

"I insist." He places both hands on my shoulders, and I freeze when his thumb swipes over the new hickey he's left on my neck.

Even though it's mostly covered with foundation, it twinges back to life at his touch, causing me to squirm.

Ever since he came down my throat two weeks ago, he's upped his methods of playing games. Now, I have absolutely no clue when the hell he'll make the toy move inside me.

I'm kept on my toes all day, waiting for the familiar vibration. The sense of the unknown adds more to the anticipation until it's almost…exciting.

Exciting—that's such a strange word in my dictionary, but if there's a definition for it then it's absolutely Kyle.

When the toy does go off, I nearly come then and there. If he's in my vicinity or calls me just to stimulate me, an orgasm is usually a given, and it's tenfold stronger.

Our dynamics are odd, and we often clash on everything. We're still both fighting for the power that will give us free rein to achieve our goals.

Me, because I want to protect my family and the legacy *Dedushka* left behind.

Kyle, I assume because he wants to climb the ladder of the Vory. *I assume* because I can never be too sure about anything that concerns him. He's still a dark tunnel with no way out.

He leaves meetings as soon as he pleases, pretending to have to work, but then he'll be typing away on his phone as if it's his lover or something. I try not to notice the subtle ways he agrees with my propositions during meetings, even if those disagree with Igor's suggestions. He does it with humor, and discreetly as to not draw attention. Kyle is smart, and the way he's been helping me cement my position in the brotherhood in the background, without speaking on my behalf, has been throwing me off.

When I asked him about his intentions, he said it's because we're husband and wife. I'm far from falling for his words, but I also can't figure out why the hell is he doing all of this.

Then, during some nights, he's been coming home late, after I fall asleep. I only sense him when he spoons me from behind and removes the toy from inside me.

In the mornings, he wakes me up with his teeth nibbling on my neck and his fingers thrusting deep inside me, then he won't let me go until I scream my orgasm.

I hate how natural this routine has become in the span of two weeks. I hate that when he didn't join me last night, I kept tossing and turning all night. The ghosts from the past crowded my space, and I couldn't shoo them away no matter how much I tried. Or that when he didn't put the toy inside me this morning, I felt something was missing.

"Aren't you going to ask where I was?" He keeps stroking my neck.

I lift my perfume bottle even though I already sprayed some. "I don't care."

"Are you saying you didn't miss me last night and this morning?"

I rub some perfume on my wrist. "Not at all."

"Not even a little?"

My lips tremble, but I mutter, "No."

"I bet your body missed me." He wraps his fingers around my throat from behind as his other hand wanders down my back before he grabs my ass cheek in his strong palm. "I bet if I checked on your pussy, she'd tell me the truth."

Tingles erupt at the bottom of my stomach and I resist the urge to close my eyes and fall into the sensations he elicits from my body. The way he grabs me by my throat, hard and merciless, stimulates me like nothing else can.

But I won't let him have his way again. He left last night, just like he left seven years ago. And this time? This time, I kept staring at his phone number, but I didn't press the green phone. When I called in the past, all I heard was the same message over and over again, and that message gives me fucking nightmares.

So even though my body would willingly surrender to his touch, I won't. He killed that part of me.

Pulling away, I coerce him to release me and turn around to face him. "I don't care where you spend your time or who you spend it with."

"I'm not leaving," he says calmly, soothingly, almost like he read my previous thoughts.

My chin trembles and I force it to stay in place. "I don't care if you leave."

"And I'm telling you I'm not. You might not want to know where I was, but I'm going to be a model husband and tell you anyway. I had a meeting with Nicolo Luciano in his club and he insisted I join him and his brothers for a drink in their house."

"I said, I don't care."

"Before that, I got myself tested for your sake and had the clinic email you the results," he continues as if I said nothing. "If I came back semi-drunk, I would've fucked you, so I chose to crash in the Luciano mansion."

I pretend his words mean nothing as I leave the room and go downstairs. The dining room door is closed, which means Sergei is having another morning meeting.

Anastasia is sitting on a sofa in the entrance while Vlad is talking to her guards. She's wearing a sophisticated flowery dress. Her hair is loose and her heels are brand spanking new.

As soon as she sees me, she stands and spins around, grinning. "How do I look?"

"Perfect, as usual." I kiss her cheek and let her place her arm in mine as I address Vlad. "We already went through the security procedures with the guards."

"There's no harm in repeating them." His gaze slides from me to Anastasia, and back again. "Do you want me to go with you?"

"No need." Kyle's voice cuts in from behind us. "I'm accompanying the ladies."

It's pointless to fight him on this. He'll just start another verbal war with Vlad, and I don't have time for that. So I simply nod at Sergei's second-in-command to communicate that I'm fine with it, then I head outside.

Kyle places a hand on the small of my back. The possessive gesture isn't lost on me. He's doing this so Vlad knows to stay the fuck away. He's been making it a habit in front of him and the other leaders in the brotherhood—especially Damien.

I try to get out of Kyle's hold, but that only causes him to tighten it further, eliciting a shudder down my spine.

He drives Ana and me to the coffee shop we rented for the brunch. It's located in a quiet neighborhood and is considered private enough that Adrian agreed to send his wife.

Still, guards, both ours and the Italians', fill the

surrounding streets and the area behind the coffee shop. The Irish have been quiet for some time now, and that's not always a good sign.

If anything, they might have stayed under the radar just to prepare for a bigger attack.

As soon as we reach the building, I exit the car before Kyle properly parks it. Anastasia follows after me, as does Kyle. I turn around to shoo him away. "It's women only. Go back."

"I'm sure they will appreciate my company."

Just when I'm about to speak, a long car stops right in front of us.

One of the Italians.

A guard comes out and opens the back door. A petite brunette exits the vehicle, wearing a huge hat and white-framed sunglasses.

Emilia Luciano, Lazlo's youngest sister, whom he raised himself.

A grin plasters on her red-painted lips as she runs toward us and throws herself in Kyle's arms, kissing his cheek. "Long time no see, you."

What the…

"I wouldn't call it long," Kyle says, not attempting to peel her off him.

"You're right. Last night wasn't that long ago, but why does it feel like it?"

Last night.

Last fucking night?

I thought he was with her brothers, but he forgot to mention the sister. My hand balls into a fist around my bag's strap, and it takes everything in me not to hit both her and him across the face.

Why should I care? I meant what I said earlier—I don't give two fucks about where and who he was with.

And yet, an acid-like sensation instantly melts my insides.

It's the humiliation. That's it. That's the only reason why I feel like I'm at the point of combusting right now.

Dedushka taught me that my honor and dignity come before anything else, and if anyone tries to tarnish them, I shouldn't let them be.

That's why I barge straight between them and offer my hand to Emilia. "Rai Sokolov, your hostess for the day."

She pulls away from Kyle to take my strong handshake with a meek one. "Emilia. Nice to officially meet you. My brothers talk about you a *lot*."

"The pleasure is all mine. I'm glad my reputation precedes me."

"They're not always good stories." She tries to hide the jab with a smile.

"Even better." I slip my hand into Kyle's arm. "I see you already met my husband."

My tongue doesn't feel weird around the word. If anything, it's natural. *The hell?*

"Oh, right." She continues her disingenuous smile. "He's a keeper, this one."

I return her smile with my own. "I know that more than anyone since I married him. See you inside."

She hesitates as if she wants to spend more time here, but then mutters, "Sure."

"Ana." I smile at my great-cousin. "Can you please show her the way?"

She takes the hint and walks beside Emilia to make sure she leaves. I keep watching her back until she disappears.

"I didn't know you were capable of jealousy, Princess."

It's then I realize I've been digging my nails into Kyle's arm with all my might. I let it go with a jerk and lift my chin. "I wasn't jealous."

"Then what do you call what just happened?"

"I was only protecting my honor. Disrespect me again and I will disrespect you in return."

"And how, pray tell, will you do that?"

"Eye for an eye, Kyle. You know I believe in that. So next time you let a woman throw her arms around you, know I'll find another man to throw my arms around. Fuck a woman and I'll fuck two men—and a woman, if I'm in the mood."

He grabs me by the throat. The motion is so quick I gasp, eyes widening. He backs me up until my behind hits a car. His usually nonchalant eyes rage with a storm so deep I feel it straight against my throat. "Don't ever, and I mean *ever*, repeat that. You're my wife—know your fucking place."

"And you're my husband," I mutter through clenched teeth. "Know your fucking place."

"Don't attempt to play with my fire, Rai. The moment a man so much as looks at you, let alone touches you, I will slice his fucking throat and watch as life leaves his eyes so he knows in every last second that he shouldn't have touched what's mine."

"Then treat me the same. I'm your wife, and therefore, your equal, not a second-rate citizen you can do with as you please. Don't dish out your double standards on me—you won't like how I react."

"Believe me, you won't like how I'll react either. I believe in retribution, Rai."

"Is that why you fucked Emilia last night?"

"I didn't fuck Emilia."

"You expect me to believe that?"

"Jealous, Mrs. Hunter?"

"I'm just asking in case I have to call someone up. Kai or Damon would be up for it."

His jaw tightens. "Rai…"

"What?" I snap. "You did it *first*."

"I didn't fuck Emilia. Why would I do that when I have you?"

"Your words won't get you anywhere. I need proof."

"My word is all the proof you need. You have to start be-lieving it for this marriage to work."

"Who told you I want this marriage to work?"

"Then would you rather we destroy each other?"

"Aren't we already?"

We continue staring at one another, gazes clashing and bodies tense. I don't know how long it lasts, but at some point, his hold on my neck turns less threatening and more…sexual. I don't know when the shift happens or if it's all in my mind, but my skin turns tingly and so do my thighs.

Kyle lowers his head so that his mouth is a few inches away from mine as he whispers, "You're so fucking stubborn."

"You knew that when you married me," I murmur back, not able to take my attention off his lips.

"That I did. I just didn't know how bloody insane it would drive me."

"You can still leave."

"I told you I won't."

My stomach flip-flops, shifts, and contracts as if butterflies are slashing straight through it. No, not butterflies. It's some-thing more potent.

I lean in close, and so does Kyle. When our lips are about to touch, the sound of a car pulls us back to the present.

Shit. I actually forgot that we're in public.

This is why Kyle is dangerous to me. He can pull me into mazes of his own making, and one day, he might not allow me out.

The back door opens and a petite woman with soft fea-tures gets out. Her dark hair is tied into an elegant ponytail. She's wearing a designer beige skirt suit and keeps the hand that wears her wedding ring on top of the other.

Lia Volkov, Adrian's wife.

A sense of relief hits me at seeing a familiar face—as fa-miliar as it gets. The last time I saw her was three months ago

188 | RINA KENT

on Sergei's birthday. Adrian keeps her hidden to a fault. She didn't even attend the wedding. In all honesty, the only reason she came to Granduncle's birthday was that it would've been disrespectful if Adrian didn't bring her.

"I have to go," I whisper to Kyle. "You can leave."

He steals a quick kiss from my lips before he releases my throat. "Tonight, Mrs. Hunter."

I don't know what he means by that, but I don't have time to press the issue since he gets in his car.

Ignoring him, I try to tame the flaming of my cheeks as I meet Lia. She smiles faintly at me, and even that appears sad. She has a generally wretched expression, like she's constantly sad or haunted—or both.

Due to not attending most gatherings, the other wives don't really like her much, and therefore, I'm basically the only resemblance of a friend she has.

"Long time no see, Lia." I kiss her cheek.

She returns the gesture. "I've been a bit unwell, and you know how Jeremy needs a lot of attention."

"I can only imagine. Is your baby boy doing well?"

Her expression lights up at the mention of her son. "He is. He's so smart."

"Just like his father."

"Sort of." Her voice is barely a whisper as we head to the building. There's something odd about the way she walks that I've never noticed before. It's mechanical, forced even.

When she catches me observing her, she blurts, "Congrats on your wedding. I'm sorry I couldn't make it."

"It's better that you didn't. It wasn't exactly safe. Didn't Adrian tell you?"

"I figured something was wrong," she says in the same forced way she's walking.

I stop at the entrance and face her. "Is everything okay, Lia?"

"What?" Panic fills her eyes and her skin turns a pale shade of white. "W-why?"

I touch her elbow and she flinches, so I drop my hand. "You don't look so well. Would you prefer to leave?"

"No. Adrian said I have to be here."

"He forced you to come?" I all but shout.

"Please d-don't yell, *please*," she whispers, her hands flat-out shaking as she watches our surroundings. "That's not what I m-meant…I…can you please forget the last couple of minutes happened?"

"Hey," I soothe, "it's okay. If something's wrong, you can tell me and I will help, all right?"

Her gaze shifts behind us to where the guards are stationed.

"No one will say anything. I outrank everyone here, and whatever you tell me will be our secret. You have my word." She still appears hesitant, so I smile. "You don't have to tell me right away. Take your time to think about it."

She nods once, and that's when I notice a red dot on her forehead—a red sniper dot.

My muscles turn rigid, but I remain calm, my expression unchangeable. "Lia, don't move."

"Why?" She sounds as spooked as I feel.

I push her down and a bullet shoots straight into the door. A body slams into me from behind and smashes me to the ground.

TWENTY-ONE

Rai

A LARGE BODY COVERS ME WHOLE FROM BEHIND, AND for a moment, I'm too disoriented to decipher what just happened.

I'm not hearing or smelling anything. My vision is blurry, and it's almost like waking up in a white room without a recollection of prior events.

"Stay low," the very familiar voice whispers in my ear, and with that, all my other senses kick into gear.

It's like being wrenched from underwater and taking the first gulp of air. As my lungs burn, I realize I haven't been breathing either. My ears buzz and my tongue sticks to the roof of my mouth.

The coffee shop's entryway, the concrete beneath us, the shot on the door…

"Rai, do you hear me? Are you okay?"

"I'm fine," I say over the constant ringing in my ears.

I attempt to roll from underneath him, but Kyle keeps me pinned in place with a hand around my nape. "Don't move."

His grip is firm, disallowing me any shift, which wouldn't be possible considering he's crushing me with his weight. Every inch of me is covered by him.

The realization of what he did slowly creeps up on me.

Kyle jumped on me. As in, he used his body as a shield for mine. As in, he was ready to take the shot for me.

My breathing hitches, cracking and turning shallower by the second. It doesn't make sense for him to do such a heroic act I would expect from only Katia and Ruslan.

He doesn't care. He left seven years ago.

I try engraving those words to memory, because if I don't? Then, I'm fucking screwed.

"Is the sniper gone?" I ask, voice low.

"Could be. I'll go check."

"Why would you go check? I'll send the guards."

"And cause a ruckus at your carefully planned brunch? None of the guards saw the bullet or the red dot. If you make sure Lia doesn't talk, we won't have a diplomatic issue with the Italians. If they know a sniper is on the loose, they will accuse you of bringing their women to be killed."

His words get past the confines of my ears and the reality slams into me.

My best option is to play it cool.

My gaze slides to Lia, who's crouching by the restaurant door, both her palms covering her ears and her eyes shut tightly as her lips move in inaudible murmurs.

Does she…have PTSD? It doesn't make sense for Adrian's wife to have PTSD. She's been married to him for more than five years, and she knows the way of the brotherhood. We're not a nice bunch, by any means, and our lifestyle is high on the danger parameter.

Even the most sophisticated Vory women, like Mikhail's

wife and Anastasia, might tremble in fear, but they don't start bawling or suffer from PTSD episodes. We were brought up on the sound of bullets.

Lia should be the same. She was there during Adrian's assassination attempt at Mikhail's birthday. She even helped Stella, Igor's wife, gather the women in the basement, while I followed Adrian and Damien to catch the attempted assassin.

We found him shot in the back of his neck. Vlad and Adrian ran a thousand background checks using the guy's picture but came up empty. To this day, we don't know who tried to kill Adrian or who murdered the assassin.

Point is, Lia was completely calm during that time. It doesn't make sense for her to have PTSD now.

"I'll count to three and you join her, okay?" Kyle says so close to my ear, drawing shivers down my spine.

"Take backup," I say.

"Worried about me, Princess?"

"You wish." My murmur isn't believable even to my own ears.

"No backup. You know I work better solo. Now, one, two…" He lifts his body over mine push-up style. "Three."

He completely stands up and I do, too, bolting to where Lia is crouching. I turn around to insist that he takes guards, but there's no sign of him.

That hotheaded man will be the death of me.

I mimic Lia's position and gently touch her hand. It's sweaty and cold. "Hey…Lia…do you hear me?"

At first, she doesn't give any sign that she does, but then, slowly, her eyes flutter open and she stares up at me with tears in them.

"Hey, it's okay." I take her by the arm and slowly stand her up with me. "You're okay."

"I-I'm sorry…I didn't mean to…"

"You don't have to be sorry for something you can't control, Lia."

"P-please don't tell Adrian about this." She grabs my hand in both of hers. "*Please.*"

"I won't for now, but he'll eventually know. We were under attack, Lia." Or maybe she was the target. After all, the red dot was on her forehead, not mine or anyone else's.

I reach into my bag and give her a tissue. "Come on, wipe your face and let's get inside, okay?"

She complies, but her expression remains half-horrified, half-shocked.

I dust my dress off, use a tissue myself, and then hold my head high and walk into the coffee shop. It doesn't matter that my legs are still slightly shaking or that my mind is still outside where Kyle ran off to God knows where.

This brunch is my way to play a role in the brotherhood, and nothing will ruin this. I shoot a message to Katia and Ruslan to go after Kyle and hope that will be enough.

Inside, the women are completely oblivious to the spy-level show that just took place outside. Thank God.

The décor is cozy with multiple soft lights hanging down from the ceiling. I had my guards rearrange the seats so it's a large sitting area instead of having separated, impersonal tables.

Everyone sits on the sofas, each cradling a drink. From our side, the women present are Anastasia, Lia, and Igor's wife, Stella. Of course, Mikhail's wife didn't join because her husband is a bastard. As soon as he heard I arranged this meeting, he said she wasn't feeling 'well', and then Damien snickered and whispered to me that he would send his wife over if he had one.

From the Italians' side, there's Sofia, Lazlo's wife, Emilia, whom I had the displeasure of meeting outside, the under-boss's fiancée, and a few new faces I'm sure are Emilia's friends or the leaders' daughters.

The gathering goes well—for the most part. Lia spends the entire evening pale and shivering while Emilia keeps acting passive-aggressively toward me, taking any chance to make a jab, like asking Stella if I'm a good daughter-in-law.

Stella, graceful as usual, rubs my arm. "She holds an important role for all of us. Being a daughter-in-law is the least of her problems."

Emilia huffs, obviously not expecting that answer.

"Thank you," I whisper to Stella.

She smiles. "We stand up for each other."

And with that, she excuses herself to go check on the kitchen. I don't know whether that means approval or what, but Stella and Igor have always been a mystery. They keep their thoughts to themselves, so I'm never sure if it's all a façade or genuine.

Unlike Emilia, Sofia seems to like me since she keeps talking to me the most among all of the women present.

Anastasia is her adorable, lovable self and is the perfect co-host. No one could hate that innocent, eager-to-please soul. She's too good for this world.

Whenever I get the chance, I check the messages in my group chat with my guards.

Katia: No traces of Kyle.

Ruslan: Same here.

Katia: Even his guard doesn't know where he went.

Ruslan: That bleached-haired kid is good for nothing.

I curse under my breath, then smile as Sofia tells me about her grown sons and married life.

Married men and women are generally more respected in the mafia. Being able to form a family isn't a duty everyone is capable of.

I quickly type a message to Kyle.

Rai: Where are you? Text me when you can.

Not expecting an immediate reply, I tuck my phone away and listen to Sofia. She's older, in her fifties, but still appears serene as she speaks. Being part of the mafia at a young age makes girls turn into women like Sofia, women who know their duties and don't deviate from them.

"Now that you're married, you can start your own family, Rai," she tells me ever so casually.

"We're still not at that stage yet." *And we never will be.* There's no way in hell I would start a family with someone as unpredictable as Kyle, someone whose past I know nothing about and whose future I can never predict.

"Why not?" Emilia slides beside her sister-in-law, slurping from her smoothie. "Trouble in paradise?"

You wish, bitch. Instead of saying just that, I choose the diplomatic road. "We just want to spend more time together before kids come along."

I hate how the lie doesn't feel like a lie when I say it.

"Oh," Emilia pouts. "And here I thought you'd toss him out."

I glare at her. "Not happening."

"I understand. He's such a charmer with that accent of his."

"Emilia," Sofia reprimands softly.

Emilia finally lets it go and moves away to the other Italian women who showed up.

Sofia apologizes on her behalf, and I pretend it's fine, even though I'm internally plotting the best way to spike Emilia's smoothie with poison.

After making vague plans to have another gathering like this, everyone leaves, escorted by their guards.

I make sure Lia is in her car before I take Anastasia and walk to where Ruslan and Katia are waiting for us in front of my vehicle.

"Any sign of Kyle?" I ask, checking my phone again. No reply.

Ruslan shakes his head once, his brows drawn together.

"How about his guard—what's his name again?"

"Peter," Katia says.

"Yes, Peter. Where is he?"

She lifts a shoulder. "He said he'd keep searching, but I don't think that kid can come up with anything useful."

At this rate, it seems Kyle has disappeared into thin air.

"Why? What happened to Kyle?" Ana's bemused gaze slides to each of us.

"Get inside, Ana." I guide her with a hand on her upper back. My limbs resume shaking from when he left me earlier.

By the time we reach home, I'm nearing the combustion point. I force myself to go into Sergei's office—the one that used to be *Dedushka's*.

Usually, I avoid this place because memories of my grandfather hit me full force. The smooth wooden desk and the neat library filled with Russian books have Nikolai Sokolov's touch to a T. He loved educating me here, sitting me on his lap to read me a book or just going about his business as I read in the corner.

Now, however, I feel numb, almost like the world is losing colors and I can do nothing to stop it. I find Sergei with Vlad going through paperwork.

I remain standing as I brief them about the attack. I'm surprised my voice is calm as I relay the facts.

Sergei stands and approaches me slowly before he takes my hand in his wrinkled one. "Kyle will be fine. He knows his way around."

"Why do you make it sound as if I'm worried about him? I'm not."

Vlad gives me a strange look, but he says nothing. I leave them and head to my room. To prove that I'm not worried, I stop checking my phone, take a shower, and go to bed.

Or try to, anyway.

In ten minutes, I'm up on my feet, checking and rechecking my texts. There's no reply. I read my emails and find the clinic's test, which says he's clean. The date at the top indicates he took it late last night and in an emergency room. I wonder how the hell he made that an emergency and how he got the results so quickly. Though, if there's someone who could make it happen, it's Kyle. I bet he flirted with a nurse and threatened a doctor. The jerk.

I stand by the balcony and call him. The standard unavailable message greets me.

Just like seven years ago.

The same message. The same circumstances.

Tears gather in my eyes. Mom used to tell Reina and me that tears are a weakness and shouldn't be in our beautiful eyes, and yet, I couldn't stop them even if I wanted to.

I'm about to call again when his scent envelops me, and then, his sensual voice follows. "Did you miss me this time, Princess?"

TWENTY-TWO

Rai

MY BREATHING SLOWS AS I SPIN AROUND.

Kyle is here.

He's…back.

I stare up at him, at how his hair is styled back, at how his shirt is still meticulously tucked into his pants like when he left earlier.

There's no visible injury on his body, no bruising or even dirt. He appears as impeccable as always.

He's back.

Those words spread through my body like wildfire, violent and potent. It's not like seven years ago when the impersonal messages were the last thing I heard from him.

His brow furrows as he glides his thumb under my eye, wiping away moisture. "Hey…what's wrong?"

Despite my need to stop the tears, the weakness, I have no power to do so. They're trapped in my lids, like a reminder of that day—the day I stood all alone in this room, when he never showed up. He never snuck up on me from behind and asked if I missed him.

"You left," I murmur.

"You knew I did." He keeps on wiping my tears as if, like me, he doesn't like the meaning behind them or the fact that I can't find the will to stop them. "I tracked the sniper, but they disappeared into thin air. They were ahead of me, and that's why they managed to escape."

"You left. You fucking left, Kyle."

He must realize I'm not talking about the present because he pauses at my cheek for a fraction of a second before he resumes stroking the skin there. "You will never forget about that, will you?"

I shake my head once.

"Not even if I'm here with you?" He smiles faintly. "Not even when you miss me? And before you say you don't, waiting for me proves otherwise…"

He trails off when I stand on the tips of my toes and capture his lips with mine. My kiss is tentative at best, the roaring of my pulse turning it a little shaky.

Kyle remains unmoving for a second, eyes widening the slightest bit.

That's all the hesitation he offers.

His hand wraps around the back of my neck as he deepens the kiss, thrusting his tongue against mine. It's nowhere near the innocent start I gave it. Kyle might be kissing my mouth, but his hold on me gets past the confinements of my lips and tongue to invade my entire body.

It's possessive, rough, and unapologetic—like everything about him.

It's a clash of tongues and teeth, as if our war for power bleeds into our kiss with vengeance.

One hand still holds me by the neck, and his other hand

digs into my hip as he pushes me until my back hits the wall. He's not the least bit gentle about it, his true colors showing through the savage manhandling of my body.

The delicious, callous manhandling.

Instead of fighting him as I normally would, I choose an entirely different route. I drown in him, in his true nature, in his scent that has become a pillar I want to hold on to and never let go of. Maybe it's because I waited a long time for this. Maybe it's because I always fantasized about Kyle losing all sense of control with me.

Maybe it's both.

Kyle's fingers curl in my hair and he expertly releases the elastic band, letting the blonde strands fall all over my shoulders.

Just when I'm focused on that, he yanks the thin straps of my nightgown down. The flimsy things rip with the savage motion, falling down my breasts and to the floor.

I yelp against his mouth, but it turns into a moan when he leaves my lips and glides skillful kisses down my neck, nibbling and sucking on the skin, no doubt leaving hickeys. He has a thing for marking my body in all brutal ways possible, and in a way, it's our point of connection. Ever since he started this habit, there hasn't been a day where I haven't stood in front of the bathroom mirror and run my fingers over the evidence of his markings.

Kyle's tongue swirls around a peaked nipple before his teeth bite down on it. It's hard enough that zaps of pleasure shoot straight between my legs and I arch my back.

Kyle holds me by the throat to keep me in place as he continues his onslaught on my nipple before repeating the same torture on the other one. My nerve endings tingle and ache, and the most frightening part is that I don't want it to stop.

If anything, it's the complete opposite.

I'm trying to get used to the sensation when his other hand

pulls my panties down and he places his palm between my clenched thighs.

"Open those legs." He speaks against the tender flesh of my breast, his breath hardening my nipple even more.

When I don't comply, still focused on the stimulation he's causing in my body, he continues, "If you don't, I'll resort to my methods. Those include 'punishing' you, as you like."

My breathing hitches at the word, no matter how much I'd like to hide my reaction. "Punish me, how?"

"I'll fuck you so hard you won't be able to move without thinking of me. I'll fill your little cunt with my dick until that becomes your only thought. But first, I'll start with this…" He slaps his hand against my wet folds. I hear the sound before the sting registers.

I gasp, my thighs trembling, but there's something different, a tingling, clenching awareness I've never felt before.

"Are you going to open, or should I repeat?" He bits down on my nipple, hard.

A whimper-moan leaves my lips as my legs fall open of their own accord.

"Good princess."

Kyle slides his fingers down my wet folds, and I close my eyes at the intimacy of it, at how well he knows my body in just the span of a few weeks, when I never took the time to learn it myself.

He thrusts two fingers inside me in one go, then curls them within me. I don't know if it's that or the earlier simulation or a combination of both, but I can feel the storm that's about to rattle my world.

"Even though I've been preparing you all this time, your cunt is still so fucking tight," Kyle says against my earlobe before he nibbles on the skin. "How are you going to take my dick?"

A moan is my only answer. All I want right now is the

thing he's building inside me: release, gratification. It's never felt this way, not by my own hand, and definitely not by someone else's.

All my life, I looked at men as rivals or allies. I never once considered any of them as someone who belongs in my night fantasies.

It hits me then, the realization that I never wanted it to be true. It wouldn't have been the same if it were someone other than Kyle.

He is the one eliciting all these foreign emotions from me.

He is the one for whom my body resurrects from the ashes like a phoenix.

And that reality is dooming.

Just when I'm about to come, Kyle removes his fingers from inside me and replaces them with his other hand.

Something musky with arousal is at my lips. My eyes shoot open to find the same fingers that were inside me at my mouth.

"Suck yourself off me. I want my fingers clean."

"Wha—" My word is cut off when he thrusts his fingers inside my mouth at the same time he scissors his fingers inside me.

I'm a goner. I come with a shudder that invades my entire body.

Kyle doesn't stop his double assault, his fingers curling inside me and his other fingers gliding back and forth against my tongue.

Tasting myself on him is a different type of intimacy altogether, but that's not the one thing that holds me hostage, even when I'm fighting with the remnants of my orgasm. It's the utter possessiveness in the sparkling blue sea of his eyes.

"This cunt and these lips belong to me. *You* belong to me."

I don't have the chance to speak with his fingers pressed against my tongue, not that I have any response to his words.

At this moment, when I'm trapped against the wall by his strong body, I can only feel.

Just let go and *feel*.

Kyle pulls his fingers from inside me, letting me ride the aftershocks of my orgasm.

The sound of a belt opening ripples in the air as he undoes it with one hand. His pants hit the ground with a *whoosh* and his boxer briefs follow. I stare down with heavy-lidded eyes, unable to look away.

Even though I've already had a full view of his cock a few times, the thing still manages to surprise me. Kyle wasn't kidding when he said he's huge.

He is, and when fully erect like right now, the veins visible with how hard he is, it's like he's ready to break something.

Not something—*me*.

He lifts one of my legs up then wraps it around his hip.

It's then that it hits me. I mumble against his fingers so he'll let me speak, but he presses his middle finger against my tongue.

Unintelligible sounds leave my lips as I push at his shoulder. I'm getting lightheaded, and it's probably because I'm not taking in enough oxygen.

He finally lets go of my mouth, my saliva clinging to his finger in a line as it separates from me.

I gasp as if I'm a newborn breathing for the first time. Kyle doesn't wait for what I have to say, though. He aligns his cock with my entrance, the head nudging inside.

My hand bunches his shirt, nails digging into the cloth. "C-condom."

"Fuck condoms." His thick brows draw over darkened blue eyes. "You just have to trust that I'm clean and would never hurt you that way."

"It's not that…" My words come out in a needy pant, and for a second, it feels like I've lost complete track of what my brain was trying to communicate just now.

Having Kyle all over me has that effect on me.

"I want to feel when your tight cunt strangles my dick," he rasps against my ear. "And I want to feel it bare."

My body heat goes up a notch at his crude words. Since I already had a preview of it, I shouldn't be so surprised that he's this filthy in bed. I should've been prepared for it, and yet he manages to suck me into his orbit, whether I like it or not.

"K-Kyle…"

"You're my wife, Rai. Your body is mine and mine alone. Get used to it." And with that, he thrusts into me in one long go.

I gasp, my mouth remaining in an O as he hits so deep I can feel him somewhere out of my uterus and so close to my stomach.

That toy is child's play compared to the force of his hips and his length and thickness. He's so big it doesn't matter how much he prepped me or played with me. It doesn't matter that I've already seen his dick, sucked it, and taken it to the back of my throat; having it inside me is an entirely different thing altogether.

It's like being split open. The pain is so fucking real, tearing at me from all directions and snatching me as a helpless hostage.

"Rai," Kyle calls my name. "Bleeding hell. Look at me, Rai!"

My eyes snap back to his at the accent he just used. It's like the other time—not entirely British English, but still sounds close.

That small distraction manages to divert my attention from the pain a little—just a little.

He opens my mouth with his thumb and glides his finger against my tongue. "Don't hold it in. Breathe."

It's then I realize I've been holding my breath since he slammed inside me. I follow his instruction and gasp for air. The moment oxygen hits my lungs, I cough at the force of life beating back into me.

Kyle, who was still as I caught my breath, slowly moves inside me. I slam both hands on his shirt with the intention to push him out of me. There's no way in hell I'm letting him fuck me with that. It *really* hurts.

Something stops me.

The pain isn't the only sensation present anymore. He rolls his hips slowly, erotically, and my body follows his rhythm as sparks burst inside me.

The sense of agony isn't completely gone, but it's mixed with a pleasure so deep it robs me of my breath all over again.

Kyle opens my mouth again. "Breathe. Don't faint on me, Princess."

I suck in air through my nose, reminding myself that I do need to breathe. That's what humans do so they don't die. It's as if I'm not functioning properly now, as if I'm reduced to my most basic form where all I can do is feel—feel so much I'm about to collapse from the force of it.

"I never thought you'd be so fragile, wife." Kyle strains with the words as he keeps his moderate pace, sparking jolts of pleasure all over my skin. "It's like I can break you with one wrong move." He releases my mouth and drops his hand to my throat, his eyes darkening when he presses. "Look at how easily your skin takes my marks, how easily you bruise."

I have no words to say—not that I can think straight, let alone formulate a coherent response right now.

Kyle pulls out almost completely then slams back in, hitting a new depth that knocks the shallow breaths out of my lungs.

My leg, that's at his hip, slides down with the force of it. The pain of being stretched is still there, but it's now mixed with a wicked type of stimulation that hits straight in my core.

He leans in so his breaths tickle my skin. "If I knew you would be this compliant when stuffed with my dick, I would've fucked you a long time ago."

I'm too delirious to respond, and Kyle doesn't let me. He wraps both hands under my thighs and lifts me up, then pushes himself all the way in.

I wind both arms around his neck and my legs wrap around his broad back. I feel like if I don't, I will drop and break to pieces.

"You're so fucking tight, you're choking my dick." He thrusts his hips up, increasing his rhythm by the second.

His speed is savage and uncontrollable. My already ragged breathing shakes and my back slides up and down the wall with every thrust.

"K-Kyle…oh…s-slow down…" My voice vibrates with how hard it is to speak.

He doesn't. If anything, his rhythm increases, and so does the roughness of his thrusts. "I've waited too long to slow down now."

"I…I…oh, God…"

"Let it out. Instead of fighting it, feel it…*all* of it."

I try to concentrate on the moment, but it's impossible. All the stimulations coming at me from different sides slam into me all at once.

My eyes clash with Kyle as I'm torn apart, literally and figuratively. The orgasm is nothing like I've had before. The ones brought on by his fingers and the toy don't even compare to this.

It's like feeling the vibration of the ground before an earthquake and knowing I'm going to be caught in the middle of it. And that's exactly what happens. I'm ripped to pieces from the inside out. The ferocity and wildness of my release scares the shit out of me, and I hold on to the only safe person in sight.

Who also happens to be the person who detonated this explosion in the first place.

The person who can break me with one wrong move, but also the person who can pick up my pieces off the floor.

The person who can build me up after being torn apart by the earthquake.

I'm still riding my wave when Kyle curses under his breath in that different accent. His back muscles stiffen beneath my legs and a warm liquid coats my inner walls.

I slowly close my eyes with a wince. He came inside me.

Not having the energy to start a fight about it, I continue holding on to his shoulders with shaky fingers.

Kyle pulls out of me, and I can actually feel the loss of it, the emptiness of not being filled. He places me on wobbly feet, and when they're unable to hold me upright, he clutches me by the throat.

Only Kyle would keep me standing by my throat instead of my shoulder or arm like a normal human.

He steps out of his pants that are still bunched at his feet and unbuttons his shirt with the other hand, revealing his lean muscles. From all the nights he's spent draped around me, I know for a fact they're hard and taut.

He has no chest tattoos except for a snake that's swirled over a dagger at his lower stomach.

The image is gruesome, but also powerful, and beautiful in its own way, which is ironically similar to the first impression I had of Kyle.

While I'm ogling him, his eyes heat with raw possession as he watches me. I follow his gaze and my cheeks burn when I make out what's getting his attention.

Now that I'm standing, his cum is dripping between my thighs until it reaches my feet. I'm all messy with both his seed and my own juices.

I try reaching for tissues on the console, but Kyle keeps me in place with his hold on my throat. "Leave it. I like watching my cum dripping down your legs. I like seeing how filthy I made you."

"Stop saying things like that." I try to scold, but it comes out as a murmur.

"Why? Turned on already?"

"N-no!"

"Well, I am." Kyle lifts me in his arms and throws me on the bed before I can even blink.

He crawls atop me, his body covering mine.

I place tentative hands on the solid ridges of his chest. "Y-you just came."

His cock nudges at my entrance. "And I'm ready for more."

My eyes widen. "Already?"

"Already. I'm not even close to being done with you."

TWENTY-THREE

Kyle

I WAKE UP EARLY.

Not that I actually slept.

I was on an adrenaline wave all night long, and the only thing I thought about was the best way to take Rai over and over again.

She passed out on me after the third round. After begging me to stop, then asking for more when I was inside her, her body lost the stamina battle and she eventually drifted off.

I lean on my elbow and drink in her sleeping naked form. She looks so docile when asleep, those tiny features and that slim body so fucking fragile it seems they can be broken to pieces like a porcelain doll.

But instead of destructive thoughts, the only thing I want to do is protect that delicate side of her—the side she only shows to me. I want to be the one she turns to when she wants to let that side loose. Because no matter how tough she acts on the outside, she's still caring on the inside. She still feels too much and hurts as much, too.

After the sniper attack yesterday, when I saw the red dot at her back, I thought I was going to lose her, thought everything would end before it even started.

My heart has never tightened as hard as it did in that moment. I didn't even think when I used my body as a shield, because right then, the only one who mattered was this fiery woman.

Neither Flame nor I could find the sniper no matter how much we searched. At first, I thought it could be Flame playing a distasteful joke, but his rifle doesn't fit the description. We never use those with laser targeting. It's not like us to make ourselves noticeable.

But I will find out who nearly snatched her from between my fingers, and when I do, he'll wish he was never born.

No one hurts Rai under my watch. Not even one of my own.

I brush my lips against her forehead, and she lets out a sigh.

It's not even a sexual sound, but my dick resurrects back to life, demanding another worshipping session at her altar.

Her lips are parted, begging for my cock between them.

Since I can't do that while she's asleep, I slide down the bed, pushing the sheets out of the way, and settle at the foot on my knees.

Pulling her legs apart, a sense of utter animalistic possession takes hold of me at the view of my dried seed between her legs.

She tried to clean herself, but I didn't let her erase the evidence of my ownership. She eventually forgot about it when she lost the battle to sleep.

I run my fingers over the silky skin of her thighs, stopping at each hickey I decorated her with. She's my canvas, and I'm the only brush that will touch her.

As I watch her, splayed out and marked, the need to own her again ripples under my skin and crunches against my bones. No idea if it's an obsession or an addiction, or both. All I know is that the urge is burning me from the inside out.

It's darkness, and it's probably wrong considering my plans, but I don't give two fucks about right or wrong now.

Not that I ever did.

I slowly slide her to the edge and place her legs over my shoulders. She's out of it and doesn't even stir.

Parting her folds with my fingers, I thrust my tongue straight inside her. She's the most delicious thing I've ever had: sweet, a bit naïve, and so bloody feisty it drives me bonkers.

Rai bucks off the bed, a moan spilling from her lips as her eyes shoot open. At first, she studies her surroundings with a confused expression. Then, when her bright blue eyes meet mine, they widen.

"K-Kyle…? What are you…oh, *holy shit*…" Her words trail off when I tease her clit with my thumb and index finger as I eat the fuck out of her entrance.

Her back arches and her glorious tits remain suspended in midair for my viewing pleasure. Her fingers latch onto my hair, and I revel in the sting of her pulling on it. She's fighting her orgasm and losing.

The faster my rhythm becomes, the louder her moans turn. She doesn't last long. She can't.

Her head rolls back as she screams my name. But then, her gaze returns to mine as she rides out her orgasm, almost like she doesn't want to break eye contact.

She's my princess for a reason.

"Did you come already?" I speak against her folds, making sure she sees me licking her sweet taste off my lips. "I was only getting started."

"A-again?" Her voice is slightly sleepy, slightly aroused, and fuck if I know why that's such a turn-on.

"Again and again." I place kiss after kiss on her pussy. "And fucking again."

Her face turns a pale shade of pink. "S-stop kissing me there."

I climb onto her body and imprison both her wrists above her head. "Then should I kiss you here?"

I capture her lips with a roughness that leaves her gasping. I don't only kiss her, I consume her. I suck her tongue, bite on it until the skin nearly breaks, then latch onto her lips until she's whimpering.

Obsession. This is so fucking close to being obsessed.

And because I am, I can't stop. I reach between us and position my dick at her entrance.

Rai tries to say something, but I don't release her lips. *I can't.* It's like my surroundings are black and she's the only light I can see, the only sound I can hear, the only bloody thing I can taste with my whole body.

I thrust balls deep inside her, causing her to slide on the bed. Her fingers sink into the palm of her hand, and she squeals into my mouth but doesn't attempt to pull away.

I try telling myself that she's sore, that I'm big, that I should take it easy on her, but the moment I have her near me, my beast-like nature takes charge and the only thing I can do is possess her, own her, tie her to me in every sense of the fucking word.

My thrusts start slow because I don't want to hurt her any more than this. While I have an impeccable record of self-restraint, all of that is null and void when it comes to this woman.

My wife.

She is now my wife.

All I want to do is unleash myself whole on her—the bad and the ugly included—but I know that will only confirm her suspicions about me and give her an incentive to leave me.

So I do the only other thing I can think of: I make her mine, because I'm that selfish, because the cards I was dealt fucking suck.

My thrusts are deep but unhurried, letting her body fall into synergy with mine as I tongue her into the mattress. She wraps her legs around my ass, caging me in.

That's my clue to increase my rhythm. I release her hands and lift her up by the nape so she's sitting on my thighs. The position gives me more room, and I power into her hard and fast, my abs tightening with each thrust.

She wraps her arms around me, mouth dropping open. I capture those lips, feasting on them as I fuck her so hard she nearly falls over.

Rai comes with a scream, her inner walls clenching around my dick, inviting me to join her.

And join her I do.

I curse as my own orgasm turns my whole body rigid. There's black magic created whenever I come inside Rai. I can't get enough of it, not ever.

Just when I'm spilling inside her, Rai tries to push me away.

"Stay still," I groan. "Unless you want me to paint your tits with my cum."

She nods frantically. "D-do it."

Fuck me. She really wants me to come all over her tits? I'll have to tuck that idea away for the future, though, because it's too late.

I empty inside her, my groans echoing in the air. She has the power to suck me dry in no time.

My hand loosens from around her throat, and I pull out to see the sticky mess I made of her. That's fast becoming my favorite view.

Rai stares down at herself with me, but unlike me, her face is pale, expression frozen.

"Hey…" I reach a hand for her. "What's wrong?"

She slaps my hand away and stumbles from the bed, falls to her knees, and then stands up again. "Asshole."

I smile menacingly. What's wrong with her all of a sudden? "Is that an invitation to fuck yours, Princess?"

She grabs a pillow and hits me with it. "I told you not to come inside me."

I hold the pillow between us, then tug on it to bring her close. "You told me to do it. 'Do it' can be anywhere, and it was already too late."

She breathes heavily, tits rising and falling and those rosy nipples begging to be sucked, bitten, and marked. I try to focus on her anger instead of how much I want to flip her under me and devour her all over again.

It's like Rai senses my thoughts. She abandons the pillow and storms to the bathroom, locking the door behind her.

My jaw clenches. That habit will have to go. She can't hide from me or lock herself away from me.

Not anymore.

But first, I need to find out what the fuck got her knickers in such a twist just now.

Desperate times call for desperate measures.

TWENTY-FOUR

Rai

I SLAM THE DOOR SHUT AND LEAN AGAINST IT, ALLOWING myself to let go.

My legs are barely able to hold me upright, and my core still pulses from the frighteningly powerful release I just had.

I'm breathing harshly like a trapped animal with no way out. I cover my face with both of my trembling hands in a hopeless attempt to calm myself down.

I need to snap out of it, and I need to snap out of it now.

How could I let that asshole, that brute, own me so un-apologetically? How could I enjoy every second of it as if I've been waiting years for that type of pleasure?

I haven't been…right?

The more I close my eyes, the harder the images from last night and this morning rush in.

I kissed him first.

I started this endless circle with no way out, and now, the evidence of my screw-up is still dripping between my thighs.

Kyle didn't hold back—far from it. He took and took, and what he gave in return? Yeah, that's my utter destruction and the reason I'm hiding like a coward right now.

For the life of me, I can't pretend I hated it, not when my traitorous insides are still begging for more.

What the hell is he doing to me?

There's a rustling on the other side of the door and I freeze, feeling him without even having to see him or hear his voice. I'm attuned to him in inexplicable ways, invisible ropes always pulling me in his direction.

"Rai...what did I say about not locking yourself away from me? Open the door." His words are measured—calm, even—but I can sense the threatening undertone beneath them.

"Leave me alone."

"If you don't open it, I'm breaking the fucking thing."

"Just...let me be," I mutter, and my gaze falls on the ring—the reason for this whole mess, the reason why my fate is sealed with no way out.

"I'll count to three. One, two..." I don't even get the chance to pull away as something hard rams into it.

I jump forward as the sturdy door bangs open, its joints nearly ripping from their locations.

Kyle stands at the entrance, naked, like some glorious warrior after a battle. I knew he was strong, but I guess I never realized just how strong he really is. Though his power in bed should've given me an idea about his insatiable stamina.

He stalks into the bathroom with panther-like agility, his feet not making the slightest sound on the white tiles. I instinctively step back. There's something frightening in the depths of his eyes. It was present when he was fucking me, but I couldn't figure the meaning behind it.

It wasn't exactly anger then, but it seems close to it now. Either way, it's a version of Kyle I don't want to butt heads with, especially since I'm naked and in my most vulnerable form.

"Didn't I say you can't lock me out?" he asks in a deceptive type of calm that knots my stomach.

The back of my foot catches on the edge of the shower's entrance. I chance a glance so I can step in. I'm probably trapping myself, but it's the only choice I have while he's advancing on me like this.

When I look up again, Kyle's height blocks my vision. I'm caged in that angry look in his eyes, in the disapproving feelings behind them.

He grabs me by the throat and pushes until my back meets the wall. My breathing is constricted and I can feel the blood rushing to my face. There's nothing sexual about his grip. It's raw and meant to threaten. "You do not get to run or hide from me. Do you fucking understand?"

I claw at his hands, but that only causes him to tighten his grip until no air seeps through. My struggles come to a halt since that will only drain my energy. He's the one with the physical power, and if I fight him on that, I will only get myself killed.

Dedushka's words about picking my battles keep me rooted in place.

"I said…is that fucking understood?"

When I remain motionless, he grabs my hair with his other hand and forces me to nod my head.

"That's yes, I understand. Yes, I won't run from you. Now, say it." He loosens his hold on my neck and I gulp copious intakes of air, choking on the life it brings me. It takes me long seconds to catch my breath.

"Fuck you," I manage, glaring up at him. "What right do you have to demand that from me when you ran away first? You left me *first*!"

"So what's your angle here? Do you plan to leave me as revenge?"

"Believe me, if I put my mind to revenge, me leaving you would be the easiest way out for you."

"Rai…don't test my fucking patience."

"Or what? Or fucking what? You took a lot from me already. If you think I will let you do it again, you don't know Rai Sokolov." I push at his chest, but his grip on both my throat and my hair keeps me imprisoned in place.

"You forgot a little something, Mrs. Hunter. You're my wife now."

"That doesn't make you the boss of me."

"We'll see about that." He strokes his finger on the hollow of my throat, loosening his hold a little. "Fuck. You do bruise easily."

I glance down my body and immediately regret it. Bruises, hickeys, and imprints from his fingertips are all over my neck, breasts, hips, and thighs. I can't even recognize my body anymore. It's like it already left me and went to Kyle.

"Let me go." I try to push at him.

He keeps me caged between him and the wall. "Not before you tell me why you left the bed that way and hid in the bathroom."

The reminder of what happened slams back into me all at once: the power, the abandon, the searing pleasure and the unbearable pain.

"Why do you want to know? You already got what you wanted."

"*We* got what we wanted. Don't try to pretend you didn't like what happened for even one second."

"I told you to put a condom on. I told you not to come inside me."

He narrows his eyes. "Is this what all the fuss is about? A condom?"

"The fuss is about getting pregnant. I'm not on birth control." My voice drops at the end and I look away from him.

Kyle uses his hold on my hair to bring back my attention to his sinfully beautiful face, his *expressionless* face. "And you hate that so much?"

"Of course I do! Who in their right mind would bring a child into this world? And with a father no one knows anything about. What if I wake up one day and you're not there, huh?" I stop before I blurt out everything inside me. That I barely survived alone the other time. That I can't do it again, especially if an innocent soul is involved.

"Is that how low you think of me?" His voice isn't angry, more like astounded, and that hits me even harder.

"What should I think? I know nothing about you. *Nothing.* All *Dedushka* said about you was that you're a reputable killer and that's it. Who are you, Kyle? Who are your parents? Where are you really from? What's your real last name? Is Kyle even your real name, or is it another 'fuck you' I have to live with once you're gone?"

"You have an awful lot of questions for someone who, according to your own words, doesn't give a fuck about me."

I purse my lips shut to not divulge all the chaos that's been building for years. If I do, he'll know how much he hurt me, and I will never give him that type of power over me again.

"Just know this, Kyle: I would never trust you. Not now, not in the future."

He continues watching me with unnerving silence but says nothing. He doesn't even attempt to answer any of my questions or get closer. He's happy with being miles apart from me while the closest moment we've ever had was when his body was sinking into mine.

I try not to let that piece of information get to me, but it slices me open from the inside like a thousand cuts. I'm bleeding, but he doesn't see it. I'm choking, but he'd never allow me air.

"Let me go." My voice is numb, monotone. "I need to shower and buy the morning-after pill."

Surprisingly, he does release me. I wait for him to say something, anything, but he turns around and leaves. He doesn't close the door, but the emptiness he leaves behind echoes in the silent bathroom.

I take a scalding shower, rubbing his dried cum from between my thighs and holding in the tears barging into my eyes.

You're not going to cry because of that man, Rai. Not again.

I close my eyes, letting the stream cover me whole as I think about *Dedushka*, Dad, and Mom, the people I lost and can never have again. Even Reina feels too far sometimes. Actually, it's most of the time.

I seem to be an expert at that—losing people I consider family. Sergei will leave, too. Then, it'll just be me and Ana. All alone.

Well, I am married, but does it even matter if Kyle remains a closed vault? Does it matter when, at every turn, I can't shake off the feeling that he'll leave?

Sighing, I step out of the shower and wrap myself in a towel.

I don't find Kyle in the room. He's inside the closet, standing in front of his small section, wearing only boxers.

My feet falter at the entrance, contemplating whether or not I should go in there.

"I don't bite," he says without meeting my gaze.

"I do." I approach so we're standing in a parallel line.

"Good to know, so if you're pregnant, you'll be able to protect our child."

"I'm not pregnant." I pull out a set of simple matching underwear.

"You don't know that." He faces me as he shoves his feet into black pants.

I slide the panties up my legs under the towel. "I won't allow it to happen."

"You know the morning-after pill isn't one hundred percent bulletproof, right?"

"A percentage I'm willing to take considering you intend on leaving."

"I didn't say that. Your trust issues did."

"Trust issues?" I throw the towel away and snap my bra into place. "Do you think they came to be without a reason? Like, one day I was just sitting there and they fell on me from the sky?"

"Point is, you have them." He slides into a shirt and takes his time buttoning it. "Don't pass them on to our baby."

"There's *no* baby."

He lifts a shoulder. "As far as you know."

"It's a fact."

"You won't know it for a fact until at least a few weeks from now when our baby is growing beautifully in your womb."

"And then what? You'll just be a doting father who will attend delivery classes with me and give me foot massages?" I mock.

"If that's what you need, sure."

My lips fall open and I pause with the sleeve of my dress up my shoulder. "Stop saying things like that."

"Like what? Like I will be there for you and our baby? Like I will read him or her a goodnight story, then come fuck you senseless in our bedroom? Those types of things?"

"Yes, those types of things. Stop lying."

He stands in front of me, shirt tucked into his pants, and runs his fingers through his hair, forcing it to submit to his will. Then, he casually turns me around and zips up my dress before he whispers against my ear, "You stop lying to yourself."

I push off him to leave the closet, but he tsks.

"Not so fast."

I groan as I face him. He's holding the toy. *Of course.*

"I'm putting a time limit on this." I jut my chin.

"Time limit?"

"In two weeks, if you don't give me the information we agreed on, you won't be putting any toys inside me."

"But you like the toys inside you."

"I do not. They're bound to make me appear weak in front of the other members of the elite group."

"And you hate that more than anything," he finishes, voice calm.

I clear my throat, but don't say anything.

He raises a brow. "But you still enjoy it."

"That's not the point. My position in the brotherhood is."

"What if I don't turn on the toy during the meetings?"

"As you shouldn't. You also need to honor the deal we agreed on."

"I already am. Why the fuck do you think I'm kissing up to the Italians' arses with Adrian all the time?"

The thought of him spending time in the Lucianos' mansion with a certain Emilia in sight bothers me more than I like to admit. "Hmph."

"What was that for?"

"Nothing."

"I'm unable to read your mind, so if you don't tell me what you think, I won't be able to act accordingly."

"Nothing means nothing."

"If you say so." A muscle clenches in his jaw before he masks it. "Lift the dress and keep it there."

"I'm sore." I try to bargain, and I mean it. I can barely walk straight with how he broke me with his merciless fucking last night and this morning.

"This will soothe you. Now, lift it."

I do so, staring at the wall so I don't get caught up in the sight of him putting the toy inside of me, a reminder that he's with me at all times.

He holds me to him by the waist, and I shudder at the feel of his erection at my stomach. The man is never satiated, I swear.

He releases me but only so he can lower my panties to my knees, then pushes my legs apart and teases my folds. I hate how familiar his touch has become, how addictive and stimulating, but what I hate the most is how much I miss it when he's gone.

He slides my wetness from my pussy to my back hole and presses his thumb against the entrance.

"W-what are you doing?"

"Testing something. Stay still."

I don't know what's going on until he presses his thumb further inside. It's a small intrusion but my bundle of nerves explodes.

"K-Kyle!" I whisper-yell, partly mortified, partly—and strangely—aroused.

"Mmm. You're too fucking tight here, too, but don't worry, I'll prep you to take my dick in the arse like a good little princess."

Before I can protest, he slides the toy into my pussy. I wince as the reminder of his dick ramming in overwhelms me. I'm hit by the memories of his ruthless thrusts and savage fucking.

I briefly close my eyes to chase away those images. When I open them again, Kyle is lifting my panties up my legs. I push away from him, finish the task myself, and go to my console.

Since we have a morning meeting with Sergei and the others, I expect Kyle to go ahead, but he sits behind his laptop while I'm doing my hair and makeup. The moment I'm done, he's by my side.

"You don't have to be my shadow," I say as we leave the room. "I don't need protection."

He raises a brow, grinning. "But our baby does."

"Would you stop with that?"

"With what? That our baby boy or girl is growing inside you?"

I'm about to hit him in the side when a presence catches my attention. Adrian is standing on the second floor's small hall, wearing his usual sharp suit, and tapping his fingers against his thigh. Only family members and their guards are allowed here. The others only come up when they have permission.

Adrian isn't the type who would do such a thing without it, and that's how I know the reason for his presence here is concerning.

We stop in front of him, and I speak first. "What are you doing here, Adrian? Is everything all right?"

His eyes flash toward me, flickering, almost like he's about to go into one of Damien's manic episodes. But then, he seals his reaction in, speaking in his usual composed tone. "What happened yesterday?"

"I already briefed Sergei."

"I want to hear it from you. Don't leave anything out."

It's not a surprise since Adrian is so attuned to details and prefers to hear retellings from the source who witnessed the event. "Well, Lia and I were standing near the entrance when I saw a dot on her forehead. I pushed her down, and Kyle pushed me as the silent bullet hit the door above her head."

"What else?"

"That's all."

Adrian grips me by the arm so hard I wince. "What. Else. Rai? Surely you saw something? Someone?"

Kyle grabs Adrian's arm and twists it off mine, his expression closed. "Do not lay your fucking hands on my wife again. She already said that's all, so that's all."

Adrian meets Kyle's impenetrable glare with one of his own. A war of gazes erupts between them with their own weapons and battalions.

"That really was all," I say in an attempt to dissipate the tension. It's the first time I've witnessed Adrian like this.

"What happened after?" He breaks off eye contact with Kyle to focus on me.

"We just went into the meeting as planned."

"And Lia didn't do anything?"

"What was she supposed to do…?" I trail off. "Wait—is she having PTSD?"

He narrows his eyes on me. "Why would you say that?"

"No reason." It seemed she didn't want him to know, so I'm not going to sell her out to a frightening-looking Adrian right now. "Let's join the others."

We find Sergei and the four kings seated around the dining table. Vlad meets us at the threshold and follows us in.

As soon as we're inside, Kyle pulls the chair out for me.

"I can do it myself," I say.

"I'm just being careful so you don't hurt the baby."

Silence fills the room and my heart nearly knocks out of its place and spills out on the floor.

"The baby?" Sergei's eyes widen with unmasked interest.

"It's not—"

"I believe we're expecting, *Pakhan*." Kyle cuts me off by placing his hand on my stomach in front of everyone and smiles. "Be good to Mommy, little guy."

Congratulations fly all over the table, and Kyle accepts them while grinning down at me. Then he whispers at my ear, "No morning-after pill. You don't want to disappoint everyone, do you, Princess?"

That's it. I'm going to kill him.

TWENTY-FIVE

Rai

A FEW DAYS LATER, SERGEI HOLDS A GATHERING TO celebrate the good news.

No joke.

I don't know why I've allowed it to go this far or how I let Kyle's manipulations lead me to this point of no return, but that single moment of speechlessness during the meeting was enough to have everyone ganging up on me with well wishes and congratulations.

Then Ana came downstairs, and she kept herself as busy as a bee in the kitchen, preparing me nutritious food and making me sit down.

Sergei won't stop smiling whenever he sees me. He may never meet his own grandchildren in this lifetime, so he's apparently living that dream through me.

No matter how much I wanted to put my foot down and scream that it wasn't true, I couldn't just wipe the doting expression off Sergei's face. He seems so happy lately, serene, almost like he's finally fulfilling the last role in his life. He doesn't even have bad coughs anymore.

I'm not cruel enough to hurt him, no matter how much I've been plotting to murder Kyle.

We're currently sitting around the dining table for the grand dinner Sergei prepared. This time, everyone else is present, including each brigade's highest-ranking guards and the 'killers', who are sitting at the far end of the table.

The *Pakhan* doesn't always invite the entire brotherhood for supper, so this means it's a very special occasion. The kitchen staff have prepared all sorts of traditional Russian dishes, ranging from sorrel soup to special types of dumplings and meaty main courses. Needless to say, the table is overflowing. However, no one touches their plates, waiting for Sergei to give permission.

He stands slowly, and I know it's so he doesn't trigger his cough. It's been getting better lately, but when he does have a fit, it can get bad. Sergei holds a glass of premium vodka in his hand. "We're gathered here to celebrate the new member that will join the Sokolov family. Our Rai and Kyle work fast."

I try not to blush, bunching my fists into my dress, but I can feel my cheeks heating. Kyle grins as he holds my hand under the table. When I attempt to push him away, he intertwines our fingers together and lifts it to his face so he can kiss my knuckles.

If my face were heating earlier, it's burning now.

Sergei exchanges a look with Igor, then laughs. "Please. Everyone, enjoy your meal."

All people present at the table raise their glasses for the toast, then dig into the food with renewed energy. It's not entirely gluttony, but rather a show of gratitude since it's disrespectful not to eat when the boss offers.

I yank my hand away from Kyle, who smirks. God, why haven't I killed this bastard in his sleep?

Well, it may have something to do with how he exhausts me every night. I pushed him away at first because of what he did, but I can't resist his touch. I tell myself that I'm using his body as much as he's using mine. It's only sex.

Just meaningless sex.

Kyle, though, makes sure to come inside me every time, as if he's really planning to impregnate me.

The joke's on him, though. Not only did I take the morning-after pill, but I also got myself a birth control prescription. My body reacted badly to the shot in my teens, so I had to resort to taking the pills.

At the end of the day, this celebration is null and void. In a week or so, I'll pretend I lost the child or that Kyle spoke too soon before we could make sure. Sergei will be sad, but he'll understand the loss.

Because there's no way in hell I'd let Kyle put a baby inside me.

There's an easy conversation at the table about mundane things. Since the wives are also here, there'll be no business talk until after dinner. A meeting that I'm invited to, per Sergei's orders. It has to do with how I've been financing the brigades over the last couple of weeks. I might not be invited to outside meetings with other organized crime leaders, but I can finally have a permanent place in the brotherhood.

Igor and Mikhail are exchanging pleasantries with Sergei. I exchange a look with Ruslan who's standing behind me. He pretends to excuse himself, and on his way, he trips and hits Igor's chair. He quickly apologizes as the older man spills droplets of his wine on the tablecloth. Igor's senior guard grabs Ruslan by the collar, but his boss discreetly motions at him to let my guard go—probably not to cause a ruckus.

One of the kitchen staff hurries to exchange Igor's glass of wine and bows in her retreat. Ruslan returns to stand behind me as the small incident is drowned out by general chatter. A few minutes later, I make eye contact with Katia who's standing across from me, near the exit, and she subtly follows the kitchen staff. We came up with this plan to have that DNA test done. I barely get direct contact with Igor or Stella, so this is one of the few chances we have. I already gave Katia Kyle's toothbrush, so she should be able to get the DNA results soon.

Now that the plan is in motion, my concentration goes back to the event.

Damien is focused on his meal, cutting through the meat with unabashed savageness. His manners are generally so bad that both *Dedushka* and Sergei gave up on schooling him years ago. He's basically the black bull of the brotherhood who's ready to murder anyone in his path.

But he's not the one who catches my attention among everyone present. It's Kirill and Adrian who keep talking to each other in hushed tones. I don't like it.

Kirill is a cunning fox behind gentlemanly behavior. While Mikhail can be considered my most vocal enemy, Kirill is the one who's able to inflict the worst damage. He doesn't stop. *Ever.* I have no doubt he's digging into me, trying to find a way to push me completely out so he can sink his foxlike claws into Sergei and V Corp.

The reason I'm threatening him with the secret he's keeping under lock and key is because it's the only card I have against him.

"You seeing what I'm seeing?" Vlad whispers from beside me, his gaze drifting to Adrian and Kirill, then back to me.

"When did those two become so cozy?" I ask.

"I told you not to trust Adrian."

"I don't." But I at least thought he was in the middle. If he chooses the other side, I'll have no choice but to attack, and it won't be pretty.

Lia isn't here, so I can't try to dig deeper into her. Judging from Adrian's reaction a few days ago, she's either his weakness or she holds something over him. Otherwise, he wouldn't have acted out of character when she was threatened. It's no surprise he purposefully keeps her out of similar occasions, but I will find a way to drag her in if I have to.

A hand wraps around my nape from behind, and shivers instantly break out on my skin before a sinister voice murmurs near my ear, "What are you two whispering about? Let me in."

"It's none of your concern." I take a sip of my soup, trying to ignore how Kyle's mere touch has awakened my whole body.

"I'm your husband and baby daddy, Princess. Everything about you is my concern."

I throw him a sidelong glare, which he merely answers with that infuriating smirk of his. I attempt to talk to Vlad so I can ignore Kyle all night, but his hand on my thigh keeps me prisoner.

His smile is still in place, but the humor behind it is gone, currently replaced by a threatening gloom. "Don't fucking ignore me for other men."

"Let me go," I hiss.

"Are you going to do as you're told?"

"You can't get in between me and my plans, Kyle."

"What plans do you have with *Vladimir*?" I don't miss the way he says Vlad's name with pure condescension.

"Plans that don't include pushing Igor for the leading position."

He pauses.

"What?" It's my turn to stare down at him. "You thought I didn't know? Your intentions are as clear as the sun."

"You're adorable to think that way."

"What is that supposed to mean?"

"Stop talking to other men in my presence—or the lack of it."

I huff and turn back to ask Vlad about the security measures. I already got my report from Ruslan and Katia, so I don't technically need to talk to Vlad about it. However, if it will piss Kyle off, I'm game.

I open my mouth, and it remains that way when humming starts between my legs.

Shit.

He set the toy at one of the highest levels from the get-go. The chatter, faces, and words start to fade into the background as the insides of my walls sparkle at once.

Due to Kyle's thorough fucking, I've become sensitive as hell, and mere friction is enough to shatter me to pieces.

"Your pleasure is visible on your face," he murmurs at my ear, then slightly nibbles on the lobe. "Makes me want to fuck you until you scream the whole house down."

Forcing my lips shut, I grab his hand that's still resting on my thigh and sink my red nails into his flesh as hard as I can.

That doesn't sway him. If anything, he brings the intensity up a notch. My thighs tremble and my stomach dips in preparation for the impact that's brewing in the distance.

"The more you defy me, the more I will wrench pleasure out of you," he rasps before pulling away to throw a piece of salmon into his mouth. He's eating leisurely as if he's not playing with me right now. I feel like the trapped mouse with no way out.

I don't loosen my hold on his hand, because, at this moment, it's my only anchor. It should be odd that Kyle is both my tormentor and my anchor, but he's always been a few steps higher than the devil. He knows exactly which buttons to push and *how* to push them.

"You want more?" He leans in again while wearing a fake smile for the outside world. "Who knew you'd be quite the exhibitionist?"

"Shut up and s-stop it." I try to scold, but it comes out like a needy moan.

"No can do, but here's what I can do." He licks my earlobe. "I can offer a hand."

"Fuck. You."

"Here?" He pretends to be astounded. "Your exhibitionist tendencies are more serious than I thought, Princess."

He pulls away to eat nonchalantly while I'm fighting with the sparks that keep invading my body. I try focusing on the food, but my hand is too shaky to grab the spoon.

"How do you feel about becoming a grandfather, Igor?" Sergei asks.

I'm too dizzy to focus very well on facial expressions and body language, but I can tell Igor's demeanor doesn't change as he says, "Stella and I are ecstatic."

His wife smiles by his side. Not sure if Kyle told them the truth or not, but either way, it doesn't seem like they're awfully happy about the news.

"Good, good." Sergei takes a sip of his drink. "This house needs kids running around."

"Weird, though." Damien wipes his mouth with the back of his hand like a savage animal, his gaze falling on me. "I never thought Rai would be the maternal type."

Everyone's attention turns to me, and I curse internally. I can barely keep a straight face right now. There's no way in hell I'll be able to talk, but at the same time, if I let Damien's provocation slide, it'll appear as a weakness.

I try gathering my bearings and swallowing a few times so my voice will come out somewhat normal.

"People change," Kyle says casually.

"Apparently they do if she's letting you talk on her behalf," Damien shoots back.

"Well, he won't have to kick your ass on my behalf," I manage in a semi-calm tone, even though I'm burning up on the inside.

Some laugh and others snicker, but Kirill smirks at me. He fucking smirks as if he knows my deepest, darkest secret and is saving it for later use.

Everyone else goes back to their chitchat, and Kirill joins them a bit too late, after he finishes taunting me.

What the hell is he hiding?

I'm about to chance a glance at Vlad to see if he noticed anything when the vibration between my legs increases. My hand instinctively grips Kyle's harder as I trap my lower lip between my teeth.

Is he really planning to have me come in front of everyone or something? My spine snaps into a line, and I can feel the tingles of the orgasm that's about to sweep me under.

I jerk upright, my voice barely audible as I mutter, "Excuse me."

The wait for Sergei's nod feels like an eternity. As soon as he moves his head, I fly out of the dining room on shaky legs. I slap my hands over my mouth so I don't release an embarrassing sound.

I continue running until I find a staff room and push the door open. After I'm inside, I sag against the wall. Just when the orgasm is about to hit me, the vibration decreases to a teasing level.

No, no. I *need* that release.

In the span of a few weeks, I've become so prone to the pleasure Kyle wrenches out of me. Even just now, in the midst of all those people, a twisted part of me wanted to come then and there.

I lift my dress up and pull my panties down before my fingers find the toy. I bite down on my lower lip as I slide the dildo out then push it back inside. My back flattens against the wall as the earlier sparks return.

They're slow-building with every thrust in. My heart crashes against my ribcage, its rate pulsing in my ear in my attempts to muffle my voice.

The door of the supply room crashes all the way open and I yelp, pausing with the dildo halfway inside me.

Why didn't I close the door? Just why?

Then when my eyes meet those dark blue ones, the reason hits me with the force of a thunderstorm.

Kyle is why I didn't close it. Did I unconsciously hope for him to follow me or something?

He steps inside, his height blocking the outside world and the light when he closes the door and leans against it. "About that hand..."

TWENTY-SIX

Kyle

A LONG TIME AGO, WHEN I WAS A KID AND HAD TO BE raised among monsters, I was taught to never covet anything.

Everything is temporary, usable, discardable. Every. Fucking. Thing.

So how come when I stare at the woman standing against the wall, all I can feel is the need to run my tongue over her cheek until I claim those parted lips?

How come she's the first thing that comes to mind in the morning and the last thing I want to see before I close my eyes?

Rai Sokolov is the forbidden fruit I should've never tasted, because one single taste isn't enough. Neither is the second, the third, or the tenth.

She lifts her chin up even though her position is the epitome of vulnerability. Her dress is bunched up to her waist, and her underwear is gathered around her ankles. Even the frail elastic causes red lines against her smooth, pale skin.

"I don't need your hand," she says breathlessly. "Get out."

I lean against the supply room door, crossing my legs at the ankle. "Never mind me. I'll just stay and watch. How does it feel to touch yourself with the toy you hated so much at the beginning? Are your walls clenching around the rubber?"

"S-shut up..." Her back visibly arches, tits pushing against the fabric of her dress. My cock throbs at the view, demanding to grab her by the throat and fuck her raw.

But the urge to play games with her is stronger, and I know she needs them too. That's why she provokes me every chance she gets.

Watching her thrust that plastic thing in and out of her pussy while I'm standing right here is both a turn-on and annoying. The former is because I love how she surrenders to pleasure. Her body relaxes, her lips part, and her eyes appear high as if she's in tune with every spark running through her.

The latter is because I don't want anything but me to touch her, not even a toy that I bought. My dick is raging hard, plotting to replace the toy and making her shatter all around him.

"Is the toy's size not able to satisfy you anymore?" I ask in the most nonchalant tone I can manage, even though I'm close to fucking her on the floor like a bloody animal. "Is your cunt begging for more?"

She traps the corner of her bottom lip under her teeth; as much as she likes to hide it, Rai gets off on dirty talk. Her walls clench around me harder whenever I describe what I plan to do to her.

"If you want the real thing, just ask. Or rather, beg for it like a good princess."

"You want this so much, too." She tips her chin toward the bulge in my trousers.

"Never said I didn't."

"Then how about *you* beg for it?"

"Women beg me, not the other way around."

"Well, maybe you should go to them."

"Maybe I will."

Her movements slow down as she pins me down with a glare. "Then maybe I will go find myself men who beg me for it too."

My jaw clenches. Even though I recognize her 'eye for an eye' principle, the thought of her with any other fucker turns my vision black. "Not if I snipe him down first."

"You can't watch me twenty-four-seven."

"Oh, I fucking can. I will murder every last man who comes within a meter's range of you. If you don't believe me, try it. Just go ahead and fucking try it."

She smiles a little through her whimpers, the expression taking me by surprise. When she speaks, her voice is breathy, needy, begging without saying the word 'please'. "Do you like exercising control so much you ignore your own bodily needs, Kyle?"

Her head tilts to my trousers again, to where I haven't bothered to hide the evidence of my fucking obsession with this woman.

"What's the matter, Kyle? Afraid to act on your urges?" She lifts her chin, still thrusting the toy in and out of her, un-hurriedly, almost…seductively. *Fuck me.* Since when did Rai become an expert in the art of seduction?

"Afraid of what?" I hold on to my control with an iron fist.

"Afraid of letting go…of feeling."

I reach her in two long strides and twist her around so her front meets the wall, then hold her by the throat from behind. Her gasp of surprise slowly turns into a moan when my fingers close around the delicate flesh of her neck, the flesh that's eas-ily bruised, easily marked as mine.

"I'm not the one who's afraid to let go, Rai," I murmur against her ear. Then I bite down on it, my voice dropping. "*You* are."

Her whimper of pleasure is the only incentive I need as I release her hair, letting it fall over her shoulders. Then I unbuckle my belt and push down my boxer briefs enough to free my aching dick.

I pull the toy out of her pussy and throw it away. She holds on to my hand that's wrapped around her throat, not to remove it, but to treat it like an anchor for what's about to come. I've become so attuned to the way she needs me. My wife is beautiful, strong, but she's still vulnerable for me.

Only me.

Her head tilts to the side, allowing my hand to completely wrap around her neck. It'd be so easy to break her and watch as she shatters to pieces.

"I won't hold back," I whisper against the lobe of her ear, nibbling on the tender flesh.

"Were you ever holding back?"

"Oh, I was. You have no idea how much I was."

"Now you w-won't?" There's a slight trembling in her voice. She's scared, but that's not the only feeling present.

My wife's excitement shows through the widening of her eyes, the way she goes completely still against me.

"No." My voice is hardly audible near her ear. "And you'll take everything I give you. Every thrust, every orgasm, and every drop of my cum."

Her shudder is the only reaction she shows as I slam inside her in one swift go. Her moan is loud, unrestrained, echoing in the small space around us.

Using my hand at her throat, I shove my index finger in her mouth. "Shh. They will hear."

She bites down on my finger, hard. I suppress a wince as I smirk. I love it when she gives back as good as she takes, when she submits to me then decides she wants to show her feisty side.

"Y-you're…you're so big," she says against my finger.

"And yet you take everything I give you like a good princess." I power on deeper into her, letting her feel the extent of my madness and the surrealness of it all.

Rai slaps her other hand against the wall for balance, her head bowing. I use my grip on her throat and angle her face up so she's staring up at me. "Look at me when I'm fucking you."

Her twinkling eyes, although filled with undeniable desire, are also projecting something different—a challenge. She's *challenging* me to give her my all.

I chuckle, the sound probably coming out manic. "If you keep looking at me with those eyes, you're fucked, Rai."

"You said you'd give your all," she murmurs as if she doesn't want to admit her deepest, darkest desire.

"Oh, you'll get my all, all right. Don't blame me if you bruise."

My hand moves from her throat to grip her by the hair as I ram inside her with a power that takes my entire energy. All my blood rushes to the space between us.

She squeals, bucking off the wall, but I hold her against it with a harsh grip on her hip. Her moans mount and rise, and she has to place both hands over her mouth so the outside world doesn't hear.

But she doesn't break eye contact, not even when my thrusts go out of control.

I am going out of control.

I have no idea what she sees when she studies my face, but it's one of the few times I show her my truest form, the one she stupidly wants to know. If she does, it'll be game over for her.

But instead of the disgust I expected—hell, fear would've made sense too—Rai removes her hands from her mouth and seals her lips to mine.

She's…kissing me.

Rai is kissing me when I'm ruthlessly using her body and showing her the monster I truly am, the monster who left her because she has enough monsters to deal with.

I bite her lower lip, a last-ditch effort to make her snap out of it, but she licks my upper lip in return.

Fuck. Fuck!

I kiss her back with an urgency that knocks the bloody breath out of my lungs. Who cares about oxygen when I'm breathing her in as my favorite type of drug?

This woman will cause both our downfalls.

Her lips part as her orgasm surfaces, but I don't stop feasting on her, not even when she's strangling my dick with her inner walls. I don't stop devouring her parted lips either, nipping on the flesh, sucking her bottom lip into my mouth.

Rai's knees buckle, failing her, but I hold her up by the hip. "I'm not done with you, wife."

At the word 'wife', she closes her eyes. No idea if it's due to pleasure or distaste, but she tries standing up on her legs.

I go on and on, thrusting into her with the same strong rhythm like a madman in search of his sanity—or probably a sane man on the verge of insanity. Because this? The way she enjoys it when I go all in? This is exactly why Rai is made for me.

Wait…made for me?

I don't have the mental space to focus on that bizarre thought when my balls tighten and my spine jerks into a line. I hold her in place, grunting as I shoot my seed inside her.

Like I told her earlier, she takes everything in, every fucking drop. I don't pull out of her for the seconds we use to catch our breaths.

Rai slumps against the wall and I crash into her from behind. If I'm too heavy, she doesn't protest, just continuing to try to catch her breath.

I give us a few seconds like that. Just me and her. Body to body. Pulse to pulse.

I stare at my watch, cursing myself for losing track of time, considering the show I plotted for tonight. Thankfully, there are still twenty minutes to go. I should keep Rai here until it all ends.

She raises a hand to wipe the corner of her eye—or more accurately, a tear that escaped.

Fuck. That was too intense, even for my level of depravity.

Feelings of regret I should never have creep in on me as I take in her form against mine. She's breakable, easily bruised, and yet I took it all out on her.

I pull out, begrudgingly releasing her. She turns around to face me, barely standing on her legs, using the wall for balance.

My eyes lock on her dark blues as I wipe a finger under her eyes. "Are you in pain?"

"I'm not a delicate flower, Kyle. Don't treat me like one."

"But you are."

She juts her chin out even though it's trembling slightly. "No, I'm not."

I glide my fingertips over the mark on her collarbone. "This proves otherwise."

"I'm fine. I asked for it."

I smile a little. "You sure as fuck did. Can you walk?"

"Just…just give me a second."

"Take a minute." My tone is amused.

She narrows her gorgeous eyes on me. "Are you mocking me?"

"Why would I, my delicate flower?"

"You're such an asshole," she mutters under her breath as she bends down to slide her underwear up her legs.

She's still shaking, her fingers barely functioning. I place her hands at her sides and take over the task of making her look presentable.

A part of me wants her to go out like this, with my cum dried on her thighs and her face looking thoroughly fucked, but the other big part, the one that wins, doesn't want anyone but me to see this side of her.

She tries to protest, but I yank her hands down. "Stay still."

I comb her hair with my fingers before I tie it with the elastic band at the back of her head.

At first, she remains as frozen as a statue, but then she starts fidgeting. All of a sudden, she grabs me by the belt. "I'll help, too."

She tucks me in, bashfully at first, like she doesn't know how to do it. My dick twitches back to life at her inexperienced touch. *Fuck me.* That thing doesn't know how to rest.

Rai zips up my trousers and does my belt as I finish cleaning up the smeared lipstick around the contours of her mouth.

Then we stare at each other, her hands around my waist and my finger at the corner of her parted lips.

"Why does it feel…normal?" she murmurs.

"What's *it?*"

"This." She tips her head between us, and I don't know if she's talking about her and me or the way we tucked each other in.

"Shouldn't it?"

She shakes her head once.

She always gets on my fucking nerves when she does that. She's still fighting and running away, even though I already have her by the throat—in every sense of the word.

"You were always meant to be mine, Rai. Quit fucking fighting it."

"Then quit hiding from me."

"I'm not hiding."

"You're running."

"Yes, Rai, I'm running, and I'll screw you over on the way. Is that what you want to hear?"

I expect her to yell back, to challenge me, because that's what she does in these situations.

Instead, her voice comes out small. "What I want to hear is something about you—the real you, not whatever image you're projecting to the world."

"What good would that do?"

"Me. It'll bring me closer to your side."

"And let me guess, you still won't completely trust me?"

"Not unless you prove yourself worthy of that trust."

I pause, considering my options and formulating the best scenario. "I was part of an assassination organization."

Her eyes widen, but she says, "I knew as much."

"No, you didn't. You only knew I was a killer for hire. The organization bit is new to you."

"And how long were you part of this organization?"

"Since I was five years old."

Her eyes droop, and I hate the look in those eyes.

"Stop looking at me like that."

"Like what?"

"Like you fucking pity me."

She shakes her head frantically. "It's not that."

"Then what is it?"

"Nothing." She pauses. "And then what?"

"Then nothing."

"Kyle!"

"What? You're not the only one who can use that word."

"Has anyone ever told you you're a major jerk?"

"You do that all the time. You have no competition in that department."

"Dick."

"I know you're addicted to my dick. You don't have to remind me."

Her cheeks heat. "No, I meant you're a dickhead."

"Does that mean you want to give my dick head?"

"Ugh. Stop twisting my words around."

"Why shouldn't I?" I smile genuinely for the first time in a very long time. "It's fun."

A bang comes from outside, and I stare at my watch. Ten minutes early—*what the fuck?*

Rai pushes away from me and runs out of the supply room, her trembling limbs long gone.

"Bleeding hell," I mutter under my breath as I jog after her toward the dining room.

Chaos unfolds in the midst of the peace as armed men barge inside with their weapons held high. Women crouch under the table, squealing as every man gets his weapon out.

Rai stops in front of them, pats Anastasia's head, and then says something to Stella and a few other women.

I think she'll join them and make this mission at least a bit easy, but then she bolts upright, and motions at Ruslan. He passes her a gun as he, Katia, and Rai form a triangle and shoot at the men.

The fucking bravery of that woman always gets me.

It's useless in this situation, though. Not only are the attackers wearing bulletproof vests, but no one in the mafia can match their level.

Rai jerks her head in Sergei's direction.

The motion happens in a fraction of a second. I follow her gaze and see the exact moment her brain decides on its course of action. There's a gunman aiming at Sergei, and Rai just decided she will protect him.

Fuck!

I run at full speed and beat her to the position at the last second. She halts at my right, her expression stunned as a bullet pierces my chest.

The force swings me back and I slump on the ground, my bones taking the impact. Hot liquid pours out of me before red soaks my chest and pools all around me.

"Kyle!" Her shrill, panicked voice reaches me despite the chaos.

An angelic face hovers over me, flashing back and forth in my blurry vision.

I raise a finger to her cheek, only my arm doesn't move.

"I knew you would be the death of me, Princess."

My eyes roll back in my head and the world turns black.

TWENTY-SEVEN

Rai

"K YLE!"
I run to him and drop to my knees beside his unconscious body, my heart hammering so loud I hear the pulse in my ears.

The chaos surrounding us, the gunshots, the whimpering sounds, the shouts in Russian—it all fades into the background. The only thing I can focus on is the man lying on the ground.

The man whose eyes are closed as blood soaks his shirt then oozes out of him at a frightening speed, as if life is abandoning him.

I place shaky fingers on the hole and press as hard as I can.

"Don't go...don't you dare go..." My voice chokes at the end, but I sniffle, focusing on my task.

He can't leave, not anymore. He promised he'd stay. He fucking promised.

"Get Dr. Putin! Now!" I shout at the top of my lungs to anyone who can hear. I can't find the will to cut off my attention from Kyle. I feel like if I take my eyes off him even for a second, he'll vanish into thin air.

Katia pulls herself from the front lines and nods, rushing to the entrance.

If it were up to me, I would take him to the hospital, but we don't have that luxury in our world, not when every gunshot is reported and will sure as hell cause a ruckus later on.

The brotherhood has its own doctor who's paid generously enough that he comes when asked to.

Ruslan stands beside me with his gun raised to protect me. "Do you want me to move him?"

"No. It could make his wound worse." My breathing is deep, controlled, but it hints at being on the verge of a breakdown. "Give me your jacket and cover my back."

Ruslan doesn't hesitate as he shrugs off his jacket and hands it to me. I press it on Kyle's chest, hard. I might not know what to do to save him, but I know the bleeding needs to stop.

With every passing second, his pulse decreases, and my heart rate picks up at a frightening speed as if it's about to stop altogether.

The gunshots halt, but I don't lift my head. I *can't*.

"Rai!"

I meekly direct my gaze upward at the sound of my name. Sergei stands in front of me, frowning. "Let's go upstairs."

"No. I'm not leaving him."

"We don't know if there are other armed men. How are you going to help him if you're hurt yourself?"

"I'm *not* leaving his side."

Sergei shakes his head, but he orders his guards to form a circle around us even though there's no more shooting.

"His pulse is weak and he's lost so much blood." My chin trembles. "What am I going to do?"

"There's nothing you can do except press down and don't release the cloth," Sergei says. "Let Ruslan do it."

"No." The idea of leaving Kyle's side, even for a moment, terrifies the fuck out of me. If I do, I will lose him, just like seven years ago—only this time, it will be for good.

This time, I won't be able to hang on to the hope that he'll come back.

I don't know how long it takes for the doctor to come, but it's long enough that Ruslan's jacket is soaked in blood and Kyle's pulse is almost non-existent.

I try to stay close by as Dr. Putin does his job, but Sergei forces me up to my shaky feet so I don't get in the way.

My gaze keeps following the doctor's movements with hawklike concentration. I'm vaguely aware of guards cleaning up the dining room and stern Russian commands from the elite group, especially Vlad. He orders two of Sergei's guards to take Ana and the other women to another room.

Everything else is a blur. For a second, I'm not sure if this is a dream or reality. I can't feel my own body or breaths.

It takes Dr. Putin a long time to get the bullet out of Kyle's chest. I don't look away from the gruesome scene, the needle cutting through Kyle's skin and the blood that's being transfused into his body.

I don't even look away from the pool of blood surrounding him as if it's his death bed.

Shaking my head internally, I continue watching the whole thing. It takes so long that Sergei grabs a chair and sits on it.

I don't.

If I move even an inch, I'll start hyperventilating.

Finally, Dr. Putin stands and addresses Sergei. "He lost a lot of blood, but he was lucky. If the gunshot was a little to the side, he wouldn't have survived. He's feverish, so it can be dangerous tonight. He needs constant monitoring until the fever disappears. I'll prescribe antibiotics that he needs to take on time."

Sergei thanks the doctor and tells one of his men to drive him back.

I snatch the prescription from the doctor's hand and shove it into Katia's. "Make it quick."

"Yes, miss." She nods and sprints out of the mansion.

Since the doctor told us how to safely move him, I order Ruslan and another of Sergei's guards to place him on a tall coffee table then carry it upstairs.

I follow after, even though my feet are shaking. I stare at the blood on my hands, a deep, crimson red. His blood...Kyle's.

As soon as I'm inside the room, I rush to the bathroom and yank the faucet on. I rub my trembling hands together over and over again and taste salt. That's when I know tears are cascading down my cheeks.

I wipe them with the back of my hand, then wash my face before I come out of the bathroom with a wet towel.

Ruslan stays by the bed on which Kyle is lying. My husband is only in his pants after the doctor cut through his bloodied shirt. A bandage is wrapped around his chest and slung over his shoulder.

"Go help outside, Ruslan," I manage to say. "And tell Katia to get in here as soon as she has the meds."

"Yes, miss."

With one last look at me, Ruslan leaves the room.

All the energy I used to remain standing abandons me. I fall to my knees at the side of the bed, then carefully wipe the blood that's marring Kyle's abs.

He shouldn't be bleeding or hurt. He's too professional and methodical for that.

And yet he is.

Because no matter how professional he is, Kyle is still human. Humans bleed and die.

Like he almost did today. His words from our wedding day rush back to me, the part where he told me not to wish to become a widow because that might come true sooner than expected.

I cup his jaw with my fingers and lean in to place a kiss on his lips, my shaking mouth lingering there for an extra second before I murmur, "You're not allowed to leave again, asshole."

TWENTY-EIGHT

Kyle

MY EARS BUZZ AS I SLOWLY OPEN MY EYES.

The first thing I see is a beautiful woman. Her hair cascades on either side of her face, the blonde strands camouflaging her expression.

The angel who came to visit me in my last moments…only, were they my last moments?

She's diligently wiping my chest, her expression solemn and her brows concentrated as if she's in the middle of the most important task of her life. I don't dare disturb her, because all I want to do is to look at her—really *look* at her, and engrave this view and her to memory, and keep her there.

With me.

At that moment when I thought everything would be over, the thing I thought about wasn't my mission or the people whose hearts I couldn't rip out with my bare hands. The only thing that came to mind was this beautiful spitfire of a woman who was finally opening up to me after hating me for years—or maybe I told myself she was opening up.

I thought about how she would be all alone again, how she would become closed off and would beat the world out of her inner circle.

And I didn't like that. I *don't* like that. She would be all alone in the world without me, without anyone to hold on to.

Deep down, I already promised myself I would protect her. I already took that vow saying she would be the only person I'd make an exception for.

The only person who would be mine.

It takes superhuman energy for me to move my arm. My hand grasps her strands, and I take them between my fingers, caressing the golden hair.

Rai jerks her head upright and stares at me with those blue eyes I never once forgot about, those eyes that sometimes visited me in my sleep and forced me to wake up in a cold sweat. Why do these eyes have a hold on me when my only purpose in life is to destroy everything she stands for?

But it doesn't matter how much I hate what she stands for. I've never hated *her*. She's the only one I've ever allowed this close.

Her lips part, and soon enough, she stares at me with that wretched expression. Then, slowly, too slowly, her mouth opens, and she smiles at me as if she's seeing me for the first time.

I guess this is the type of reaction I wanted when I came back, but she wanted to have me punished. She wanted me killed. Now she's smiling because I woke up.

This woman is a paradox.

"You're awake."

I nod, and the simple motion holds me hostage. Pain explodes in my chest and spreads all over my body.

"How are you feeling? Should I get the doctor?"

"No," I say in a voice so hoarse I doubt she heard the word. "I'll survive."

"Don't you ever, and I mean *ever*, do that again!" Mixed emotions are evident in her voice: relief, desperation, but most of all, she appears to be on the verge of a meltown.

"Do what?"

"Why the hell did you run in front of Sergei that way?"

"Because you were going to do it. You were running to use yourself as a fucking body shield. Did you expect me to let you sacrifice yourself?"

"That's my duty as part of the brotherhood."

"It is not your duty to get yourself killed."

"And it's not your duty, either. Since when do you give a fuck about Sergei?"

"I don't. The only one I ever gave a fuck about is you."

Her lips part and I expect her to say something, to shoot back a retort, as usual, but she continues wiping my chest. Her expression is solemn, and I can see the tears that are gathered in her eyes.

"I thought you left again." Her hand continues wiping my arms, my hands, and even my biceps. While her touch is gentle, the expression on her face is anything but. "I thought I lost you and you would never come back."

"Did you really think it would be so easy for me to leave? After all, I still haven't put a baby in you. Not officially, at least."

"Shut up, asshole."

"I see your tongue hasn't changed, so you can't be *that* worried. I'm wounded."

"Stop joking around!" Her chin trembles. "You have no idea what I've been through. You had a fever last night, and I couldn't sleep a wink in case I needed to stop it from going up."

"Sorry."

She wipes her face with the backs of her hands. "Just focus on getting better."

We remain silent for a bit as I drink in her presence. Who knew having her by my side this way would feel so fulfilling?

"What happened last night?" I ask.

"I don't know. We were attacked by armed men. Adrian and Vlad think it was the Irish, but I'm not sure. They didn't look Irish."

"And how do you know what the Irish look like? Did you hear them talk?"

"No, but the Irish aren't stupid enough to attack the *Pakhan*'s house. That's like a direct declaration of war, and they wouldn't do it."

"Maybe they didn't do that in the past, but now they've changed their minds."

She shrugs, neither denying nor confirming that option. I opt to not push the idea because it will appear suspicious. It's the only time I'm glad most of the other men don't take Rai's words seriously. They can't suspect that it's not the Irish.

"Either way…" Rai continues wiping my skin as she speaks. "Sergei told Damien to prepare for battle. I bet he's the most ecstatic about this turn of events. You know how he gets when it comes to the word 'war.'"

"What is your role in all of this?"

"I'm just financing for now. I can't fully participate."

"Why not?"

"Because I'm taking care of you, genius."

"You don't have to take care of me. I have that guard, Peter. Where is the useless kid, anyway?"

"No." Her tone brooks no argument as her determined eyes swing back to mine. "I will be the one who takes care of you."

"Do you really want to?"

"I'm your wife. It's my duty."

"I didn't think you took our vows so seriously. Speaking of which, there's that part that says to love and to cherish."

"Don't get ahead of yourself."

"Well, at least I tried."

There are still tears in her eyes, and I don't like it. I don't like that those beautiful blues are marred with something as painful as tears, because I know Rai's not the type who would show her emotions to the outside world this easily. She's not the type who cries just because she feels pain. If anything, she's the type who would hide her weaknesses with all her might. So the fact that she can't right now, means those emotions are too strong for her to control.

"I'm in pain," I murmur.

Her head snaps up from her task and she checks my wound, then my face. "What? What is it? Is there anything I can do?"

I extend my arm on my non-injured side and point at it with my head. "Come here."

"No. You're wounded."

"Come here, Rai."

"Why?"

"Because I want you close."

"Why do you want me close?" Her voice is small, as if she doesn't know how to ask that question.

"Because at the moment when I thought it was the end, that's the only thing I wanted."

She doesn't release the wet cloth as she slowly climbs into my side, carefully trying not to disturb my injury.

Her head lies on my bicep and she watches my face with her hand slung around my abdomen.

For a moment, she stares at me and I stare back. Tear streaks break the layers of her makeup, and she's still last night's dress. She really didn't have the time to leave me if she's wearing clothes from last night.

"What are you thinking about?" I ask.

"You have another gunshot mark on your shoulder."

"Have you been touching me inappropriately, Princess?" I tease.

Her cheeks gain a red hue, but she stands her ground. "What are you talking about? I'm your wife—I can't touch you inappropriately."

I like how she calls herself my wife. I like how she's finally coming to terms with that fact.

"I was shot at."

"You're lucky to have survived two shots."

"It's probably because I had you this time, and that's why I escaped the afterlife."

"Stop joking around about death. You were almost gone."

"I'm right here."

Her breathing, which was hitched a few seconds ago, returns to normal as she strokes my abdomen. Then, her fingertips slide up my chest to the mark of the gunshot. "What happened?"

I can't tell her the truth because that will reveal who I really am, but I can at least show her the side of me she has never seen before. It's so selfish of me to try to keep her close when I know her stance on what I have in mind.

"A long time ago, I was with my friends."

"Friends?"

"They weren't exactly my friends, but my colleagues from the assassination organization. In a way, they were like a family to me. It's somewhat like the brotherhood, only we barely had any loyalty to each other. We just co-existed. The head of the family, whom I considered my godfather, was slipping away from me."

"Godfather? Is he from the mafia?"

"Sort of. I wouldn't consider him part of the mafia, but the concept is close enough."

"Then, what happened?"

"Some rivals in the territory we ruled in London wanted

my godfather dead. Of course, I couldn't allow that to happen, so I took it upon myself to draw out the culprit."

"That's how you got shot?"

"That's how I got myself shot." Or close enough, anyway. She doesn't need to know about the details.

"What is the difference between getting yourself shot and being shot?" Her question takes me by surprise. She really focuses on the details others wouldn't even pay attention to.

"Getting oneself shot means I brought it upon myself."

"What did you do?"

"I was overprotective of my godfather."

"And that's a bad thing?"

"Sometimes, yes, but that's how I was able to learn that I shouldn't be overprotective about anyone. Because in the end, they have their own life, and I have mine."

"I don't think that's true. I don't think protecting people makes you a bad person or someone who shouldn't be trusted. I think it takes a lot of courage to not only protect oneself, but everyone else around you."

"Believe me, Princess, that wasn't my intention, but if you take it that way, I won't mind."

"Didn't you just say you were being overprotective?"

"Yeah, but not of everyone around me. We don't do that where we came from. Not like you do."

"Me?"

"Yeah, you make sure your family is well taken care of."

"It's my duty."

"Using yourself as a fucking body shield in front of Sergei isn't duty—it's reckless."

She stares at me for a beat, then sighs. "I had to. That's the only way my family could survive. If Sergei dies, both Anastasia and I are fucked."

"No, you're not."

"Yes, we are. Don't you see how the others are plotting

against me? Mikhail will have my head on a platter the moment Sergei dies, and have you seen that fox Kirill? He has something up his prim-and-proper sleeve, too."

"Neither of them will hurt you."

"How can you be so sure?"

"Because you have me now. There is no way in hell you'll be hurt under my watch."

She's silent for a second, and I think she's falling asleep. But then her words fill the silence. "Why did you leave?"

It's the first time she's spoken to me with that vulnerable voice outside of sex. It's not only due to the question, but also about how she felt when it happened back then.

I consider my options and what to tell her without pushing her away. I'm enjoying having her around me so much right now. Or any time, basically.

"I was on a mission," I say.

"What type of mission?"

"The type you shouldn't know about for your own safety."

"You left me, Kyle. I have the right to know why."

"What do you mean I left you? We weren't in a relationship back then. We weren't sexual, or anything."

"You were the closest guard I had, and you were the only one I ever allowed to know about my twin sister. You were the only one I shared my past with. And yet you just up and left as if nothing happened, as if we didn't have those things together."

"You told me you didn't need me, Rai. After we saved Reina, you stood in front of me and said you were your own person and didn't need someone to do things for you. You said those words, so don't sit here and pretend as if you begged me to stay."

"*Begged you?* Do you realize how that sounds? You know me, Kyle, or at least you did back then. Did you really think someone like me would ever beg? I'd just lost my grandpa back then, my only anchor, and the only person I needed by my side fucking left."

"I didn't know. I don't exactly have the capacity to read your mind."

"So you decided to leave as if nothing happened?"

"I told you I was on a mission."

"What type of mission? And don't tell me I shouldn't know for my safety. We're already married. There's no wall that exists between us."

Yes, there is, and she's the one who has been building it since the beginning. I'm no better myself considering everything I'm hiding, but the barrier does exist, and all I want to do is to fucking eradicate it.

"The mission was for that organization I told you about. I had to go back to England."

"And that made you unable to answer my calls or send me a text to let me know?"

"Yes."

"But why, Kyle? Just why the hell did you erase yourself from my life that abruptly?"

"Because that's what I do. I disappear. I couldn't stay in touch because that would've made me want to come back, and that was out of the question."

"You just wanted to leave."

"Yes." *And I didn't want to think about you.* "You'd already chosen your life path, and I didn't have a place in it."

"Idiot," she mutters.

"What is that supposed to mean?"

"You don't need to know for your own safety." She repeats my words from earlier in a mocking tone.

"You never give up, do you?"

"No, and if you leave without notice again, it won't be pretty."

I brush my lips over her forehead as my form of an answer.

We remain like that until exhaustion takes its toll on her and she falls asleep. As soon as she does, I reach for my phone and unlock it. I have several messages.

One of them is more important than the others.

Flame: The attack tonight went smoothly.

Fucker. Of course it did.

Shouldn't it be ironic that I'm shot by an attack I initiated?

I type.

Kyle: Were there any casualties from our side?

Flame: None aside from your embarrassing shot.

Kyle: It was part of the plan.

Flame: Bullshit.

Kyle: Why the fuck did one of us take aim at Sergei?

Flame: You said to hurt them enough to start a war.

Kyle: If Sergei is gone, who the fuck would start that war, genius?

Flame: All the others. Genius.

Kyle: Don't take aim at Sergei without telling me first.

Flame: Yawn.

Bloody arsehole.

Kyle: How is it with the Irish?

Flame: They're trembling in fear.

As they should. Because while the Russians were holding back before now, they will never allow one of their own to be shot and stay quiet about it.

That in itself is worth being shot for. Not only that, Sergei will also have his full trust in me, and everyone will respect me for protecting their boss.

I will use all those privileges to my own advantage.

Flame: Oh, and Ghost knows you were shot.

The phone nearly slips from my fingers as I read and re-read Flame's text. I'm not imagining things. He just said my godfather knows.

Kyle: Why did you tell him?

Flame: Passing conversation.

Kyle: Bollocks.

He doesn't do anything without a prior plan, and the reason he told Godfather isn't a coincidence, either.

Flame: He asked me about you.

Godfather asked about me? But why? When we parted ways ten years ago, he made it clear that he didn't want to see my face again.

Kyle: And?

Flame: And what?

Kyle: And what did he say?

Flame: Nothing. You know he's a man of few words.

The hope that rose in my chest from earlier withers away and perishes. Of course he would say nothing after that betrayal.

Shaking my head internally, I get myself back in the game.

Kyle: Keep me updated about your side, and next time, kill one of the Russian leaders.

If one of them is gone, the war will be stronger and more furious.

The only miscalculation in my plan is this woman who has her hand wrapped around my waist as if she doesn't want to let me go. This woman is my only loose end, but I will find a way, and I will get her where she belongs.

Right next to me.

"Sleep," I whisper. "Your life will never be the same in the near future."

TWENTY-NINE

Kai

TWO WEEKS HAVE PASSED, AND ALTHOUGH IT'S A significant amount of time, it doesn't feel like it.

I think it's because of how little has happened, but at the same time, it feels like a lot.

As promised, Sergei had Damien start his attack on the Irish. It was savage and merciless, like Damien's character. We only lost two men, but the Irish lost more.

The Italians are currently by our side, but the Yakuza and the Triads are still reluctant about a war they don't belong to.

Vlad asked me to talk to Kai since he seems to be open to negotiation. However, Kyle wasn't very fond of the idea. He didn't like the thought of me having a one-on-one with Kai.

For now, I will just agree with him because he is recovering, but in the long run, I know we can't survive on our own. If the Irish bring in their allies, the Luciano family alone won't be enough.

Other than the attack, we've been somehow blissfully living our lives. Kyle and I wake up early and take walks, or we go through V Corp's numbers with Ruslan and Katia. I'm surprised by Kyle's way of conducting business; he knows the ins and out at a level that rivals mine. When I asked him how he learned these things, he said it was from his 'family'.

The one he told me about the other day. For the first time ever, he talked about a part of his life I had no idea about.

In the midst of our uneventful days, I'm far from relieved. If anything, I feel like it's the calm before the storm.

Anastasia told me the storm already happened during the shooting at dinner, but why do I have a premonition like that's not even the beginning of it?

Two days after the attack, Katia told me that they couldn't get a DNA sample from Igor's glass of wine because she was interrupted during the attack and wasn't able to preserve the DNA. I was too preoccupied with Kyle to get another sample of Igor's DNA during his recent visits, but I'll eventually have it.

That moment when I saw Kyle lying in his own blood, all I could think about was that I'd lost him right after I had just gotten him back.

So, during these past couple of weeks, I've been at his side as he slowly recovers. I haven't gone to the company a lot, and even when I do, I bring my work back home with me.

It's not easy to juggle two lives at the same time, but I make it work so Kyle can get back on his feet again.

His recovery has been going smoothly. Even Dr. Putin said he has a strong immune system.

Last night, during a dinner with the leaders of the brotherhood, Sergei officially named him as his honorable councilor.

Though there was no formal ceremony, the fact remains that Kyle is now part of Sergei's closest circle. If it were a few weeks ago, I would have been suspicious of how close Kyle has gotten, but after he put his own life on the line to save mine and Sergei's, it's not possible to.

Little by little, the bridge that was already broken between us has started to build again. For the first time since our marriage, it feels like there's something to salvage between us, a connection of sorts that's not directly connected to the physical department.

Don't get me wrong, there's inexplicable energy about having sex with Kyle. It's freeing in a way words can't describe.

Only a few days after being shot, Kyle insisted on fucking me—he wouldn't stop talking about it every time we were in the same room. As a result, I attempted to get on top and ride him so he wouldn't hurt his wound, but he suddenly flipped me over onto my back and fucked me until I screamed his name.

It's become a habit since then. I try to ride him, and he goes with it at first, giving me a sense of power, just to snatch it away a few minutes later. It's not really about the power anymore—for me, at least. I'm more interested in the tension and the connection that blossoms between us whenever I'm in his arms.

For Kyle, it's most likely about the power and the control that comes with it. He likes it when I fight him in bed just so he can subdue me.

He gets off on seeing me powerless. He gets off on holding me by the throat. He gets off on having me underneath him, screaming or moaning his name, begging him to stop or go faster and harder. He gets off on those things, and he's not ashamed to admit it.

I've become so addicted to that side of him, the side that lets go completely even though he's injured. On one of those nights, he didn't stop; he literally had the stamina of a youngling on Viagra. I was less concerned with the delicious soreness between my legs, and more scared that he would rip his stitches out and we would have a bloodbath on our hands.

Thankfully, that wasn't the case, but I overestimated my endurance ability and was barely able to walk the following morning. Kyle teased me about it during the entire walk. His eyes twinkle with amusement whenever I rise up to the challenge. Our banter can last for an eternity if we're not interrupted.

Our morning walks around the garden started as a sort of physical rehabilitation for Kyle, but with time, it's become something I look forward to every day. There's a peace in having my arm around Kyle's waist and just talking, even if we clash most of the time.

Today, I woke up early so I could help prepare breakfast. It's been a long time since I cooked, but I try my hand with the kitchen staff and ignore the weird glances Katia and Ruslan keep throwing my way.

So what if I'm doing something out of the norm? It's true that I haven't done it since I came to live with *Dedushka*, but I used to cook just fine when I was living with Dad. That was sixteen years ago, so my memories aren't exactly that perfect, but it will work.

I make some pancakes and toast with jelly. Well, some of the toast is a bit burnt, but Kyle doesn't have the right to complain after I did all this for him.

No—I'm not doing this for him. I'm just doing it because I feel guilty about what happened to him because of me. That's it. That's *all*.

After preparing the picnic basket, I hold it and attempt to go upstairs, but I find Kyle already waiting for me at the entrance. He's wearing his usual black pants and a white shirt.

The clothes and the bandage hide his injury, but I can almost see the hole currently lodged in his chest.

The images of him being shot rush back to the front of my mind, and I have trouble getting them out. It's not until his very distinctive scent overwhelms me that they slowly dissipate.

Kyle places his hand on my arm as he usually does every day. "Morning, Mrs. Hunter."

"Morning. Are you feeling better today?"

"Are you still asking that after I fucked you till you tore the sheets yesterday?"

"Kyle!" My face burns, and I instinctively check our surroundings in case someone heard.

"What?"

"What if someone is listening?"

"Then they have voyeuristic tendencies. Is auditory porn a thing?"

"You're hopeless."

"For having sex with you? I'll take that badge with honor."

"For being this shameless about everything."

"We're already husband and wife. It's universally known that fucking is included in that holy union."

He is incorrigible. There is no way I can get him to stop saying these crude things. The more I try, the more creative he gets about getting on my last nerve.

But is he really getting on my nerves if I secretly enjoy this side of him?

"Can we go now?" I ask.

"Not yet. I need to know how my beautiful wife is today." His voice drops with seduction. "Did you have a good night's sleep with my cum inside your tight cunt?"

"Stop it."

"Why? You didn't mind when you were moaning 'harder, Kyle' in that fucking sexy voice of yours."

My blood flows to my ears and my core at the same time, and even though I try to fight the effect, I can't. Truth is, a strange sense of arousal invades me when he talks in this brazen way that has zero cares about the world. The only people who matter to him are the two of us.

"So?" He nudges me with his elbow. "You didn't answer my question. How are you this morning?"

"Sore," I whisper.

"You'll be sorer as soon as I get you in our room."

"You're still recovering, Kyle."

"I'm as immortal as the devil. You don't have to worry about that."

That's the problem—I *do* worry. I worry he already escaped two bullets and that the third will definitely take him away.

I push those ominous thoughts out of my head by focusing on him.

My husband.

My previous guard who turned into my husband.

I don't know if it will ever be normal. After all, we're not a normal couple. We didn't start the ordinary way, and our world is anything but a fairy tale.

However, after he told me why he left me—because he thought I was cold toward him—something inside me softened. It might have to do with that or the promise he made about not leaving me again, or the fact that he put his life on the line for me—not once, but twice.

He was ready to face death on my behalf.

A part of me, the part that was trained by *Dedushka* to be naturally doubtful of everything, tells me I shouldn't trust Kyle this readily. I shouldn't put my life in his hands like I did once upon a time.

But the other part—the twisted, screwed-up part that falls into his arms every night—wants me to stay with him every second of the day. That part misses him when I don't see him for a few hours. That part lets him consume my body like it's always been his to feast on.

And he does feast on me.

Kyle's stamina knows no limits, not even when he's wounded and bandaged and far from being entirely healed.

It doesn't matter whether he brings me pleasure with his dick or his toys. Both have the ability to provoke sides of me that were hidden, up until now.

I know people say the physical and emotional aspects are separate, but they're not for me. I never once thought my body was disconnected from my heart, so ever since the first time Kyle stimulated my body, he touched something inside my chest, too. With every unapologetic fuck, he lodged himself in even deeper.

We sit at a bench underneath a large Ailanthus tree, and I place the basket between us. The sky is clear, the occasional cloud blocking the sun now and again.

"Is there poison in it?" he asks with a playful gleam.

"If you want poison, I can gladly get it for you."

"Hey." He pinches my cheeks and keeps his hand there as he speaks. "Don't be offended—I was only kidding. Has anyone ever told you you're uptight, or are they too scared of you to say the words?"

"I'm not uptight. I'm just realistic."

He releases me, but not before stroking my cheek. "Which is another word for uptight, but I digress—only slightly, though."

"Stop being passive-aggressive."

"I'm British, Princess—passive-aggressive behavior is in our nature."

Shaking my head, I retrieve the pancake container and slide it toward him. Kyle takes a bite, and I wait with bated breath for his reaction. He doesn't wince, so that's a good sign. However, he pauses chewing.

"What? You don't like it?"

"No. It's just…it brought back a taste from a long time ago." He smiles a little. "My mum used to make these and even had her own special recipe."

"Dad used to make them. He said that before he made his fortune, he was a broke student and pancakes were a luxury breakfast he had whenever he got paid from his part-time job. In a way, they became special to me, too."

"Do you think you would've had a different life if you stayed by his side?"

"Probably. But if I had, Reina wouldn't have survived here, and I wouldn't have met *Dedushka*. I spent the most exciting days of my life with him, and I wouldn't change it for the world. At the same time, I missed Dad and Reina all the time. It doesn't make sense, I know. On the one hand, I loved *Dedushka*, Sergei, and Ana, and on the other hand, I wanted Dad and Reina."

"It makes perfect sense. You just wanted your entire family with you. That's why you can turn heartless when it comes to protecting them."

I stare at him for a beat, incredulous. I never thought he'd be able to figure out my angle this easily.

He's too observant sometimes, and it's both scary and comforting. Right now, it's definitely leaning toward the latter.

I retrieve a piece of pancake to stop myself from reaching over and hugging him. We silently eat for a few seconds. The sun peeks out from between the clouds and glares down at us. Kyle places both his hands in front of my face, shielding it from the rays until the sun disappears behind another cloud.

His way of protecting me can be over the top, but I can't help smiling at his serious expression as he does it.

We continue eating in silence, enjoying the nature, the calm, and the birds singing in the distance. A few guards bow upon seeing us, and we greet them back—well, I do. Kyle keeps glaring at each and every one of them.

I pour myself a cup of juice and take a sip. "Why do you seem like you're plotting the best way to kill them?"

"Because I am."

"Why would you?"

"They look at you funny."

A chuckle escapes me. "I'm their boss. They don't look at me funny."

"Yes, they do."

"You're just being paranoid."

"And you are being so unaware of your beauty."

I pause with the straw halfway to my mouth. It's not the first time Kyle has called me beautiful, but it never feels normal. "What does my beauty have to do with this?"

"If it weren't for your fucking beauty, I wouldn't want to rip out the heart of every bastard who looks in your direction."

I lower my head, not knowing how to answer that. I have no clue what to say when he talks in this possessive way.

"So don't make their fate worse," he continues.

"How so?"

"Don't talk to them, or flash them your smiles—those should only belong to me."

"You are too much."

"And you are mine."

I'm stunned into silence again, so I gulp my juice in one go, which makes Kyle grin.

He then takes my hand and places it on his thigh before he intertwines our fingers together. His thumb strokes the back of my hand in a rhythm that makes me breathless.

"How was it?" he asks with complete calm.

"How was what?"

"How was it after I left?"

"It was fine."

He gives me a funny look.

"What?" I puff my chest. "Did you expect me to explode in tears and tell you it was a tragedy?"

"You're being defensive."

"No, I'm not. I'm merely answering your question, and the answer to that question is that I was just *fine*."

I hide the fact that my life seemed to have lost something crucial: meaning. I might have reached every goal I set, but there was no excitement.

At some point, I realized something was missing, but I didn't know what that was until he showed up again in the dining room claiming to be Igor's son.

Kyle brushes his lips against my temple, and I shiver as if I'm standing in the middle of a snowfield during a freezing storm.

"I wasn't fine," he confesses against my skin. "In fact, I was miserable. I missed you."

A mixture of emotions clogs my throat. I clear it before I speak. "Why would you miss me?"

"Well, let's just say I got used to your stubbornness and your take-no-nonsense attitude and how much you challenged me every step of the way. I missed waking up every day to find you at my door demanding that I teach you something. I missed how you looked out for everyone around you, even though you tried to make yourself as discreet as possible so they didn't feel uncomfortable with it.

"I missed how you treated your guards as family members and how you never made them feel inferior. But most of all, I missed your smile." He grins. "As rare as it is."

This time I can't control the feeble sound that escapes my throat. This time, I feel like I will fall to pieces in his arms.

"Did you miss me?" His voice is low, and is that a hint of vulnerability I hear?

When I don't answer, he continues, "Are you ever going to forgive me?"

I manage a smile. "Keep trying."

"Well, I am trying every night, though for different reasons."

"What are you trying to do?"

"Hello? I'm obviously trying to put an actual baby in you. Imagine everyone's surprise when they find out there was no baby in the first place."

"That would be impossible."

"Why's that?"

"You really haven't noticed that I use birth control pills?"

"Of course I have."

I laugh. "Then how the hell do you expect me to get pregnant?"

"A little thing called a miracle."

"*Miracles* won't be happening any time soon."

"We will see about that."

I narrow my eyes at him. "What the hell is that supposed to mean?"

"Nothing." He feigns nonchalance. "But I promise you that one day you will have my baby inside that womb of yours while I worship you."

"Not if I have a say in it."

"Hmm."

"What does 'hmm' mean?"

"I have another promise for you."

"What type of promise?"

He raises my hand to his lips and brushes them against the skin. "The type where I will never leave. And if I do leave, you're coming with me."

THIRTY

Kyle

I NEVER THOUGHT THERE WOULD BE A DAY WHEN RAI would lie peacefully in my arms this way.

She's too hotheaded and individualistic to succumb to my hold like this.

At one point, I realized there would be a day where she will leave me and never look back.

But that was before I decided I won't lose her.

I wasn't joking when I told her she's coming with me. It was said in the heat of the moment, but it's the truest decision I've ever made.

Rai is coming with me.

When this whole thing is done, she will be by my side when we go to live somewhere far away from here.

Far away from the tragedy I'll bring to the place she loves so much. The wound in my chest is nothing compared to the one she'll suffer once I'm done.

She's currently changing my bandage and telling me about Mikhail's latest screw-up. That's what she's been doing for the past couple of weeks. I try to focus on her words instead of the urge to flip her underneath me and fuck her.

It doesn't matter that we just came out of the shower and I took her against the wall until she was screaming at me to stop.

I *can't* stop.

Not when she looks at me with those eyes. I wish to be able to keep them safe somewhere. I wish I could hide them so they wouldn't see the monstrosity of what I truly am or what I'm capable of. If she does see, she won't only want me dead like the other time I disappeared on her. This time, she will shoot me with her own hands.

I would probably deserve it, but still, I won't let it happen, even if I have to resort to methods she won't approve of.

Once finished with the bandage, she helps me put on my shirt and buttons it. Her black-manicured nails look so feminine against the fabric, elegant and full of finesse like everything about her.

Her face appears younger, probably because she's not completely alert like when we're in the company of others. She's starting to gradually let her guard down around me.

I wouldn't say that's a very clever choice on her part, but it's better than having her always fight me—though she does still fight me whenever she feels the urge to. I love provoking Rai and causing her to blush or squirm before she tells me to take her against the closest available surface.

"All finished." She smiles at her handiwork.

"I wouldn't say it's all finished unless you're bouncing on my dick, Princess."

She sucks in a harsh breath. "Do you ever stop talking like that?"

"I do."

"Yeah, right."

"I really do."

"When have you ever, pervert?"

"When you're riding me, Mrs. Hunter."

She rolls her eyes. "You say that as if you let me."

"I will now." I tap my thigh.

She hesitates for a second too long before she shakes her head. "No, we're supposed to go meet Kai, remember?"

"How could I forget?" I mutter.

We have a meeting with the Japanese fucker who looks at her in a way that bugs me. That's an understatement. It's not only that I dislike the way he looks at her. Whenever his name is brought up, I have the urge to finish his miserable life and start a diplomatic problem between the Yakuza and the Bratva.

However, the other fucker, Vladimir, has been urging Rai to go talk to him for a possible alliance. He knows Kai has some sort of an agreement with Rai, and I don't like that type of agreement.

Needless to say, there was no way in hell I was going to let her go meet him on her own. So either I go or we ditch him. I prefer the second option, or better yet, I'd rather option zero where I should've had Flame snipe him down.

"Kai can wait," I say.

"No, he can't."

"Yes, he can. In the meantime, you can ride me. Come on, you know you want to."

She pulls her bottom lip between her teeth and peeks at me through her thick lashes with a seductiveness I'm sure she doesn't know she has but still manages to exude, anyway.

She might not be a natural seductress like her twin sister, but she has these hidden tendencies that appear every now and then, and they sure as fuck work on me judging from the bulge in my trousers.

"Later, okay?"

"Why wait for later when we can do it now?"

She sighs heavily but doesn't push away from me when I grab her by the waist.

Rai stares at me. In the beginning, I hated her eyes. I thought they were too cold, callous, and impenetrable, but now they're anything but closed off. She's soft, peaceful, and I might be too addicted to that side of her.

"Do you realize just how much you've screwed up my schedule?"

"And is that a bad thing?"

"Of course it is. I have work to do, and it's not only about the brotherhood. I'm an executive manager in V Corp, where many people's livelihoods depend on me. I have the directors to answer to and the employees to look after. I also have to keep an eye on Ana's internship so she stops being too sheltered, but I forget all about that when I'm with you. Would you stop distracting me?"

"Why would I when it's the best distraction you will ever have?"

"Kyle…" she pleads. "Let's just go, and when we return, I will let you do whatever you want."

My interest is piqued at that. "Whatever I want?"

"Whatever. You. Want," she says emphatically. "But now promise you'll be good."

I narrow my eyes. "Good to who?"

"To Kai."

"Why would I when he threatened to kill you on our wedding day?"

"Because we want an alliance with the Japanese. We have to practice diplomacy sometimes."

"You're the contact, not me. I don't see why both of us should play nice."

"What is your problem with Kai exactly?"

The way he looks at you. But I don't say that because it'll make me a pathetic fool, and I'm anything but. If anything, I'm the villain of this tale. I'm the reason her beloved brotherhood will be wiped away.

When I don't say anything, Rai considers the subject closed and places my leather shoes by my feet. "Do you want me to help?"

"I can at least do that myself. Go before me. I will follow."

"Are you sure you don't want me to help? It'll be quick."

"You're becoming a wife way too fast, Rai."

But I feel like it's only because she feels guilty that I took a bullet for her great-uncle.

That's the reason why she wouldn't leave my side all this time. It's gratitude. I hate that fucking word. I don't want her to feel gratitude toward me. I want her to be with me because she needs my presence as much as I can't breathe without hers.

But there will be a different time and place for that. One day, she will snuggle into my arms, not because she feels grateful for my 'heroic' acts, but because she can't stay away from me.

After making a face, she leaves.

I make sure the door closes behind her before I put my shoes on, grab my phone, and go to the balcony. It's rarely open due to the fear of snipers. The late boss, Nikolai, was overly cautious, and Rai takes after him in more ways than one.

I dial the number on my phone and wait a few minutes before Flame picks up.

"How are things from your side?"

"First of all, fuck you—I didn't sign up to be within the Irish. Feigning their accent is a nightmare."

"Stop moaning. Did Damien's attack work?"

"Magically. They're anxious and kind of know they're doomed because of the Russians and the Italians joining forces to crush them."

"As they should," I mutter under my breath.

"I believe Rolan will either reach out to Sergei or Lazlo or both."

My fist tightens at the sound of that name. *Rolan Fitzpatrick*. There's no way in hell I would ever forget it.

"And what does he intend to do exactly?" I ask Flame.

"Ask for a truce? Or a whore? How the fuck would I know?"

"Doesn't matter, anyway. Both Lazlo and Sergei think the Irish sniped at my wedding and came to Sergei's special supper."

"To give them credit, the Russians did try to catch us that night, especially that bearded guy and the one with the glasses, but we escaped in time."

I stare down at the guards stationed near every entrance. "No matter how much the Russians think they're strong, they don't compare to professionally trained killing machines."

"Speaking of those killing machines, they're waiting for their second half of the deposit."

"I'll send it over as soon as they finish the entire job."

"Just give me a name."

There's a pause—from my side, not his. Why the fuck am I hesitating? After all, this was the reason why I returned to the States in the first place. This is why I've been staying alive.

"Kyle?"

"I don't care who you have to kill from the Russians as long as it's an elite and not Adrian or Sergei."

"Why not Sergei? He would've been my first choice."

Adrian is off the list because he knows some of the story. My secret kills for him in the past are the reason why I got in the brotherhood in the first place. Nikolai didn't question my background when Adrian gave him a fake one because he—and Sergei—trust him that much. Adrian wants me close because he likes having one of the best professional killers in his arsenal, and for that, we have a mutual understanding. Of course he doesn't know that I intend to ruin the entire brotherhood, though.

Sergei, however, should've been game because his position allows for greater impact if he suddenly dies.

Rai's words from the other day are what's stopping me from finishing him.

If he does die, she'll be thrown out of V Corp and everything she worked for. The brotherhood is a harsh world for a woman, especially a very opinionated and outspoken woman like Rai.

So, I choose not to kill her fantasies yet, even though she'll eventually leave them behind once I whisk her out of here.

"I still need Sergei. He prefers me now, and I'll use that to my advantage," I say. "Choose one of the others."

"And then?"

"And then stop asking questions and make it happen. After all, I'm paying you in fucking favors, and you know how much I hate them."

"Fine, fine. I was just wondering if you had a plan for that blondie wife of yours."

You don't fucking talk about her that way. In fact, don't bloody mention her at all.

That's what I want to say, but if I show my weakness to Flame that way, he won't hesitate to use it against me in the most brutal way possible. I might have him as an ally right now, but there will be a day when he will return to being my enemy.

"Rai is nothing," I say in a casual tone. "I'll just leave her behind."

"Which is the smartest thing to do, because if she knows what you're doing, she'll murder you."

She would.

But I'm still taking her with me. I don't care if she kills me as long as she's by my side.

"We're close to the finish line, so get your head in the game, Flame."

"Always is, punk."

"By the end, I want both the Irish and the Russians destroyed."

This is my vengeance.

THIRTY-ONE

Rai

I STAND FROZEN IN PLACE, NOT SURE WHAT I JUST HEARD or if I heard it correctly.

Maybe my mind is playing a trick on me. Maybe none of this is real and I'm dreaming.

I'll wake up soon, right?

I close my eyes so hard they sting then I open them again. Unlike what I foolishly hoped for, I don't wake up.

Instead, my mind is assaulted by the words I heard as I stood by the door.

By the end, I want both the Irish and the Russians destroyed.

Kyle said that, among other things I'm unable to wrap my mind around.

He usually notices my presence even before I step into the room. Not this time, though. He hasn't shown any sign that implies he knows I'm here. It could be that his medication has dulled his senses, or that I'm too silent.

Or maybe he's too focused on his destruction plan to notice I'm here.

The fact remains, he said those words.

This is not my imagination.

This is not a nightmare.

This is reality.

The man standing on the balcony, the one I took as a husband and whose ring I'm wearing, has been plotting my family's demise.

For a second, I'm unable to breathe or think. Should I barge in there, confront him, and possibly get myself killed? Or should I step away and pretend I heard nothing?

Pretend I didn't come back because I got the DNA tests from Katia and they said in big fat letters that he's not Igor's son.

Pretend I wasn't stupid enough to fall for his games all over again after seven years of swearing to never be a fool.

I was doing just fine, getting used to him being my husband. I was ready to forgive him and put everything behind us.

But how long would I have lived in that pipe dream before the bubble burst? Before I saw Kyle for what he truly is?

A mastermind of destruction.

A man who will ruin my family.

Unlike what I thought, Kyle didn't marry me to help make Igor the boss—he did it to destroy the entire brotherhood.

The bitter taste of betrayal explodes in my mouth, and I bite my lower lip until I taste metal.

While he's still speaking on the phone, I step back and try to be as quiet as possible.

He told me once that I shouldn't trust him, that when I trusted him, I would be dead. Did I listen to that? Did my foolish heart listen to that? It didn't. Instead, I fell deeper into his web of secrets and lies. He dragged me with him into a darkness so black, it's impossible to see the light anymore.

I don't close the door because the click might alert him to my presence.

If he knows I heard everything, he'll change his plan, and I won't be able to thwart it.

As I stand in front of the room I'd started to call 'ours', tears sting my eyes. I wipe them away with angry hands.

It's all over now.

He thought that he could hurt my family and me, but it would've been better if he'd just disappeared. It would have been so much better if I hadn't seen his face.

But he went ahead and committed the most unforgivable sin of all.

Fuck my heart. I will crush it and Kyle before anyone is able to harm my family.

A rustling sound comes from behind me before a male voice speaks in a noticeable accent. "Looks like you heard something you shouldn't have."

And with that, he grabs my throat from behind and twists my neck.

My vision gradually goes black as I fall to the ground with a thud. Large hands grab my feet and drag me away.

My eyes slowly close and a tear slides down my cheek as a frightening type of void grips me in its clutches. While I blackout, Kyle's words keep playing at the back of my head.

Rai is nothing. I'll just leave her behind.

TO BE CONTINUED

Kyle and Rai's story concludes in *Throne of Vengeance*.

You can read Rai's twin sister's story, Reina, and Asher's in *All The Lies*.

WHAT'S NEXT?

Thank you so much for reading *Throne of Power*! If you liked it, please leave a review.
Your support means the world to me.

If you're thirsty for more discussions with other readers of the series, you can join the Facebook group, Rina's Spoilers Room.

Next up is the conclusion of Rai and Kyle's epic mafia romance,
Throne of Vengeance.

When vengeance strikes…

You don't know me, but I know you.
I'm the shadow that creeps behind you without notice.
The moment you see me, you're dead.
An assassin. A killer. A nobody.
Until I became somebody.
I'll make everyone who reduced me to a shadow pay.
To do that, I'm willing to risk everything.
Everything except for my reluctant wife.
Rai Sokolov can show me her worst, but this will only end when death does us part.
The road to the throne is paved with loss, betrayal, and blood baths.
To win, we go all in.
Our lives included.

ALSO BY RINA KENT

For more titles by the author and an
explicit reading order, please visit:
www.rinakent.com/books

ABOUT THE AUTHOR

Rina Kent is a *USA Today*, international, and #1 Amazon bestselling author of everything enemies to lovers romance.

She's known to write unapologetic anti-heroes and villains because she often fell in love with men no one roots for. Her books are sprinkled with a touch of darkness, a pinch of angst, and an unhealthy dose of intensity.

She spends her private days in London laughing like an evil mastermind about adding mayhem to her expanding universe. When she's not writing, Rina travels, hikes, and spoils cats in a pure Cat Lady fashion.

Find Rina Below:

Website: www.rinakent.com

Newsletter: www.subscribepage.com/rinakent

BookBub: www.bookbub.com/profile/rina-kent

Amazon: www.amazon.com/Rina-Kent/e/B07MM54G22

Goodreads: www.goodreads.com/author/show/18697906.
Rina_Kent

Instagram: www.instagram.com/author_rina

Facebook: www.facebook.com/rinaakent

Reader Group: www.facebook.com/groups/rinakent.club

Pinterest: www.pinterest.co.uk/AuthorRina/boards

Tiktok: www.tiktok.com/@rina.kent

Twitter: twitter.com/AuthorRina